MW01593250

THE AGENCY FILES

BOOK FIVE

HASHTAG ROGUE

CHAUTONA HAVIG

Copyright 2019 Chautona Havig

ISBN: 9781690962755

Chautona Havig lives in an oxymoron, escapes into imaginary worlds that look startlingly similar to ours and writes the stories that emerge. An irrepressible optimist, Chautona sees everything through a kaleidoscope of *It's a Wonderful Life* sprinkled with fairy tales. Find her on the web and say howdy—if you can remember how to spell her name.

Edited by: Haug Editing
Fonts: Palatino Linotype, Clatens Serif, Alex Brush
Cover photos: FotoMaximum/thinkstock.com
Cover art by: Chautona Havig

The events and people in this book are purely fictional, and any resemblance to actual people is purely coincidental. I'd love to meet them!

Connect with Me Online:
Twitter: https://twitter.com/Chautona
Facebook: https://www.facebook.com/chautonahavig
My blog: http://chautona.com/blog/
Instagram: http://instagram.com/ChautonaHavig
Goodreads: https://www.goodreads.com/Chautona
BookBub: https://www.bookbub.com/authors/chautona-havig
Amazon Author Page: https://amazon.com/author/chautonahavig
YouTube: https://www.youtube.com/user/chautona/videos
My newsletter (sign up for news of FREE eBook offers): https://chautona.com/newsletter

All Scripture references are from the NASB. NASB passages are taken from the NEW AMERICAN STANDARD BIBLE (registered), Copyright 1960, 1962, 1963, 1968, 1971, 1972, 1973, 1975, 1977, 1995 by The Lockman Foundation

TERRY

I don't know you, but your interest in this series is such a blessing to me. The kindness you show my girlie doesn't hurt, either. Thank you for serving the Lord in all the ways you do. Many are blessed by your ministry.

PERRY

Thanks for the inspiration for Keith's new dream car... he's no Brent, so he can keep on dreamin'.

CLARK

Without your brainstorming brilliance, this book would still be languishing in St. Louis. Thank you for being the awesome friend you are.

NOAH

Especially to Noah—the *real* Noah who made sure "his" scene was realistic, believable, and fun.

ONE

The steady *snap-clink-snap-clink* of a Newton cradle provided percussion to the steady drone of half a dozen news channels played out on the screens. A single finger tapped a key on the keyboard, and the volume rose for the center top screen. "—sources say that the bio-terrorist threat is over. With fifty-seven confirmed dead and thirty-seven in critical condition, as well as hundreds still being tested, it is being called the widest-spread act of terrorism on American soil..."

Snap-clink-snap-clink. The balls continued their steady swing as a finger tapped again. Another screen's volume rose as it pulled into the foreground. "—in protective custody from the Malakov organization located in Portland, Oregon. West and the man assigned to protect him, Secret Service agent, Keith Auger, were gunned down at a safehouse. There are no ties to the Malakov organization for this attack on the safe house, but law enforcement assumes..."

A finger crooked around two of the balls swinging in the Newton's cradle and let them go. *Snap-plink-snap-plink.* Another screen's volume rose and fell. Another. Most received no more than a moment or two, but three stories—anytime they showed up on a channel—received full attention.

The Secretary of Homeland Security filled the screen

again. *Snap, plink, snap, plink.* There had to be a connection. *Snap, plink, snap, plink.* To the Malakovs and their Russian connections? *Snap, plink, snap, plink.* To the North Koreans? *Snap, plink, snap, plink.* Both? *Snap, plink, snap, plink.* Time to discover. Time to act.

Snap, plink, snap, plink.

0000 01 000 0000 1 01 110   010 111 110 001 0

Same make. Same model. Same color. Same car.

No one could argue it. Flynne Dortmann, assistant extraordinaire to The Agency, stared at the screens she'd captured over the past month. A third of them showed the same man sitting in the same spot. Waiting. Watching.

Flynne's gaze slid to the doorway that separated her from her boss's office. Would Mark listen this time? A sigh escaped. Probably not. Why change his modus operandi?

Listen or not, Flynne's job was to check and report on Keith Auger—Shafter now that he was officially dead—and report anything that looked like someone might be watching him. Mark took good care of his men, and though Keith wasn't an agent anymore, he'd given everything to keep The Agency and its clients safe.

While Erika Polowski wasn't Keith, as his girlfriend, she was Keith's weakest point. And this car was watching Erika Polowski. She just knew it.

If I was, like, going to try to find someone who's hiding, it's so obvi that I'd just find his favorite person and, like, make her take a permie vacay.

That did it. Mark could ignore the facts. Flynne couldn't. She grabbed her iPad and stormed the citadel also known as Mark's office. "Got a minute?"

"For you... two."

She couldn't help a grin. "Aw... I'm getting me a coolio graphic tee that says, 'I'm Mark's Fave.' The agents will be *sooo* jellie!"

The new, oversized chair jumped out of position and attacked her toe. Again. "Next time you redecorate, do it one piece at a time!" Flynne scowled at the chair until she was confident it felt her displeasure.

"I was going for the Band-Aid approach. I didn't know you were so clumsy."

"I'm not!" At the look he gave her, she added, "Okay, so I pay more attention when the room's a new place—then I totes go on auto-pi."

"Auto-pi?"

She sighed and popped imaginary gum. "Pilot? Like airplanes? Anyway, I have that statement transcribed and something to show you. Statement's in your inbox and..." Flynne took a deep breath. "I've been watching this for the last month. I think it's something to pay attention to."

Swipe after swipe, Flynne showed the car parked outside the coffee shop in Dolman. "He's there. All the time. Every day that she is."

When Mark took the iPad and gave every picture his full attention, she relaxed. Of course, Mark would take a threat against Keith or his friends and family seriously. She'd been totes ridic on that one.

"I see why you're concerned," he began.

Oh, good.

"But I don't think it's actionable, and even if it were, Erika has Keith. They're probably going to get married. She's in the best hands possible as it is."

"Will he be on his guard if he doesn't think she's in danger?"

At that, he shut down. Oh, he acted engaged, but she saw it... total shutdown. "Thanks for bringing it to my attention, and I want to see any more that you find, but we'll mark this as insufficient for now." Mark gave her a perfunctory smile. "I will let him know you had some concern."

"I think—"

Mark sent her off, insisting that he had to read that statement.

"But—"

"Not now, Flynne."

She turned to storm from the room in a brilliant display of displeasure and did a front-flip over the stupid blue chair. *Way to go, Dortmann. Supes Ridic.*

"You okay?"

Some things you don't dignify with an answer, and that was one. Three seconds later—maybe four, if Mark was lucky—Flynne made up her mind. After a glance at the surveillance cameras, she jerked her Burberry backpack from the desk drawer and flipped the flap open. A glance inside showed two refillable bottles of water. Against everything she believed in, Flynne set them on the desktop. *I can put a whole lot of cash in that space.*

Her phone came next. That took a bit longer to decide, but she eventually sent out a group text message telling friends she'd be gone for a bit, pulled the SIM card from the back, and reassembled. That, she left beside the water bottles.

After much deliberation, only her license and one credit card were hidden in the RFID tucked in a hidden pocket. The wallet joined the rest of her rejects. Three books and a Kindle. She dumped them all. *Too tempting when I need to be on my game.*

At last, she'd pared down to bare essentials. Brush, toothbrush and floss, retainer and case, a note from her boyfriend, Tyler, and her car keys—for now. With all that decided, the rest became almost automatic.

Five thousand dollars in cash dropped to the bottom of the bag—and filled it a third of the way. Flynne grabbed a couple of bundles of hundreds and several more twenties. Ten thousand. After that, three burner phones—charged and ready to go, of course—and two tranq pistols, complete with as many darts and CO_2 cartridges as she could stuff into the bag. One cartridge lay abandoned on the desk when she finished.

Instinct said to repack with the tranq stuff on the bottom of the backpack, but she didn't have time for that. *Besides, my instincts could be mallow fluffs.* A glance at her monitor told her she'd spent enough time already.

The logbook of inventory went into Keith's personnel file—the paper one. If Mark had any brains, he could find it. If not, well, that wasn't her problem.

A sound from the employee room nearly sent her through the roof. *Tyler and Raina are sleeping just one door away, and you're over here banging drawers.*

Shadows appeared where there were none, and Flynne could have sworn that she tasted V8 Juice. *Probably bit the inside of my cheek again. It's like every sense is in hyperdrive.*

With everything set, Flynne zipped a message to Mark through the office system. GOING TO LUNCH. WANT ME TO BRING BACK SOMETHING? MEXICAN TO GO WITH YOUR COOL NEW LAST NAME? PAPER CLIPS?

The reply came swifter than usual. I'M GOOD, BUT THANKS. TAKE YOUR TIME. SLOW WEEK HERE SO FAR.

Until someone makes off with Erika... But Flynne didn't

say it. Instead, she assured him she'd see him ASAP and dashed from the building with the backpack swinging over one shoulder.

0000 01 000 0000 1 01 110   010 111 110 001 0

The Chevy Volt rolled to a stop a mile south of Hearthfield Way—beside a field of early-blooming wildflowers. A curve in the road would hide Keith's '39 Packard when it turned, but she'd see it moving to that curve and could count from there. With that in place, Flynne swapped out the SIM card from one of the burner phones with her SIM card and made the call.

Keith answered on second ring. "The answer's no, Flynne. I'm retired."

"You're still training newbies, so technically, you just had a demotion."

"*Promotion*," he argued.

"Those who can't do, teach." Guilt wracked her as she said the words, but it's what Keith would expect.

Keith's low rumble of a chuckle told her she'd made the right call. "Well... you guys will thank me when your new recruits actually save a life instead of hasten their earthly extraction."

A dozen comebacks surfaced, but her lips refused to allow any of them to pass. She tossed out a, "Ha!" before jumping into the purpose of her call. "Look, I'd love to have a word fight, but Mark needs you to come in—like now. It's supes important. He didn't think so at first, but I convinced him. Hashtag Flynne for the win."

It was sort of true—or would be ten minutes after Keith got on the road.

"What's up?"

"Possible danger to Erika. It's why I'm calling on my own phone. I'll have to ditch my SIM, thanks to this. He said not to call. Just come in. Ready for today's code?"

A short huff told her he was either ticked or concerned—or both in one. Probably that. "Give it to me."

"9-2-2-0-6-3-5-5-8-4-3. I can repeat..."

As expected, he rattled the numbers off without a hitch. "9-2-2-0-6-3-5-5-8-4-3."

"Yes."

"Got it. Heading in now. Erika's getting ready for work. Do I tell her to call in?"

She hesitated. Would it be easier to grab Erika in HearthLand where they had friends or in Dolman? In town there'd be more people who might try to stop her, but would they even care? "I've got Tyler en route to her cafe just to watch over her while you guys talk. If you think there's a threat, he can get her out."

"Excellent. You're awesome, Flynne. Bye."

You won't think so later. It only took a minute before she saw the speck approaching the curve. It grew until Keith's '39 Packard tore around that corner and shot out of sight. Flynne started her car and eased it into position. The counting began. *One... two...* Not until she hit sixty did Flynne pull out onto the highway and gun it. Just as she rounded the curve, she saw Keith ahead, already streaking down the Dolman Highway.

"Phase one: complete. Now if Erika just cooperates..."

She'd considered just putting a gun to Erika's head and demanding the woman do what she said. The thought prompted a snort. No one with half a brain would believe Flynne would shoot at close range—if at all.

"Okay, Plan K... or is it L?"

After taking a deep, fortifying breath, she shot down Hearthfield Way and zipped past the growing town square to the road leading to the newest development in the small, planned community. What looked like a freshly-tilled field signaled the corner to turn to Erika's house. *Keith'll live there soon enough, too, I bet.* For now, however, he lived in a trailer on empty property—between training runs, that is—just across from Erika's micro house.

The adorable little house seemed to rush toward her as Flynne considered a dozen ideas and settled on the one she liked least. "I've gotta do what I've gotta do," she muttered and slammed on the brakes.

Minutes ticked past as she struggled to see if she had the gun loaded properly. Of course, she didn't bring instructions, but it looked loaded… ish. She kicked open the car door and stormed around to the passenger side in an attempt to block anyone seeing what she planned. One shot, and the dart flew out and hit the dirt. Flynne retrieved it, tossed it in the back seat, and climbed back in the car.

With the chamber reloaded, Flynne drove up to Erika's house and pulled her car as close to the front door as she could. The sky-blue trim and red geraniums in the tiny window boxes of Erika's house mocked her. *I'm totes gonna turn a tranquil scene into a nightmare with a tranquilizer. So not cool.*

Movies said to put the gun in her back waistband. Gang bangers stuck them in front. She'd thought that was just to be macho, but Mark had said it was actually more efficient—a faster draw. *Not using any waistband.* At that thought, she shoved the gun back in the backpack and hefted it. The thing nearly gave her a one-way ticket to the chiro, but Flynne kept walking as if it was nothing.

The door opened and Erika stood there, staring. "You

14

just missed Keith. He shot out of here a minute ago. I'm just waiting for his call now."

"He's gone to talk to Mark..." If puppy dog eyes and exaggerated innocent smiles could do it, Erika would invite her inside in five... four...

"Come in! Sorry. I thought you were here for Keith."

"I came to be your escort if they find the problem credible."

Erika blanched. "Problem?"

"I found some anomalies in the surveillance at your work. It's probably nothing, but..."

Flynne found herself escorted to the mini couch and nearly shoved into it. The backpack jabbed her side. "Oof!"

"Something wrong?"

Lies—they flowed. *I'll be cray cray if I don't get to stop with the lies like... now.* "Nope. So, how do you like it out here?"

"Takes getting used to, actually. It's really quiet. All. The. Time. You don't get that in the city. And dark..." Erika sighed. "But when summer gets here, we'll have fireflies right out my front door. That's cool."

Half a dozen sentences of chit-chat ended with Erika fumbling for her phone. "I should call and see if Keith has spoken to Mark. Excuse me."

Despite every effort to get the gun out of her bag and aim it before Erika could stand, it didn't happen. Instead, Erika had taken three steps away before Flynne felt ready. She aimed at the upper thigh and squeezed the trigger.

The dart landed in Erika's right butt cheek. "Hey, wha—?" A glance behind her made Erika roar. Eyes flashing, she demanded, "What'd you do *that* for?"

Flynne did the only thing she could think of. She fired again. Two for two—aimed for thighs both times and

15

managed to hit cheeks of the posterior area.

"I can't believe you! What's wrong with you, Flynne?" Erika's eyes widened and she jerked out the first tranq dart as she growled, "Is Keith really going to see Mark?"

Flynne stowed the gun and rose. "Yep."

As she fumbled for the second dart, her movements just a little less precise, Erika began swearing. Beginning with the mildest epithets, she cursed Flynne up one side and down the other. By the time she extracted the second dart and dropped back to her chair, Erika had run out of curses and gone into hyper-vocabulary mode. Her voice slurred as she fumbled for her phone. "—can't believe some rogue agent got me. It's insane."

This time, Flynne smiled at the words. She stood and confiscated Erika's phone. "I'll take that."

The ten minutes she expected it to take her to get Erika into the car and on the road stretched into twenty as she taped, tied, and dragged their best agent's girlfriend out the door and into the backseat of her car.

With a duffel bag of Erika's clothes and all the food she could pack quickly from the cupboards and fridge, Flynne started for the door. The sight of Erika's phone on the counter prompted a new thought. She snatched it up and sent out one tweet from Erika's Twitter account.

TWO

The dossiers of three potential clients lay open before him. Mark leaned back in his chair, fingers templed under his chin, eyes riveted on the one tiny spot where the painting crew had either missed or wiped away fresh paint. About the size of a dime, he often found himself staring at it. Thinking. He thought of it like the "spot" a dancer uses to keep herself balanced and keep dizziness at bay.

It worked, too.

Well, it worked until Flynne's knock interrupted his thoughts. "Come on in. Back so soon?"

Keith Au—um... *Shafter* walked in. "Flynne isn't out there."

"She's out to lunch." He sat up and grinned at his favorite agent. "What can I do for you?" Mark gestured toward the blue chair Flynne hated so much and then froze at the look on the man's face. "What is it?"

"She said you needed me here to check out—"

Every foul word in every language he knew rose to the surface, but Mark respected Keith too much to let even one fly. Something deep inside niggled, hinting that he should respect himself that much, but he managed to remember that he didn't have time for introspection. "She did, huh?"

Mark ripped the handset from its cradle and punched

a single button. *"Hey, hey, hey! Leave a message. No promies, but maybe it's your lucky day and I'll call you back."*

His scowl must have been telling. "Went to voicemail?"

He nodded.

Keith's lips thinned and his jaw went rigid. "Could that be because it's sitting on her desk?"

"What?"

Without a word, Keith stormed from the room and returned before Mark could even step away from the desk. He wiggled the Anime-cased phone. "Sitting right there… on her desk. Next to a pile of books, a Kindle, water bottles…" He stepped forward. "And how did she go to lunch without her wallet?"

Dropping back into the chair without looking might not have been the smartest move. Mark fumbled and nearly landed on his backside instead of in the chair. He pulled up office monitors and scrolled back until he saw Flynne exit. Slower, he slid the bar all the way back to the moment she'd exited his office for hers—unnecessarily, of course. Seeing things in reverse doesn't hide facts.

"You'd better come see this."

The minute Flynne reached for the first bundle of cash, Keith barked out two orders. "Pull up that surveillance she was so worried about and unjam my phone."

Mark complied… and sent messages to Tyler and Raina. GET IN MY OFFICE NOW.

The two agents burst through his door and nearly ran over Keith as he paced in front of the desk. Erika's phone rang… and she obviously *didn't* pick up. In one fluid move, he made another call. Mark listened.

"Hey, Ralph? I need you to do something. *Now*. Go to Erika's place, and see if her car's there—if she's okay. Call me right back." Keith paused before nodding an answer "Ralph" couldn't see. "Yeah. Emergency. Go."

"You don't think—?"

Keith nodded. "She took cash, tranq supplies, and what did she do in that corner?"

Mark scrolled back, but no matter how close he zoomed or which angle he looked at, he couldn't tell. "I don't know." Both men pushed their way into Flynne's office, and only when Mark nearly bowled over Tyler, did he hear the younger man shouting.

"What's wrong? Where's Fly—?" Tyler froze. "Why does Keith have Flynne's phone?"

At Keith's glance, Mark nodded. *He'll handle this better than I would, anyway.*

"Tyler, you used to work in this office." Keith pointed to the empty area. "What would Flynne put over there?" He cleared his throat. "Or rather... what would she *hide* over there?"

His gut sinking into his shoes, Mark stared at the space. It looked empty enough—to the untrained eye. But artwork hid seams in uneven panels that slid aside. Behind them—office supplies, the office's shredding and recycling area, and locked files. Agent files.

While Tyler rattled off these things to Keith, Mark slid open the panels and used his access codes to get into the firesafe file boxes. Not one looked askew. He counted. Every agent had two sets—by year and by surname. All but one were there. That one was in his desk—he thought.

Keith dug through shredded bits of paper that couldn't be reassembled if you wanted to for any sign of what had most recently been shredded. A hopeless attempt, but Mark understood why he tried. Meanwhile, he sent Tyler for the missing file. "I just need to be sure it's there."

Their new agent stood there, arms folded over her chest. "Can someone tell me what Flynne *did*? The girl's a whiz with tech stuff, but c'mon? She speaks in emojis or something. Is she smart enough to—?"

The three men spoke in unison. "Yes."

Keith added. "Just smart enough to know how to create a nightmare for the rest of us."

Tyler returned with the file. "It's here—looks complete to me."

A tingle ran up Mark's spine, but he had to hide all signs of nerves. "Tyler, sit."

Her cocked eyebrow showed Raina's thoughts. "Does he speak and roll over, too?"

One of the men said, "Stuff it." The other, "Shut up."

When Tyler asked what to do next, Mark answered with the only thing he could think of while his mind worked out other problems. "Go over every bit of that desk and tell me what's wrong—including why you think Flynne would leave each of those items there and fill her backpack with cash—need to know how much is missing—tranq gear, and burner phones."

"If she took all that, there wasn't room for any of this." Tyler flipped open the wallet. "She's missing her VISA card and her driver's license." One by one, he checked every item on, in, and near the desk. "Something's gone... He closed his eyes as if trying to remember. When he shook his head, Mark's heart sank into his shoes as well. "Sorry... can I see the surveillance footage? I might notice something there that isn't now. Or vice versa."

Keith's phone rang. He grabbed at it with more desperation than haste even. "Yeah? What'd you find?"

It only took a second before Mark knew what Keith

would tell him. Erika was gone. Another second passed before Keith quit staring at the screen and turned it to face him. There Erika's phone lay on the tiny counter. Abandoned. Fear, amazement, and confusion swirled in what once had been his gut. The full reality of the situation hit him. *She's done it. She's actually done it, hasn't she?*

He hated to say it, but Mark had to. "Tell him how to grab it with a Ziploc bag." Keith hesitated, waiting… and Mark knew why. He closed his eyes and gave the order. "Keith… find Flynne. Take Raina."

0000 01 000 0000 1 01 110   010 111 110 001 0

As if oblivious to the cold storm raging in his heart, spring wildflowers dotted green meadows on each side of the Dolman highway. Keith gripped the steering wheel with unnecessary force as he inched the speedometer past sixty-five to seventy. The engine informed him it wouldn't go much faster, but he accelerated just a smidge anyway.

"Don't kill your car, or we'll never get there."

Keith shot Raina a sidelong glance, scowled, and held the car at seventy-five. As much as he hated to admit it, she was right.

"Sweet ride…"

Maybe you're not so bad after all.

"But I'd have thought you'd have a car with decent speed in your line of work."

"Instructors don't need fast cars to get to and from their jobs." If he bit the words between gritted teeth, who could blame him?

Another two miles passed before she spoke again. "Why do you live way out here?

They crested the rise in the road that hid the stretch of Hearthfield Way from southbound traffic, and he relaxed just a little before answering. "Privacy. I'm dead, remember? I can't be seen by anyone who knows me."

"So, that's what's up with the beard. I don't get guys and their beards."

"I don't either, but Erika loves it." If he closed his eyes, Keith knew he'd be able to feel her hand stroking it before kicking him out the door at night. Only the knowledge that he'd probably total his car kept him from indulging.

They took the corner to Hearthfield Way much faster than he ever had. Gravel flew in an arc in his rearview mirror. *Right out of a movie. Erika'd like that.*

"Keep us alive, Shafter."

Keith started to inform her that he'd never lost anyone. His jaw clamped shut at the memory of a tiny woman with a ferocity to intimidate any man. He'd failed *her.* That knowledge still rankled. "I've never made a reckless driving mistake." There. At least that was true.

"You're about to now. And for what?"

That question nearly got Raina ejected from the moving car. *I really need to invest in some cheesy spy gear—a button I can press that opens a secret panel in the roof and ejects unwanted, mouthy passengers.*

When she pressed again, Keith just said, "I need to get there, okay? This is serious."

"Didn't say it wasn't, but kill—"

Maybe it was wrong—he didn't even know anymore—but Keith just demanded she be quiet. "Look out for kids." Despite every intention of shooting past the entrance to the town square without slowing, he crawled past the stores and streets until he entered the empty area between settlements one and two. He shot forward again, spinning his wheels as he rounded a corner.

"Keith!"

"I meant it. Shut up."

Erika's tiny house did its level best to loom in the distance, but nothing the size of a modest storage unit could be that imposing. When he slowed, Raina gasped. "Is that like a temporary place until she builds—?"

"It's her house. Stuff it."

"Stop treating me like some—"

Keith jerked into the drive and came to a jarring stop. He turned to face Raina and almost didn't blast her. Almost. "Then stop disrespecting my friend, our client, and the woman I love."

Her hazel eyes glared back at him. *Will I ever get used to those light eyes with her mahogany skin?*

"What?"

"Sorry… I can't wait for you to meet Erika. She's going to love you."

The scowl returned and Raina turned to open the door. "Whatever." Despite her display of nonchalance, by the time she caught up to him at Erika's door, Raina asked, "Why?"

"Why what?"

"Will your girlfriend like me?"

He unlocked the door before answering. *Glad Flynne locked it anyway…* "You are a lot alike, I think."

After that, she could have told him she'd hidden Erika away herself, and Keith wouldn't have heard it. He stepped inside and pulled out his gun in one smooth movement. Unnecessary—perhaps, but Keith didn't know what to expect.

His phone buzzed—Ralph. "Yeah?"

"Sorry, had to go. I can come back if you need me, but

I think Annie ate some bad chicken. I'd like to stick around here—"

"We're good, but thanks. Say hi to Annie for me. I'll pray for her."

The moment Keith disconnected, Raina pounced. "Who's Annie?"

"Ralph's wi—"

"Wife. Fine. Who's Ralph again?"

This is a total waste of time! I have a girlfriend I want to call wife someday to find and you want to know about my neighbors? It wasn't fair, of course. In the same situation, he'd be asking the same questions. They were valid—solid.

And wouldn't help him a bit right now.

"He started the town. That's all." And that's when Keith remembered the phone. He shoved his at Raina and asked her to call Ralph and ask where it was. "I'm going to start looking around."

It took exactly thirty seconds for him to see it—a tranq dart in the chair. Just as he would have groaned, Keith spied another on the shelf above the chair. Blood on the tips told a story. "Oh, no you didn't…"

"What?" Raina stepped up, Ziploc bagged phone in hand. Then she saw the tranqs. "No way… Two?"

"Flynne's not field trained."

"Erika could be *dead* by now! What was the potency of those darts?"

Why her words soothed, he couldn't have explained, but Keith just gathered the darts and moved on. A couple of market totes were gone… and food. Salad bags from the fridge—and cheese. The Doritos Erika had brought home the night before—and bananas. One small, empty cubbie confused him. "Why'd she take the trash bags?"

"Maybe she killed Erika? Two tranqs could in a small

woman. How big—?"

"If Erika was in medical distress, Flynne would have gotten help and called. She did this to keep Erika *out* of danger—"

"Then why tranq her? Why—?"

What else she said, Keith didn't hear. He ignored it and made a mental note *never* to work with her. *Raina makes me miss Corey at her worst.*

His phone rang again. Tyler's name flashed on the screen. Never had Keith Shafter... *or* Keith Auger answered a phone faster. "Whatcha got for me?" He set the phone on speaker and began examining Erika's. Had she tried to call him before Flynne shot her?

"I found what Flynne hid. Pretty smart. We've got the numbers of the phones she took, and something else..."

Just at that moment, Keith powered on the phone and stared at the screen. "Oh, no..."

"—posted to her Twitter. It's just a hashtag, but a weird one."

"#HASHTAGROGUE—with the word hashtag spelled out." Keith sank into the chair, staring at the phone. "This is bad, Tyler..."

Tyler's next words confirmed his suspicions. "I'm pretty sure Flynne wrote it, though. That's just the way she'd do it to make a point."

"Thanks Tyler. I've got to go. I'll check in when I'm done here, and I have a plan."

But he didn't get up. He just stared at the silly, silly tweet. #HASHTAGROGUE. Keith's mind churned. *Flynne, do you even realize that Erika knows more about protection detail than you do?*

"So, where do we go now?"

Eyes closed, Keith took a deep breath and tried to

remain as calm as possible. "I need a moment, all right?"

"C'mon, Keith. You really don't think that little miss 'unicorn dust and rainbow farts' is going to hurt your girlfriend, do you?"

Not laughing—impossible. When she kicked his ankle and demanded he take her seriously, he gave her a look that prompted an apology before adding, "I'm more worried about Flynne. Erika's going to kill her."

THREE

The sign announced the on-ramp to the Rockland loop a quarter mile ahead. Flynne glanced back at the still-sleeping Erika and racked her brains to figure out what to do. *You're dead.com! All the times you ignored strategy sessions because you thought, "Well, this isn't my circus, so who needs these monkeys?" Yeah. Bet you're regretting that now, aren't you, Dortmann?*

Instinct said to stay away from any place the Agency might know she knew about, and home obviously fit that bill. Flynne gripped the steering wheel and stared straight ahead as the ramp to the loop entrance appeared. The wheel jerked right—almost as if by itself and late enough that she barely missed the exit marker in the process.

Traffic surrounded her, and something about it felt strangely comforting. Cars zoomed by on her left, as she zipped past ones on her right. Blissful normalcy. *Totes underrated.*

As her exit neared, two sides of herself warred like angels and devils on cartoon shoulders. If only the halo didn't keep bouncing from one side to the other. *Which one of you creepy things is the creepiest?*

The idea that they might not expect her to go home so soon... or even that they might not know she'd "gone rogue" yet, prompted her to signal like a reasonable driver, shoot across two lanes in six seconds flat—not like a reasonable driver that time—and zip down the off-ramp. Her ideas formed and transformed as she worked her way through the city to her duplex three streets off Wharton Drive.

Her street—empty. Just the way she wanted it. Flynne made sure Erika was still asleep and breathing and climbed from the car. Though it probably lasted a good thirty seconds, Flynne stood at the back of her car and deliberated—planned. If she left Erika there—a big risk, but a huge time saver—and went to retrieve...

Risk or not, it was a plan and the only one she had. Flynne bolted from the car and began jogging. Four duplexes down, she froze. Backtracked. With the car doors locked, she raced back down the street.

On the other side of Wharton sat the Elmhurst neighborhood and the Detweiler's house—a key item in her still-forming plan. As if a beat, she ticked off each street as she jogged past. Arthur, George, James, Oliphant, Quaker. At Rosewood, she jerked right and raced to the fourth house down.

Fumbling for the right key, stumbling inside, punching the numbers into the keypad—it all took longer than it should have. Duty trumped desperation as she dashed for the mail, grabbed every plant in the house, and put them all in the bathtub. Two inches of water later, she shut off the tap and froze at the sight of a row of prescription medications on the counter.

"Should I take my Ambien, Roger?"

"You're due for a refill, and I forgot to stop for it. Let's get them there so you have plenty when you get home."

The conversation replayed itself until she made her decision. A glance inside showed about ten tablets. Flynne took five. In the kitchen, she fumbled through drawers until she found a snack baggie.

Most of the houses on Rosewood had detached garages, and the Detweiler's did, too. But theirs was a double, and Flynne had seen the inside often enough to know that they had bicycles... and a bicycle *trailer* with a canopy. Sure, it was meant for kids, but asleep, Erika could fold up enough to make it a couple of miles. Right?

It took four trips to the key cupboard in the kitchen before Flynne found the one that would open the garage door, but inside three minutes, she zipped back down 42nd Avenue to Wharton. Riding *back* would not be as easy.

Getting an unconscious woman into the trailer—not easy either. Flynne opted for leaning through the trailer, hooking her arms under Erika's underarms, and pulling. That landed Flynne across the trailer, her chin slamming against the bar. "That's totes gonna bruise."

Using her elbows for leverage, she propped herself up and pulled again. And again. The bicycle shifted and scratched her car door. "Mark's gonna pay for that."

Every grunt cost her boss fifty dollars, she decided. By the time she finally got Erika mostly into the trailer, he owed her four hundred-fifty dollars. By the time she was neatly tucked in and zipped up tight, the total was six hundred even.

Flynne pulled her car into the carport, dropped the screen she used to protect the back from summer sun, and bolted into her duplex. One backpack later, and a quick check to see that Erika was still out for the count, she began the long, miserable ride back to the Detweiler's house. *Gotta be grateful for Christian schools that save spring break for Easter week, or I'd be sunk right now. Hashtag go God.* She winced. *Is that sacrilegious? Probably.* Her gaze shot up to a fluffy cloud overhead, and she whispered, "It was meant as a compliment—if you really are up there."

Despite the perfect sixty-seven-degree temps, the sun beating down on her, the effort required to pull her own body weight plus trailer, and the adrenaline of being totally out of her element conspired to perspire. She soaked a shirt enough to do any pro ball player proud. Lungs screaming, legs burning, she pulled onto Rosewood in twice the time it had taken her to get there and back the first time.

Pedaling up into the driveway—nearly impossible. Even jumping off the bike and pushing it proved little better. Only the idea of having to leave Erika exposed kept her going until they pulled into the garage.

Flynne rolled down the door and collapsed on the floor next to the bike and trailer, panting with the desperation of a dog and none of the enthusiasm. Cool concrete next to her cheek. Bliss.

Erika ordered her eyes to open. They declined the offer. Once more, and with as much of a mental drill sergeant tone as she could muster, she demanded the possibility of sight.

Neither eyelid gave so much as a twitch.

Resigned, she then tried to ascertain the reason for said uncooperation by the lids of her eyes. Her brain, too, had gone AWOL. White noise replaced rational thought, grit replaced natural eye moisture, and if the sensation coming from her tongue could be trusted, she'd transformed into a cottonmouth.

Except that I can't slither. I know I can't.

That, Erika decided, was improvement. It just had to be rational thought. *Oh, God please.*

A question arose. *Do I pray?* The moment she asked, Erika nodded — inwardly, anyway. *I do. Not sure since when... maybe that'll come next.*

Clarity formed when a voice broke through what might or might not have been consciousness. "Oh, thank whatever you're supposed to thank — don't want to be, like, totes offensive if I'm not supposed to say, 'God,' but I was afraid you had flat-lined."

"Flynne?"

"Yay! She lives!"

Why do I feel like that's supposed to be "He lives?"

"So, can you, like, sit up if I help you?"

Bile churned in Erika's gut. Her eyes felt like they bugged, but she wasn't even confident she could see anymore. Then Flynne's purple, green, and blue hair came into view. She glared, wrestling her mouth into contortions and fighting back the urge to vomit. "Please!"

It came out more like, "Mmmweeeeeeffff"

"Can't understand you." Flynne's eyes narrowed.

Perspiration formed on Erika's forehead, neck, and in every other uncomfortable place. Cold, clammy perspiration.

"Do you promise not to scream if I take this off?" She tapped the tape.

Erika just nodded with vehemence that nearly lost her what breakfast she'd eaten.

Again, Flynne's eyes grew even narrower than the first time. "Okay..." Eyes wide, the girl ripped off her high-top converse and pulled a sock from her foot. "So help me, if you scream, I'm stuffing *this* in your mouth — supes gross." She wriggled it for effect — just in case Erika didn't catch the utter disgustingness of it.

Once more, Erika nodded and pleaded. *You're so going to regret threatening me with that.*

If Satan wanted to recruit torturers to relieve demons, Flynne would have been perfect for the job. She worked the tiniest corner of the duct tape free. Erika choked and grimaced. She jerked her head hard to the right. Flynne stared. Once more, she jerked it.

"You want me to rip it off? That'll hurt!"

But the moment Flynne said "rip," Erika began bobbing her head fast enough to ensure she'd drown in vomit within seconds. Flynne had mad ripping skills, however. In less than three seconds, the tape jerked free — and so did the contents of Erika's stomach.

All over Flynne's bare foot and Converse shoes. The moment she stopped heaving, Erika glared up at the girl and moaned, "That's payback for this."

The battle of the glares began. Flynne broke the silence that followed first. "If you weren't Keith's girlfriend and religious, I'd swear at you. Consider yourself cussed out." Before Erika could choose between the half-dozen scathing remarks fighting for preeminence, Flynne froze. "Wait. You called *me*, like, every name in the book. I thought you religies couldn't do that!"

The churning began again. "I did?" If she could have gagged, she would have. If she could have *puked*, she might have. "Do I want to know what I said?"

Without hesitation, Flynne rattled off every inappropriate word Erika had spent the last six months working to eradicate from her vocabulary. "Then you got all sesquipedalian on me."

"Sesquatch-what?"

Flynne turned a little green herself as the stench of

partially digested breakfast assaulted her olfactory system. "Sesquipedalian." At Erika's doubtful look, Flynne went into action. She removed her other shoe, disappeared outside, and returned with clean feet and ready to do business. "For your information it's a big word that means, 'a big word.'"

"No offense, Flynne, but you aren't exactly known for your erudition."

The girl gave a fine imitation of a puppy cocking its head—a blue, green, and purple-haired puppy. "That's not one of the word-of-the-day words I've had. C'mon... let's get you cleaned up and inside."

She peered around the garage door, scanned the area, and looked back at Erika. "No one's in the neighborhood—not that I can tell, anyway—but you'd be smart not to go all screamo on me or anything that would call the cops."

"And why's that?"

Flynne tried to be surreptitious, but Erika caught her eying a white Camry on the other side of the garage before answering, "Because I can get you out of here before they arrive, and you don't want to be awake when I'm driving fast."

Something deep in her gut—something *other* than the renewed churning that hinted she might lose what was left of the contents of her stomach—hinted that Flynne might not be exaggerating. *But I'm not going to let her know that. It'd serve her right if I puked all over that car. What'd she do with hers, anyway?*

After throwing a dark look at her, Flynne stalked from the garage and returned a few minutes later with a roll of duct tape slid over her arm like a grunge bracelet gone wrong. "You're already in hot water with the Big Guy for your potty mouth, so don't add lies. Stuff it or stick it?"

"If you tape my mouth and I vomit, you'll be responsible for my death. Just sayin'."

"Then don't make *noise*." Flynne glared at her. "I'm just trying to help here. *Just sayin'.*"

Didn't know you had that much grit. The woozy, stomach-revolting-on-every-side feeling returned in time for Erika to make a decision. "I'm not going to scream. I don't want to puke in a cop car, either. But if you don't get me inside where I can be comfortably horizontal with a bowl by my side, I'm going to puke all over you and enjoy every second of it." Her stomach rumbled. *Mostly.*

That perked Flynne up for reasons Erika couldn't fathom. She hooked her tape-free arm under Erika's and said, "Then let's go, Kokomo!"

That's way too old-school—like fifty years old school. A vague memory poked through the cloud cover of her mind. "I think Keith gave me vitamins or drugs to combat aftereffects. I think I need those."

Not until Flynne had her tucked up on a couch in the family room, a bright red mixing bowl on the floor beside it and a glass of water on the coffee table, did Flynne bother to answer. "Sorry. I was freakazoiding when I left The Agency and just got what I thought I needed to get you safe. I'm not trained for this."

"Then call Keith. He'll come. He *is* trained, and he'll take care of me."

Even as she said it, Erika knew it was futile. Flynne had it in her head that this was necessary. So, she could wait. The Agency would take care of her job, her bills, and Flynne could learn that being an agent wasn't a good career choice. Everything would be just fine for a few days—until Flynne got over herself.

The first epithet marched across the stage of her mind,

34

stepped up to the mic and tapped it, ready to let loose. Erika groaned.

As if propelled by itself, the red bowl appeared at her lips. "I'm sorry! I don't know what I'm doing. The stuff these guys have to do—totes amazeballs!"

"I was groaning at my language. Can you be quiet for a minute or two while I pray? It's totes impossible to take repentance seriously when you're puffy hearting your cray-cray amazeballs."

"Coolio. Sure thing."

I just lost fifty IQ points. I know it. Let's start with prayers for rejuvenated little gray cells and move onto repentance after that, okay, Lord?

FOUR

Angled with a perfect view of the front doors of the Mayflower Building, he watched. One by one, agents arrived. Tyler and Raina met at the doors and entered together. *She cleans up well. You'd never know she lives in yoga pants, sports bras, and oversized muscle shirts.*

Keith stormed the doors as if he considered it his own personal citadel—determined to conquer. Karen arrived thirty seconds later in heels, pencil skirt, and carrying a designer bag that had probably come out of her expense account. He grinned at it.

Good for you.

Doyle and Brian entered only ten seconds apart, but Doyle was so preoccupied with his phone that he didn't realize he'd allowed the door to close in Brian's face. *Unless they had a bad detail—or disagreed on calling it complete... should have debriefed first.*

Should have or not, there wasn't time. Keith and Tyler had searched every place they imagined Flynne going and found only her car—at home. No sign of Flynne anywhere, and no neighbors around to see things they didn't even know they had. *If I wasn't so ticked at her, I'd be impressed. She won't last long, but to make it out of her own neighborhood without a car and with a "client..." That's impressive.*

Sam wore slacks—no skirt. He'd have to talk to her about that. For their gatherings, they needed to balance

37

blending and standing out as individuals instead of a group. She blended great—not so much the standing out bit.

Tim, Jude, and Darryl strode up one after the other. *It's a good thing we've got a full crew now.*

Just as he reached for the door handle, a red car that looked much too much like a west coast agent's for his comfort tore into the parking lot and stopped in front of the double glass doors. As the car door flung open, Mark climbed from his car, slipped his hand into his suit coat, and reached for the holstered gun. He took a step. The man bolted for the doors. Mark took two steps... three. Cautious, but deliberate

Too short for Henry... Could it be Will Rickwood?

Mark made a dash for the door, but moments later, two security guards escorted the man—clearly not Will, no less—from the building and stood there until he peeled out of the parking lot. Then they turned to look at him. Mark pretended not to notice. He patted himself down and returned to the car. A moment later, he made a show of putting his wallet in his pocket and striding from the car.

"Everything all right, sir?"

Mark jerked his head to the left at the stockier guy's question. He infused a trace of a Spanish accent into his voice as he asked, "Pardon me?"

"I asked if everything was all right?"

He stared at the guy with as much attitude as he could muster. "If forgetting my wallet is a crisis, no. Otherwise, yes. Are you here to take care of that...?" Mark scanned the area. "Well, I guess you did. Good work getting rid of that fool. Thanks."

Without another word, he strode into the building and stood in the security line. The moment Mark stepped up for his turn, the security guard pounded his wand, shrugged, and grabbed another. "Dead battery or something," he muttered to the guy next to him. It blipped, showed green, and the guard waved him through. As usual.

0000 01 000 0000 1 01 110   010 111 110 001 0

The phone's camera clicked without a sound. Despite a vague familiarity to the man, who it was proved elusive. Still, with the arrival of every new face, one finger tapped a screen and held it down—continuous shot. All the way inside.

Repeat. Repeat. Repeat.

The count and photography continued. By the time the number reached six, a foot slid across the brake pedal before tapping once. *Zzzttth... thop. Zzzttth... thop.*

At ten, doubt crept in. Which ones belonged to Marco's crew, and which worked in the building? At fifteen, a fire-engine red Audi TT ripped into the parking lot. The finger tapped and held until the man entered the building. Ten seconds later, the process repeated in reverse—a waste of time, probably, but still...

Zzzttth... thop.

The man who stepped from his car... difficult to tell. He froze, patted himself down, returned. A moment later, the guards stopped him. Waiting... watching... pictures.

Zzzttth... thop. Zzzttth... thop. Zzzttth... thop.

After following Karen Stenano to the building, it hadn't taken much effort to pull in first and park. Still, a meeting right as everyone arrived back from lunch— genius on the new owner's part. But why...?

The new owner... Mendina. Too bad it wasn't Cho. *He'd* been spotted entering Subsix, the underwater nightclub in the Maldives, less than an hour earlier. A glance at the photos — side, back, hint of a profile... But was it? The foot dragged and tapped again.

Zzzttth... thop.

A second look at the Maldives photo confirmed. Definitely Cho. Poor Claire. She'd be devastated to hear of Mark's new interest. A smile formed. *A weak spot.*

Zzzttth... thop.

New owner, unbalanced former employee, devastated current employee... *Very nice.*

A moment later, another car peeled into the parking lot and came to a sharp stop in the next parking space. The hair, the half-run, half-hop as heels replaced flip-flops... *Speak of the devil's angel... Claire Auger.*

The smile became real, warm, content.

Zzzttth... thop.

Let's play.

0000 01 000 0000 1 01 110   010 111 110 001 0

In a secure room in the sub-level of the Mayflower Building — a level most thought was part of the foundation, Mark stood at the head of the table, hands relaxed in his pockets. Only the faintest twitch of the corner of his left eye belied the truth.

He's agitated. Why? Just *Flynne and Erika, or more? I guess we'll see...*

Keith sat at the opposite end of the table and watched the agents. A hand squeezed his. He smiled at his cousin and nodded. Claire squeezed again. "Flynne wouldn't hurt her."

"She shot Erika—used tranqs. She's not trained for that."

From the other end of the table, Doyle sat up. The man looked nothing like the rest of their agents. Short, scrawny, glasses. Anyone who saw him would assume he belonged upstairs with the actuarial department. *And he's the best we have.*

"Keith, did you say *Flynne* shot Erika?"

"Yes."

Doyle removed his glasses and polished them with a square of cloth from inside his suit jacket. "Tranq, correct?"

The low murmur around the table ceased. All eyes turned to Keith first before shifting to Mark. All but Doyle's. He shook his head. "Doubtful that one of even the highest dose cartridges would—"

"Two." All Keith said was that one word. *Two.*

Claire squeezed again and dashed to the empty chair at the front.

Everything in the room shifted. Mark broke into the conversation. "We'll discuss this in a minute. First, we need to look at a few potential cases."

Keith had only been to one other briefing with so many agents present at once. Usually, there were too many detailed to cases to make an all-hands meeting. Only Sol and Wylie remained on a case in the UP, and seeing who remained showed just how much of a hit The Agency had taken in recent months.

I don't even know half of these guys. We've been decimated—squared. Seven agents. Gone—eight, if you count me. That's more like cubed. Ugh. Irrelevant thoughts tried to crowd out the fear in his heart. *Is there a word for thirty percent? Tri... something.*

41

"After the mess with Helen Franklin, I've become even more vigilant to cross-check all requests, but even still, too many of our agents have left us—not to mention Jill and Tony."

A hush fell over the already mostly silent room at the mention of the agents Franklin had killed over a year earlier. "So, before we continue, if anyone would like to exit now, please do so. I have two private party security positions and one with Secret Service waiting for anyone who is no longer comfortable or confident in our ability to send you into reasonable scenarios."

Every eye in the room stared at Mark. No one moved. "All right, then. I'll be splitting the salaries of the agents we've lost between the rest of you for the next three months—even if I manage to replace them. You may count on the salary adjustment to last at least through the end of July. I'll reevaluate then."

His jaw twitched, despite himself. Keith shoved his hands in his pockets to keep his fingers from tapping out Morse code or at least the beat to "Eye of the Tiger."

A few people nodded. Doyle scribbled something on a paper and passed it to Mark. Tension thickened until it became difficult to breathe. Was that—did Mark swallow hard? Keith couldn't be sure. A glance at his phone showed fifteen minutes shot. Fifteen minutes that they could have used to find Erika before Flynne did something dangerously stupid.

"Doyle has pointed out that with continued attacks on us, we need to accept that *we*—and by we, I mean *you all*—may become targets. If you'd rather not leave now, please just let me know *before* you take your next assignment. Your contracts *are* valid, and I will prosecute anyone who abandons a client during an assignment."

Tension relaxed a little when Claire leaned back, propped her feet up on the table, and crossed her arms and ankles in one fluid movement. "Like any of us would do something so selfish and stupid. You pick good people." She tossed a sassy wink at Mark and said, "And that's not just because you picked *me*."

Claire… really?

But it seemed to buoy Mark again. "Okay, then." Mark lifted a stack of files from the floor in front of the table. "Take one and pass them…" He set half in front of Doyle and the other half in front of Claire. "I need to know who we're accepting, if anyone. I have my thoughts, but I want your input right now."

A low murmur began as people discussed the contents of the first file. Keith flipped through and made an instant decision. *Nope. Excessive. This guy heard about the Agency and wants to brag about using it.* That done, he concentrated on *not* jostling his heel or tapping his knee.

Mark sent out the next dossier… and the next. Unanimous opinion came in to accept the last two. Only Doyle agreed to the first. Keith made a mental note of that. *Of anyone, Doyle should know better.*

Still, the man might have his reasons. Keith raised his hand. "If the first comes in after we find Erika and Flynne, and if Doyle wants someone with him, I'll work that one. I don't think he should go in alone or with anyone who doesn't *choose* to."

Mark nodded, and with that nod, Keith felt confident his warning had been received. *Now, can we find Erika before I lose what semblance of self-control I have left?*

"Okay, before Keith comes unglued, we need to get on the main reason we're here. First—assignments." He turned and gave an apologetic glance to the left side of the table. "Sorry, Tyler. You're in the office until we get Flynne back. I need someone who knows the business."

"I was going to request it. I want to try to find her from there—cameras and such."

"Great." Mark scanned the room. "Raina and Sol—be ready for the Langat case." Doyle's displeasure radiated through the room. "Sorry, Doyle. You're too politically minded for this one."

"I understood it, but that doesn't kill the desire."

"Understood. Okay. Doyle and Sam will handle the Schmatloch case."

Appeasing? Really? I didn't think you could stoop to that. You're more nervous than you want to admit. Great.

"Okay, so this is what we know about the Flynne situation."

Every person in the room sat up and leaned forward. Keith relaxed just a little. Taking it seriously meant they'd have Erika home today—likely within hours. *And then I give Flynne a piece of my mind.*

"Tyler, can you tell us what we know?"

Tyler pulled out his phone and began talking without looking up. "The timeline I've created shows Flynne approaching Mark with a surveillance concern at approximately nine o'clock. She'd been working since five this morning, so it is not unreasonable that she left for lunch fifteen minutes later. Before leaving, she packed ten thousand dollars—"

A gasp went up from Sam. "Flynne *stole* ten *thousand* dollars from The Agency?"

Keith couldn't let that pass, even as ticked as he was. "I imagine she considers it expenses for her protection. She'll likely return anything she doesn't use."

Several other murmurs started, and Mark stepped in.

"Let Tyler finish before we become sidetracked with things that aren't important."

"Right. So, she also left with two tranq guns and enough CO2 and cartridges to hold out for quite a while. Additionally, she took three phones and logged everything in our hardcopy log. That she filed in Keith's agent file, which I think was a challenge to him. I think she wants to be found, because she knows she's in over her head."

"Then why not just ask—?"

Mark stepped in again. "Okay, just hang in there. Tyler's almost done."

"Right. Well, at ten-fifteen, Keith got a call to come in. We know that by eleven-thirty, they were long gone. Two tranq darts were found in Erika's living room. Additionally, clothing and food were found missing, and Erika's phone was left on her counter."

"Hashtag," Keith growled.

Tyler gulped down water from a bottle Keith hadn't even seen him bring in. "Right. The last thing on the phone was a tweet sent at ten forty-seven. It said, 'pound sign, hashtag rogue.'"

This time, Sam commented. "Wait... she used the hashtag and then *wrote* hashtag rogue?"

"Yes. Mark called this meeting immediately, and while we waited for everyone to arrive, I went to Flynne's duplex. There, I found her car in the carport. I *think* clothes are missing from her house, but I can't be sure. I don't pay much attention to what she wears. It also feels like some food is gone, but not much—lightweight stuff like chips, microwave popcorn, salad bags, and stuff. All the heavy fruit, canned food, frozen food, and such are still there. She obviously just went shopping."

Murmurs filled the room as they realized Tyler had

finished. Keith scanned every face and stopped at Doyle. He toyed with a pen and his pad of paper. A moment later, he elbowed Tyler. "Think she's going hiking? Did she have trainers or hiking boots that are missing?"

"Her not-broken-in running shoes are gone, from what I can tell. Why?"

"Because," Keith interjected. "Lightweight food and shoes with traction hint at hiking."

Doyle nodded.

"Flynne hates nature."

"That's"—both men began in unison. At Doyle's nod, Keith finished for both of them. "What she'd want you to say."

"How could she go hiking without a car to get there? Is she really going to get Erika to walk to… what? A tour bus? A friend's house with a camper?"

Without hesitation, Keith pulled out his phone and punched Ralph's picture with force enough to put an eye out if it had actually been the man. "Ralph, check the treeler for me. Be careful, though. Don't let Rory or Andre go out there right now."

The entire room stared at him now. Keith shrugged. "A tornado flung a travel trailer up in a huge oak. It's been secured there as a tree house. Flynne knows about it, and it's near where we live. Flynne would try to divert our attention, so…"

"Good thinking."

Keith nodded at Doyle and turned back to Mark. "I want permission—although, I'm going to do it anyway, just so you know—to go check out this surveillance guy Flynne was worried about. Perhaps if we let her know we've cleared him, she'll return."

Mark nodded. "Go. I'll update you once we're done

here."

With that, Keith bolted from the room. *I'll find you, Flynne, and then you'd better be glad you're not a Christian. If you were, I'd be tempted to give you a one-way ticket to those pearly gates.*

FIVE

Large, over-stuffed, clunky furniture filled the Detweiler's family room. Flynne recognized and could name every piece in there. Pottery Barn, circa 2000. She'd drooled over the catalogs until her mother had banned them from the house.

And now it's all outdated. Everyone wants the equivalent of a skinny jean couch now.

Still, Mona Detweiler could rhapsodize about the superiority of her new West Elm living room, but the old couch was twice as comfy as the new one. If Erika's snore meant anything, even she agreed. Of course, the denim blue canvas wore better than the thin, dove gray linen that had replaced it.

Flynne grabbed the upholstery brush and worked some more cleaner into the arm where Erika had missed the bowl. *Easier to scrub, too.*

As Flynne rose and cracked her back once more, a car rolled down the street—at less than five miles per hour. The driver craned her neck to peer at the houses on the opposite side of the street. Five doors down, it pulled in front of a blue and bleached brick house and parked.

Flynne dumped the bowl, rinsed, washed, and rinsed again, dried, and put it away. A second glance out the door showed the woman sitting there still. *It's not Karen, Raina, or Sam. Ergo, it's either innocent or worse than one of them. But*

49

which is it? A second look prompted a second thought. *At least if I have to borrow the Detweiler's car, she won't know it until it's too late. It's almost dark, so maybe keep the lights off...?*

A glance at the giant train clock in the corner told her sundown would be soon. *I need to plan... but how? Why? Where can we go? And no one knows I'm house sitting, so...* Staying put would be ideal—if Erika continued to cooperate with the whole not screaming bit, and if Tyler hadn't ever heard her mention going to the Detweiler's house.

The car still sat in place when Flynne looked out again. A scan of the street showed about half the residents home—but not the ones in the blue and brick house. *I need a plan. In case we have to go fast, I need a plan.*

Taking the Detweiler's car was a given. She'd already been given permission to use it. Okay, so they hadn't meant for days and days, but with them in Bavaria through May, they wouldn't know until Erika was home safe and the whole thing settled. *I should start with a note. Yeah. A note. In case something happens to me.*

An inexplicable sense of urgency prompted her to scour the house for note paper until she gave up and grabbed a sheet of printer paper. With it folded in half, she grabbed a pen and tried to figure out how to explain that she'd taken their car and would try not to ruin it without making promises she didn't know she could keep.

In the end, she wrote a blunt, no-excuses note that would definitely get her fired.

Mona,

I had an emergency that I can't explain. I used your house for a little while, took five of your Ambien tablets, and borrowed your car. I did clean up after myself, and I'll be back with your car as soon as I can. I'll also pay you back for everything.

50

If anything happens to me, I hope this counts as a legal document, because I'm willing my bank account and my car to you as compensation for the loss of yours.

Thanks for giving me fun money these last few months. You've been totally eptastic.

Flynne

It sounded like a suicide note—except for the paying back part, anyway. Still, it made her feel better. And it was a plan. *Anything gets weird, and we're outta here.*

The car still sat out front, waiting. If the head bopping meant anything, at least the driver was listening to something fun. *Assassins don't listen to fun music, right? They're more death metal, aren't they?*

Soft stirring sounds from the couch sent Flynne into proactive mode. *We're eating. Then, I'll clean up....* From what to pack first to how to get Erika into the car, Flynne decided everything but the most important thing. How to get Erika to cooperate. *That* would take some serious skills.

She pulled a salad bag from the fridge, rinsed off the lettuce, and dug in the freezer. Chicken nuggets might not be as good as grilled, but they'd both need protein.

She'd just popped a dozen into the microwave when Erika's moan reached her. "Flynne?"

"You okay?"

"Get dizzy when I sit up. I think you overdid the tranqs."

Heat flooded her as she peered around the corner and saw Erika sitting with her head in her hands. Flynne raced to grab a glass of water. The way Erika grabbed it and held on with a death grip unsettled her enough to prompt a confession. "It might be the half an Ambien you had after you fell asleep."

"You..." Erika growled the word into about six

51

syllables. "You gave me *more* drugs?"

"Drink? I think you need to flush your body. And you wouldn't stop ranting, so I thought maybe it would just put you to sleep while I figured out..."

The rest of the words faded as the car she'd been watching started up and did a U-turn. Five seconds later, right in front of the Detweiler's house, it paused. Flynne jumped back behind the curtains and pointed to Erika. "Get *down*."

Erika flopped over, spilling water all over herself, the floor, the couch, and the coffee table. "Ugh! What?"

Seconds passed until the lights grew bright enough to make it obvious that a car was coming from the other direction. "I can't see without showing myself, but I think someone is coming this way. Hang on...."

A moment later, the first car made yet another U-turn and pulled up to the blue and brick house again. The woman flew from the car and met a guy at the end of the drive. "I think we're clear," Flynne continued her commentary as a kiss to rival all movie kisses commenced. "Either they haven't seen each other for a while, or this is the beginning of a makeup-slash-make-out session."

"Meanwhile, I'm drenched."

The microwave beeped—probably for the tenth time. Flynne hadn't even heard it. She grabbed one of the tranq guns from her backpack and went to cut the duct tape shackles she'd contrived for Erika's ankles. "I'll cut your wrists when we get to the bathroom. Go."

"Do you know how creepy that sounds?" Erika groaned as she stood. "Don't forget dry clothes. I'm not standing naked in a weird bathroom while you try to do fifty things at once."

Despite her words, Flynne scooped up Erika's duffel

bag and carried it to the bathroom. There, she ripped the duct tape with her teeth."

"I hope I got vomit on that."

Flynne huffed. "Stop mocking me. I'm trying to *help* you."

"Then get me to someone who could actually protect me if I really was in danger. This..." she wriggled her wrists at Flynne. "This doesn't inspire confidence."

The stress of the day combined with Erika's total lack of appreciation for the exertions expended on her behalf and a dash of low blood sugar "hangriness." The result was the tranq gun pointed at Erika's gut. "Get changed."

"You know it'll take ten to twenty minutes for that to make a difference."

"Probably eight to fifteen," Flynne countered. "It's probably not all out of your system."

Erika shrugged. "It's still not fast enough."

The sneer that used to make Flynne's cousins quake in their Keds didn't faze Erika in the slightest—not until Flynne added, "No, but you won't like the feeling of a tranq dart or two in your stomach."

A flicker of something—was it surprise?—appeared in her eyes. The way Erika began stripping right there in front of her hinted she'd made her point. With that threat in her hip pocket, Flynne turned to go. "I'll be in the kitchen. Don't try anything funny. Mona is totes big on cast iron, and I'm not afraid to use it."

"Wrong person."

She turned back. "Huh?"

"Flynn gets the frying pan over the head—not the other way around."

The words made no sense. "You're just trying to confuse me."

As Erika jerked a dry T-shirt over her head, she muttered, "In *Tangled*. Rapunzel uses the frying pan to protect herself *from* Flynn Ryder." At Flynne's blink, she added. "I'm the prisoner here, so that makes *me* Rapunzel. I get the frying pan. You get the goose egg."

"Shut up and change your pants." She stormed down the hall and would have felt rather proud of herself if Erika's laughter hadn't followed. *This is soooo way harder than I thought.*

0000 01 000 0000 1 01 110   010 111 110 001 0

Flynne knew about his penthouse at the Harbinger Building, so to ensure he actually slept, Mark went across town, almost into Westbury, to the Wexfield house. Property records showed it belonging to Ivy Trent—a name he'd stolen from an old Gene Kelly movie. Ivy Trent, however, was actually a DBA he used for a few private holdings he didn't want traced to himself.

Privacy is under-appreciated in today's world.

The moment he disarmed the interior alarm, the outdoor cameras were armed, and fifteen seconds later, a green light began flashing—the surveillance crew was on it. Blissful sleep awaited.

First, the gym. Two slow laps in the pool. Four moderate. Rest. Ten fast. Rest. Four moderate. Rest. Two slow. Mark clung to the side, panting. When his arms were willing to support him, he hoisted himself up and stepped into the corner shower. Hot water… shampoo and rinse. Warm water, soap up and rinse. Cold water—stand until he couldn't take another drop.

With a thick terry robe around him and a towel to dry

his hair, he made his way into the kitchen and peered into the fridge. Nothing looked tasty—nothing that wouldn't take an hour to fix. "Protein shake it is."

An hour after he arrived home, Mark climbed beneath the covers and snapped off the light. With a tap, the white noise machine came on at his usual low setting. Five minutes later, he bumped it up a few notches. Fail.

That left a conundrum. If he flipped on the light, the surveillance crew would check in on him. If he didn't, he'd either need to take something to make him sleep—not possible with the Flynne and Schmatloch situations—or lie there until boredom ate his soul.

Soul… Mark sat up, flipped on the lamp, and waited with fingers hovering over the intercom button. It blipped. He tapped it. "All's well. Can't sleep. Reading instead." All two-word sentences. If he used three words, they'd mobilize. *Can't even remember what it's like not to have to think about it. Would Claire be able to stand it?*

That was all it took. Mark pulled the Bible from his drawer and flipped it open. Acts… he'd start there. Again.

One chapter, two… five. Fifteen… Two hours passed and he'd nearly finished when his phone blipped. Mark turned the page with one hand and swiped his screen with the other. His gut churned at the name that glowed back at him. *Nick Fahrina. What prompts this one?*

"Hello."

"You have a problem."

Interesting choice of words… None of his usual disconnected responses would work with that one. He hesitated, but there wasn't any way out of it—not if Fahrina called. "What kind of problem?"

"I have a gal dogging me everywhere I go. She's convinced that her sister was murdered, and it's being

55

covered up."

"And this is my problem because…"

A huff sounded more like an arctic blast through the airwaves. "Because I finally gave her ten minutes to convince me to look into her concerns. She did it in one."

"And *her* name is…?"

Nick Fahrina's voice deepened as he said, "Olivienne Todd."

Oh, no…. Without bothering to deny it, Mark asked, "What convinced you?"

"She said, and I quote, 'My sister supposedly died while hiking in the woods up by Lake Vienna. Here's the thing. I found out she paid her gas bill the day she died. You can't get cell reception up much past the lake once you start hiking—not since they upgraded the tower…'"

Changing the date of death bit us this time. A few choice words bubbled over.

Fahrina didn't sound amused when he said, "Glad you find it funny. I have a girl who is on a mission to prove a cover-up."

"Sorry. Made the wrong call that time. Should have stuck with the actual date of death."

"I can trust you to handle this?"

"Yes." Mark disconnected the call and stared at the empty bed beside him. "With any other woman, she'd be there—now. When I want her." He picked up the Bible and glared at it. A moment later, it smashed against the wall beside his bathroom door and landed in a heap on the floor.

SIX

A keyring hung suspended from one finger. Another finger flipped the far-right key up… It fell over to the other side with the slow swing of a hammer-head carnival ride and landed with a *plink.* The next key didn't make it to the top before it clattered back into place. *Plink!*

Nondescript. It was the best description *for* the house on Rosewood. Nondescript. Gray siding, painted white brick, manicured landscaping that looked ripped from a Playmobil set, obligatory welcome mat.

Two days they'd hunkered down in the house belonging to Karl and Mona Detweiler. That silly peacock of a girl, Flynne Dortmann—another German name. There was Schmatloch, too. Three. Interesting how that worked out.

Another flick to the last key. This time it spun around as it should. *Plink!*

How long could they hole up in the Detweiler's house before fear sent them running? That would make a mess of things. Too much hassle to look when one could just follow.

Alert The Agency somehow? The tech guy-turned-agent… *Tyler.* Yes… he and Flynne had a thing going.

Another key couldn't quite make the crest and fell back into place. *Plink!*

As tempting as it might be, the simplest solution, as

usual, was the most obvious. *The brother*. A bozo picture appeared, and with a tap everything changed. "Rosewood Court. Slow pass once an hour." A moment later, a picture zipped its way across cities and countryside in the space of a second. "Slow in front of that one."

"For how long?"

"You'll know."

At the disconnect, a flick of the hand sent all keys spinning over the finger, caught in one movement.

Splink!

0000 01 000 0000 1 01 110   010 111 110 001 0

Thirty-six hours. Twice as long as she'd expected—and twice as irritating. If Keith hadn't found them yet, then she needed to act herself. As it was, Erika knew more about how to do the protective detail than Flynne did. The girl alternated between cowering in the house with all drapes and blinds closed and practically announcing their presence to the world.

"Hey, Flynne?"

The girl turned the tranq gun on her again. "Yeah?"

"If you want to keep the cops at bay, you might not want to do that where anyone can drive by and see you."

"Do wha—oh." She turned her back to the window and kept it pointed. "Tape your ankles."

"What?

Flynne glared. "Choose. Taped up or in the bathroom with me. I gotta pee."

"Can you just grab some zip ties from the kitchen trash or something? What if I promise that I won't move? There's not a landline in here, anyway, so it's not like I can call for help."

Flynne got a *look* on her face—one Erika didn't like. The girl waved the gun at her. "Go on. I have an idea."

"What's that?"

"What my mom did when I was little. It works great, and we don't have to, like, trash the planet with wasted duct tape."

At the bathroom, Flynne entered and pushed the door mostly shut. "Grab the handle on the inside and hold on. If you let go, I'm chasing you down and shooting you in the butt with this thing again, and I don't care who sees."

"I'll promise not to go anywhere if you'll find a way to show me the guy you think is stalking me."

Flynne spun in place and stared. "Pinky promise? On like, Keith's grave—or better... *Jesus'* grave?

"Not allowed to do the swear thing, Flynne. I'm pretty sure that's one of the things we *can't* do. But, seriously, I don't want to be where someone can get me if they're after me. I'll stand there, hold the dumb doorknob, listen to all the things I do not want to hear going on in that bathroom, but then you've got to find a way to show me this guy."

It took twenty-seven seconds—not that Erika counted or anything—for Flynne to enter the bathroom and empty her bladder. It took triple that time for her to exit—wiping damp hands on her yoga pants. At Erika's prodding look, she just said, "If you're going to dress one-handed, you shouldn't wear anything with Lycra."

She held the gun the whole time. Why? So she could shoot my fingers? Really? So as not to antagonize the girl with the gun, Erika reduced her sarcasm level to Defcon 5 and said, "I'll try to remember that. Where's a computer?"

The home office—impressive. With dual, large-screened monitors and a desktop that booted in ten seconds flat, if Erika had a job that required any techiness, she'd want *that* room. "Nice."

"It's not bad. I tried to get Mona to let me make a few security tweaks, but she said no." The sigh that followed sounded just like a toddler doing his best to sound as grown up as possible to show his mother how ridiculous she is.

The first password failed—as did the second, third, fifth, and tenth. Lucky eleven, however, got her in. "Interesting," Flynne muttered.

"What's interesting?"

"I threw out her boss's name and it got me into her computer. Why her boss's name? That seems weird."

"What's weird is that you not only remembered that name, but you thought to use it."

Flynne began typing, and as she did, she explained. "Always start with levels of contact—not knowledge, contact. Spouse, kids, pets, favorite things—and move out. Since merlot didn't make it, I tried her boss because he was next. I suspected her personal trainer. At least he's eptastically hot."

Ignoring the eptastic word, Erika brought the conversation back to some semblance of normalcy. "How would you know?"

"Instagram."

Who could argue with that? Some women posted their breakfasts of coffee and muffins, clearly Mona Detweiler liked to post her crunches and stud-muffin. Before she could comment, a third, incognito window prompted Erika to ask. "Why are you using those? You of all people should know that they're not any safer than a regular window."

"And you should know enough about computer stuff

to know that people have to know that they can look and *where* to look to find it. It's the best I can do from this site without messing with stuff that wouldn't be right."

Like kidnapping, drugging, and holding me hostage is the epitome of moral excellence. A wince followed. *Ouch. Salty, much?*

"Okay... here..."

One by one, pictures of a man, usually hidden from view, appeared on the screen. "I dated each one—that's a month ago... and that's—"

"So, you've found how many pictures of Brent Knupp outside Java the Hut?"

"Brent..." Flynne turned and stared at her. "Brent, who?"

"Knupp. He's a regular—comes in with his girls sometimes." Erika took over the mouse and tried to find a picture with one of them, but there were none. "Odd... that parking space."

Flynne huffed. "It's like he *knows* it's the only one in the entire place where I can't read the license number. I can get a partial on the one next to it, but—"

"That's just it. He always parks on the east side and comes in the side door. I don't think I've ever seen him out there. He must come in when I'm gone, too."

Flynne's fingers flew over the keys. Backspaced, tried again. A wail that Erika couldn't understand at all filled the office.

In fact, she became so engrossed in her search that Erika could have snatched the gun from her. However, just as the thought occurred to her, a list of files came up on the screen. Erika recognized the website name. Java the Hut's security service. And the files... .WAV. "Are those?"

"Yeah. What time does Brent Krup—"

"Knupp. He usually shows up around eleven-fifty. Unless he brings his girls. Then it's more like ten after seven—almost on the dot."

Two days showed nothing, but then it came. Same car. Brent getting out. Zooming in... License plate blurry but readable enough to make a start. She opened another incognito window and passed the keyboard to Erika. "Log in to your Twitter. I need it."

"Why not use yours?" she asked, but she logged in anyway and stood back. "Why mine?"

"They'll be watching yours if anyone there has any brains left."

As the screen pulled up, Flynne typed in one word— sort of. A hashtag.

#hashtagrogue2B7B92H

What?

Erika's silence screamed for answers.

With a huff, Flynne clicked on Erika's Twitter name, EriKaff2, and pointed. "See. I left your phone open to that. All they have to do is turn it on, and they'll see it. Then, if they're smart—if they've got *Tyler* back in the office, anyway—they'll monitor that hashtag."

"Why'd you write out hashtag if you put one in front? Isn't that redundant? And will it come up in a search if the number is attached?"

Flynne gaped. "I don't know! I've never actually searched one. I don't use hashtags or Twitter. Social media is a security nightmare. I just look up names and stuff and make, like, fake accounts for people."

"Well, I'm pretty sure you have to search for the exact hashtag to find it—and they'll never know to put those numbers behind that."

She floundered until Erika asked what she was doing. "Trying to find the edit button. Where do you edit these things?"

In a huff, Erika took over the mouse and copied the post. She deleted it and a moment later, posted it again—this time with a space between rogue and the license plate number. #HASHTAGROGUE 2B7B92H

"Thanks."

"I still don't think it's a big deal, but it is odd that he'd be parked there when he's usually on the other side..."

Flynne closed out everything, turned off the computer, and shooed Erika from the room. "Let's go eat something. I'm starved."

As they passed through the family room, Flynne noted a car passing. Something about it felt familiar. *Probably just someone who lives here. I've probably seen it drive by like a million times. This protection detail stuff makes you supes jumper cables.*

A new idea hit her. "Erika..."

The woman glared. "If you tell me I have to take a pill *before* I eat, I'm going to kick you—even if I land on my butt afterward."

"I'll buy you anything you want for dinner if you let me tie you up so I can go—"

"Let you? *Now* you're asking?"

Probably a dumb idea, anyway. I'll just give her a tiny bit of the wine in the fridge to go with an Ambien. That'll knock her out long enough.

"You're right. Sorries."

Of course, getting Erika to drop the subject and onto

something else proved detrimental to sanity. Finally, Flynne blurted out, "So, what made you go all relige? It all sounds nice, but then I read about Corey, and she was a nut job with crackers to spare."

That worked—bring up all the religious stuff *and* Erika's most disliked agent in one move. She launched into a rant on why Corey personified what people hated about Christians, Christianity, and Jesus—in that order. Then she went on to talk about comparing Corey to Keith and her father. Flynne listened, asked intelligent questions, or so she hoped, and kept the conversation going all through dinner, clean up, and a gab fest on the couch.

"Do you really think Jesus did that?"

Erika nodded.

"But I thought wine is bad—like really bad. Alcohol and stuff. That's bad, right?"

It worked. Erika launched into an argument in favor of casual, light drinking and how people didn't have safe drinking water. Flynne insisted she keep talking and raced to fill two glasses of wine. Erika would balk at the Ambien later, but it had to be done. *Even if I have to lie about it.*

"—then a big-wig in the early church—a guy named Paul—told another guy to drink wine for something wrong with his stomach. So, I don't think you can make the argument that wine is bad."

Flynne offered a glass as she entered. "All this talk made me crave it." She forced a giggle that sounded real enough. "I think I'm too rebbie to be a churchie."

Though Erika had been set to refuse the wine, Flynne's words seemed to make a shift. She reached for the glass and took a sip. "Oooh… good one. Very nice." After a third sip, she asked, "Okay, so I get churchie. What's rebbie?"

"You know, with or without a cause? Rebs.com."

"Rebel. Rebbie. Great." Erika took another sip.

Flynne smiled inside. *This is gonna work.*

Fifteen minutes after Erika finished her drink, she held out her hand. "Give me the Ambien. Is it safe with this much wine? Did you make sure of that?"

"I—"

"I'm not stupid, Flynne. You *never* drop something as fast as you did earlier. I figured you had another plan. Alcohol and Ambien, though..."

With greater success than she expected, Erika accepted her assurances that, as long as Erika didn't drink *much* alcohol, not on an empty stomach, and didn't plan to operate machinery, it would only accentuate the effectiveness of the meds. *And if her god is a thing, maybe he, she, it—whatever—maybe I could be right about that, so I don't totes fry her brain or anything...*

Erika was out in less than thirty minutes. Flynne tried to rouse her, and even saying, "It's over. We can go home!" got her nothing more than a moaned, "Great."

Flynne grabbed the Camry keys from the hook, locked the doors behind her, but didn't set the alarm. If Erika woke up and the motion sensor went off... *Not good.*

It took only a minute to hop into the car, start it up, back out of the garage, and roll down to the street. There, however, with the taillights glowing in the gutter, Flynne waited. She stared at the darkened house with only a light in the kitchen glowing through the family room. Was it safe to go?

The picture of a more comfortable Erika blended with the expectation of less antagonistic interactions and spurred her to shoot out into the street and zip up Rosewood Court. FreshMart closed in twenty minutes, and FreshMart carried gift cards—great, heaping gobs of them.

Including ones for Amazon. With one of those, and same-day shipping in Rockland, she'd be set.

I'll get their Danishes, too. She'll like that.

Shaking the sense of foreboding—of being followed or watched—that proved impossible. Flynne parked out front, dashed inside, stacked all four kinds of available Danishes, and stood before the wall of gifting shame, searching for the familiar, black, Amazon-with-an-arrow smile. It didn't appear.

A kid pushing a dust mop sidled up and asked if he could help. "I need Amazon. Fifty bucks."

"Forget a birthday?" He reached for it—white, of course.

Flynne could have sworn that they did it deliberately—swapped out white for black and vice versa—just to keep her sanity on the brink of no return. "No... I just don't put my card online. Supes stupes with how easy it is to hack into databases and steal identities." She grabbed another one—just in case she needed it later. "You never know... and what's with changing the color so we can't find it?"

"It's like when the store moves stuff around. They want you to have to look for it, so you see other things you missed before."

Something shifted in him—the way he shuffled his feet and couldn't quite look at her again—and Flynne backed away before the miserable moment occurred. *"Don't let them have the moment."* Her mom said it every time, and Mom was right. If Flynne didn't get away, she'd be making a date to meet the kid and tell him she was ten years too old for him. Stupid, but true.

"Thanks! Bye!"

"Wait—"

She rushed up to the counter, peeled a hundred and a twenty from the small wad in her pocket, and slapped them on the counter. "Can you hurry?"

The checker nodded. "Jordie's a nice—"

"I'm too old for him. Don't want to hurt his feelings."

That's all it took. She had her change inside twenty seconds and was out the door and in her car before another minute passed. A look through the giant windows showed the checker talking to the kid, him shaking his head, her nodding. Slumped shoulders.

Bet you just ask anyone who's nice to you—on the off chance. I remember… Wait, kid. Going out with someone just to be going out is, like, the dumbest thing you can do. Flynne sighed. *Life isn't over when you haven't had a date by sixteen. It just feels like it.*

Nothing could have made her feel more like a philosopher than that thought right then. She pondered wisdom she hadn't possessed at fifteen and sixteen all the way back to Rosewood Court. Up the drive. Back to the house.

And just as she reached for the door, a car drove past—slowly. Not uncommon during the day on Rosewood, but after ten o'clock? She shrank into the shadows and watched. *If it slows or stops, we're outta here.*

But it didn't. It drove to the corner and turned right. Even then, it crept along as if the car only had one speed— school zone.

Must be some insomnie grandpa or something.

SEVEN

Three hundred miles—that's how many he'd put on his Packard in less than twenty-four hours, and it didn't include the back and forth to Rockland. No, Keith had burned three hundred miles on it just going back and forth to Dolman to check the coffee shop. And all for nothing.

Hour after hour, he sat there feeling more conspicuous each time than the last. This time, he called for a replacement. Tyler apologized. "I don't have anyone who can bring you a rental. Would Erika let you use hers, do you think?"

Hers... she'd not had it long—less than a year. Still, it was to find her... "I'll figure out something. Guess that means the Langat case just escalated. I'll be praying."

Why he said it, Keith never knew. It wasn't as if most agents cared, but he did. Every time. "Lord, any foreign political target is a huge risk, but Kenyan? Please give me wisdom to know how to help them if I can. I ask that You keep Claire safe if she's on this one. Clarity, discernment, instinct—I pray that You will keep these in perfect balance with courage and grit."

Prayer covering complete, Keith raced back to HearthLand, almost forgetting the speed trap five miles outside of Dolman, and pulled into Ralph's drive. Annie met him at the door. "Whatever you want, get someone else to deal with it. Ralph's finally asleep. He stayed up all

69

night praying for whatever's going on."

"Can you drive me to Dolman and drop me off at the mechanic's?"

As she reached for something, presumably her purse, Annie asked, "Is something up with your car?"

"Nope. Just need to rent one, and I saw they offer cheap rentals for customers."

"Oh… why don't you take yours in for an oil change. You've been—"

"I do those myself, but thanks. It's kind of important that I hurry, Annie."

She stared at him. A grim line formed around her lips, and the effect made her look twenty years older. "I see. Let's go."

If Ralph was praying, you had to have guessed….

"—knew, deep down, I did, but I hoped I was being paranoid."

A miserable, awkward silence hung heavy in Ralph's truck until Annie pulled up in front of Mid-State Towing and Repair. Keith leaped from the cab, but she called out to him. "Keith, wait."

He paused, gripping the door frame with more force than necessary. "Yeah?"

"If this is like me… and Erika is—" He didn't even try to hide his expression. "Yes, well," she continued, "get her safe. We want her back in one piece."

"She would be if she was with me, but—"

Annie cut in. "I don't care who is 'protecting' her at some undisclosed location. Find the threat. Neutralize, or whatever you call it. She's safe as long as whoever *he* is can't get to her. Make *that* happen and come home."

"Don't get dead?"

She grinned. "That's right. Don't get dead."

70

Her not-so-peppy talk spurred him on anyway. Keith convinced the owner of the repair shop to rent him the plum-painted Civic for half what a new car would have cost and with more camouflage properties. The crunched rear quarter panel added a nice touch. *Easy to find in a crowded parking lot, too.*

Set with new wheels and certain he hadn't been followed anywhere, Keith parked himself in sight of *the* space and waited. Again.

0000 01 000 0000 1 01 110   010 111 110 001 0

Two weeks earlier, Mark had almost considered bringing in a partner—again. *Who are you kidding? You wanted to promote Claire so she wouldn't have to go out.* This latest issue proved why that wasn't a good idea.

Still, he'd added three more monitors to his desk—five in all—and watched, listened, or read the details of three separate cases, all while taking notes in three separate notebooks. Weariness built upon weariness until he couldn't remember if A team had secured a location for Langat or if they were still on the move. "Tyler!"

The door flung open a pair of seconds later. "Yeah?"

"Update on Langat."

"Sent them to the Oregon place. They'll leave soon. Paris and Henry are close if we need them to take over."

The words were normal enough, but something about the way Tyler spoke them—or perhaps it was the obvious absence of what he *didn't* say—painted the air in ominous colors. "What is it, Tyler?"

"I'm not sure it's real. I didn't—"

Tyler didn't deserve the blast, but Mark delivered it

anyway. "Just *tell me.* I can determine credibility on my own."

"I found an account—in the Caymans."

His gut soured to vinegar. "What name?"

"It's probably just—"

"Name!" Why he bothered, Mark didn't know. Tyler would never be able to spit it out, and that answered the question. "Flynne Dortmann?"

Only the faintest of nods followed.

One carefully chosen curse dropped in the room and wreaked the verbal carnage it deserved. Tyler stepped back. Mark dropped another. And another. With each choice epithet, Mark's voice grew louder, and Tyler withdrew altogether.

The catharsis lasted only until Mark had exhausted his supply of swearing—both foreign and domestic. With excess calm and precision, he returned to his desk, pulled out a drawer, reached up above it, and withdrew the handset to a line Flynne didn't know existed. He called Keith's phone.

"Hey... did you know that Java the Hut sells approximately *half* what Erika's old place did? It's better coffee, too. I think that's because Erika—"

"She's got a Cayman account." Tyler entered the room and dropped a slip of paper on the desk. The top number was obviously an account number, but the bottom... Mark swallowed hard. "Are you sitting down, Keith?"

"Yeah... why?"

He swallowed the bile that tickled the back of his throat and balled his hands into tight fists to stop the tremble. "We've been had, Keith. Flynne has a two-point-six-million-dollar Cayman account—as of..." Mark's fingers flew over his keyboard, and a minute later, he puked in his wastepaper basket. "Sorry—the pills I take…" A lame excuse, but his pride clung to it with all the ferocity of a toddler with a teddy bear.

"Mark?" The tone said it all. Fear, rage, and disbelief mingled in that one-word question. "Mark?"

"The account was opened the day she started with us. This was a set up, but I don't know by whom or why."

Pacing, ranting, stomping, sagging into the chair—none of it clarified anything for him. What had he missed, and *how* had he missed it?

"I've got to think adversary now…"

"*Now?*"

Peeling tires hinted that Keith was on the move—back to HearthLand or to Rockland? Mark didn't even ask. "Yes," Keith insisted. "I *was* trying to anticipate the moves of a scared but determined, inept techno-geek who thinks her job is 'totes amaze' and agrees to everything with, 'awesomesauce.' Now…"

"Right… of course, right… Sorry. Get back here."

"Already on my way." Silence hung there, waiting for Keith to say whatever it was that he hadn't yet. Thirty seconds… a minute—possibly two. "Mark?"

"Yeah?"

"Erika trusts Flynne. She's going to be ticked, but she's going to trust that Flynne believes whatever story she tells."

He could only say one thing, so Mark said it. "We'll find her. I promise."

It was the first time he'd ever made a promise to any of his agents, much less one he wasn't confident he could keep.

She paced. Nervous energy erupted in random wall scrubs, a window job that left streaks to rival mascara after a sob fest, and a freezer defrost. That's when Erika put a stop to it. "You don't have to defrost new fridges—haven't needed to for decades."

Flynne scanned the piled-up hunks of frozen foodstuffs that probably had long outlived their freezer life. "Now you tell me."

"I thought it was a joke!"

The car passed again, and Flynne almost didn't wait for the delivery of her Amazon order. She began throwing things back in the freezer, repacking everything she could fit into bags, and taped Erika to a chair when she couldn't keep an eye on the "client" anymore. *I so need to remember she's a client. Gotta take care of her like a client, not a coworker's girlfriend.*

Coworker. Not anymore. The cushy job with Burberry bonuses was probably gone. No excuses would make any difference—not now.

Those thoughts would have sent her into despairing depths, but Flynne shook her head. *I just have to talk to Mark—make him understand. When Erika gets back safe... yeah...* A glance Erika's way prompted another thought. *I can't let anyone get to her—even if it costs me. Then maybe I can earn his trust again.*

The doorbell rang, and Flynne nearly jumped out of her skin. "Who—?"

"You ordered something. One day. It's supposed to be here by three. Remember?"

Flynne bolted for the door. The delivery guy was

strolling down the walkway again by the time she jerked it open. She started to call out, but a champagne sedan rolling past and then parking right in front of the house did her in. She bolted inside and slammed the door shut. Overly dramatic? Maybe. But who cared? A peek through the side of the front window showed the car sitting there. Waiting.

Action became imperative. Flynne gathered every bit of their stuff and set it outside the back door. One step… two… five. At eight, she knew he'd see her if she went even one more step. Go anyway? Try to lose him on the streets of Rockland? Pretend to leave and come back? Call the police and turn themselves in for safety? Call the FBI?

She'd go to jail with the last two. *No way.*

Erika met her at the door. "What's going on?"

At the sight of the package she'd dropped on the floor, Flynne picked it up, ripped it open, and fumbled with the interior packaging, too. She pulled out a few police-grade zip ties and threw them at Erika. "Cuff yourself."

"Wha—? You ordered *zip ties*?"

"I need to be able to function without worrying about you trying to take over. So, get your ankles cuffed."

"There's a frozen ice cream bowl in there. I so could whack you with it." At Erika's scoff, Flynne added, "It's, like, the most awesomest saucy weapon. You hit, it gives you a goose egg, but it's cold, so that takes down the swelling. All in one thump on the noggers. Supes effish." When Erika just glared, Flynne threw out her second-to-last threat. "Now put on the zip ties, or I'll do it and drag you out by your hair."

To herself she added, *Please, just do it. I so don't want to have to go get the guns.*

"I'm not going to—"

Flynne stormed out the back door, grabbed the tranq

gun, and marched back in. "Do it."

"You're not going to—"

Flynne aimed, fired, and missed—likely due to her hands shaking with barely repressed anger. It did, however, accomplish her purpose.

Erika created a chain of links and tied her ankles together. At first, Flynne nearly made her scale back, but the very real likelihood of them needing to run at some point prompted a change of mind. *I'll just hook her hands behind her. That'll work.*

A glance out the window turned into a stare as Flynne watched the car. "It's just sitting there!"

"Then tell him to leave!"

She started to protest—to insist that was the stupidest thing she could do, but something she'd read about human nature prodded her out the front door and onto the lawn. She stood there, arms folded over her chest, glaring. Whoever was in the car didn't look her way at first, but the moment he did—and it *was* a he—the car shot off down the street and around the corner.

If she'd had pompoms, she'd have waved them. Instead, Flynne bolted through the house and carted everything to the trunk. In less than a minute, she had Erika as comfortable as possible in the back seat—and complaining the whole way.

"You're seriously tying my hands *behind* my back?"

"I have to. It's not safe to have you able to use your hands to resist. I remember *that* much. Now let's go!"

Erika pulled her feet out of the way so Flynne could close the door. "Where are we going?"

Without even the slightest pause for breath or consideration, Flynne shot back, "No idea!"

EIGHT

"Obama Langat arrived in Rockland yesterday. Cheers arose as he and the rest of the Kenyan delegation strode into the Harbinger Building for talks on the Kenyan refugee crisis. Much of the world is unaware of the flood of refugees that pour into Kenya every year, sometimes returning after being sent home…"

With one flick, the tiny "wheel of fortune" spun on the desk. *Ffftttthhhttttthhhttttzzz…*

"Today, Langat is said to be resting from his long flights and two back-to-back meetings. The summit begins tomorrow morning at nine o'clock and is expected to last the week. Two former presidents and first ladies are expected to attend as well. Local law enforcement has been brought in…"

Zzzzttth…

A tap to the keyboard silenced that screen, while a few more taps turned on another. "… in other news, a semi overturned just off the Rockland loop this morning. Witnesses at the scene said it was one of the most invigorating crashes they'd ever seen." *Zz zzt tth…*

"—smelled like you got trapped inside a coffee grinder or something. I've been hyper ever since I stopped." A woman with short, frowzy, strawberry hair giggled into the mic.

A smile formed as the wheel slowed and the story of

the coffee crash played out on the screen. *Fftht... ftht... ftht...*

One more screen popped up after a few clacks. Between the *ftht... ftht... ftht...* of the ever-slowing wheel, the senate minority leader stood before Congress and decried the move toward helping Kenya by bringing more of the Somali refugees to America.

That smile grew and the wheel of fortune slowed. *Fftht... ... ftht... ... ... ftht...*

0000 01 000 0000 1 01 110   010 111 110 001 0

No matter how many times he tromped through muddy fields and meadows to get to the "treeler," Keith always found it empty. The boys of HearthLand who used it as their combination clubhouse-tree house asked every other hour if they could return. Twice, he'd caught them sneaking that way. This time, he'd let them make it inside.

Keith made a show of walking back to town after checking on it, but instead of staying in his trailer, he crept out and made a beeline for the trees along the creek to the west of town. It took three times longer to make it back. A few times, he had to scramble to stay hidden from Rory and Andre, who also attempted stealth-like, evasive movements.

He nearly broke his neck jumping from a tree to the one that cradled the old travel trailer in its branches, but once inside, all was well. With arms behind his head, Keith lay on the bed and waited for them to arrive. It didn't take long. They could have alerted enemy fire with their constant admonitions to "shhh."

Rory spied him first—the big, black geek glasses

framed wide eyes. If he'd had an Adam's apple, it would have bobbed worse than apples at a harvest party. "Um…"

Andre stopped mid-sentence, bragging about how they'd done it and gaped. "How'd you get up here?"

"It's my job. If I was a bad guy, I'd have a gun on you. Do you get that?"

"There's no bangers in HearthLand." Andre's scoff did little to return color to Rory's pale face. "That's why Mom moved us here."

You think you're so worldly wise. Poor, foolish kid. Keith sat up and leaned forward. "I agree. HearthLand doesn't have a single…" He tried not to cough or smile over the word, "—*banger*. But that doesn't keep people we don't want here from coming."

This time, comprehension brightened Rory's face. "Okay. We're going. You'll tell us when we can come back?"

"Wha—?"

Rory elbowed Andre and growled his opinion. "Shut up. It's like Annie. We're going."

Keith rose and walked back to town with them. Andre may not have understood, but Rory's willingness to stand up to him said all it needed to. They'd stay away until given the green light.

So, bring her here, Flynne. This is safe ground. Just bring her here.

While the boys went off to check out the creek, Keith kept walking… back to the new settlement. Back to Erika's house. Back to where he'd failed her.

In a slow arc, Keith walked every inch of her property—property she hadn't even made a dent in owning yet, because Ralph was too much of a softie to stick to his own plans. Only a footprint that had to be Flynne's

79

looked out of place.

Sweeping the house—much faster. He started at the front door and scanned every inch of wall, surface, floor. The lack of dust hinted that Erika really had ducked out of their tentative date to clean and decompress after the workday from the nether regions. It wasn't that he hadn't believed her, but... well, he hadn't believed her.

This time, he paid close attention to every item of food, article of clothing, toiletry, and even her books. The Bible lay on her pillow—proof Erika hadn't packed for herself. It also explained why her makeup bag was gone. Erika would never bother to pack it. She knew the protection drill—no time for that nonsense.

His phone buzzed the moment he opened the fridge. Mark. "Hey, I'm checking out Erika's—"

"Need you on the Langat case—now. The idiot thought he could notify his security detail of his location. They're ready to move, but if you sweep in and take him, we can round up the detail and then send Sol and Raina in to relieve you again. No one else is close enough."

"Where are they?"

"I'll send coordinates with... " Mark hesitated. "Let's go with Biblical protocol."

You're worried... about what? Keith didn't even need to ask. The answer—obvious. "Tyler?"

"Probably clean, but we can't risk it. Um, and there's even more bad news about the Cayman account."

"Yeah?" Mark should be impressed that his voice sounded as calm as it did.

"Tyler also found copies of tax returns...."

All self-assurances that Flynne would make rational decisions fluttered to the floor of his gut. "She reported the interest income?"

"Yeah."

So much for my theory on it being a setup. It took a few huffs—he sounded like a bull snorting in the ring—before Keith managed to stamp down enough fear and anger to say, "Mark. Do me a favor."

Mark agreed.

"After I disconnect, swear for me."

0000 01 000 0000 1 01 110   010 111 110 001 0

Nestled among tall trees and a few random rhododendrons, the cabin emerged as if grown there rather than built. Keith crawled past slowly enough that Sol and Raina couldn't miss him. No cars on the highway when he turned off, and still no sign of them now, meant he'd beaten the security detail. With the way he'd thumbed his nose at every speed limit sign, it's a wonder he hadn't racked up a dozen tickets and been an hour behind instead.

Keith parked just past a tree break a few hundred yards from the edge of the property and worked his way back through to the back door. Raina met him there. "You got here fast."

"Yes." They didn't have time for chit-chat. He passed the keys to his plum Civic and held out his other hand for keys to the commercial minivan.

"A Honda?"

"2000—plum. Bashed back quarter panel."

She sniffed and made the exchange as she stepped aside. "You travel in style…"

"Yeah, because every girl's dream car is that thing over there."

That brought a smile. "You don't love the lack of side

windows and PIPER'S PLUMBING & SEPTIC painted on all sides?"

"I wouldn't… except it at least has the name written in reverse on the front, too. That's class, baby."

Sol appeared—six and a half feet tall, broad enough shoulders to do serious damage to narrow doorways, deep honey-brown skin, and bleach-blond hair. The enigma of him rivaled only Mark when he'd been "Cho" and looked like he had been ripped from a Norwegian clothing catalog. "Langat is ready. You?"

He nodded. "Let's go."

Obama Langat was an imposing man for someone just under five and a half feet. Scrawny, with thick glasses, his piercing gaze swept over Keith, and he nodded. "I will go."

Like you have a choice. You signed, buddy.

A blip from the other room sent Sol dashing away. "Incoming!"

Trying to induce Langat to run—impossible. After the third, "C'mon!" Keith hoisted the man over one shoulder and did his best to run to the tree line. "Better… be… glad… you're… light."

"Put me down!"

Keith did not. Instead, he broke into the trees, dashed left, and promptly tripped over a log he'd forgotten about already. Almost too late, he clamped his hand over Langat's mouth to stifle a roar of protest. "Shut. Up. We're paid to keep you alive, and we can't do that if you keep dragging us down and announcing our presence. So, shut up, and *run*."

This time, Langat ran.

That slight concession to cooperation ended the moment Keith pulled out zip ties and a large bandana. "What is this? Are you the one—?"

Keith whipped the bandana into a strip of fabric and gagged the man before he could spew the rest of his indignation. Zip ties took a bit more effort, as Langat fought to free himself, but a trip, a knee to the back, and a face full of dirt was all it took to have the man ready to stuff into the van.

A long, agonizing wait followed. "I wonder if your security team is better than Sol and Raina thought. It's taking longer—"

A shot rang out.

"Nope. There it is. We go."

He helped Langat—shoved, more than anything—into the van, tied the man's wrists to a loop by a low seat, and slammed the door shut. Taking the direct route to the highway would shave half an hour off their trip back to HearthLand, but that would beg for a tail. Not something he could afford.

His thumbs hovered over his phone. *Is HearthLand the best choice? Well, not exactly HearthLand, but the fields to the north... there's a perfect landing spot over there hidden by the trees...*

Keith went for it. He typed in the last four digits of the longitude. Count to twenty. A single period. Twenty seconds. Then the first two. To Tyler's phone, he sent the last four digits of the latitude. A single period. And then the first two—all separated by twenty seconds.

The helo would be waiting by the time Keith and Langat arrived. They'd go off to Oregon, and he'd go back to the treeler—just in case Flynne really did think she was saving Erika from something.

Just in case God gave him some direction on where to start looking.

Just in case...

0000 01 000 0000 1 01 110   010 111 110 001 0

The texts came in one after the other. Tyler burst into the room with the first, and seconds after he'd left, he raced back. "Do you have the rest?"

Mark just reached for Tyler's phone and added the numbers to the coordinate list—Dolman Highway— probably close to HearthLand, if he recalled the numbers correctly. "Get the helo to…" A few clicks and a dozen taps later, and he found it— "Yes. Mile marker forty-two, north of Hearthfield Way. Now."

Only the soft snick of the door as it closed hinted that Tyler had listened. Mark opened the office messenger program and tapped out another request. GET THAT REAL-TIME SATELLITE THING FOR ME. THE LINK. Guilt prompted him to add. PLEASE.

The link came through half a minute later, along with a message. REMEMBER. UNLESS SOMETHING CHANGED IN THE PAST YEAR, IT STILL HAS A THREE-MINUTE DELAY.

Movies acted like anyone could watch anything as it played out, but that wasn't true. Still, Mark had never told the team that the so-called three-minute delay was actually ninety-seconds. Not perfect, but better than waiting for updates sometimes.

A moment later, Tyler reentered with only half a knock's warning. "Okay. Helo sent. They'll be waiting." He set the office iPad on the desk and stood back. "Have a minute to go over my plan for finding Flynne?"

"Pop it up on the screen," Mark said.

A list of places appeared a few seconds later. "I've ranked these by probability," Tyler explained. "First, she has an uncle with a lakehouse in Grand Haven. I don't think she knows I know that, so that's my first guess."

"What makes you think she doesn't know?"

Tyler went on a long explanation that would have confused Rube Goldberg, but Mark finally got the gist. A photo on Flynne's fridge, a mention of summers at the lake house, and a little digging had turned up property records. "I thought it was her dad's, but no... not that place."

Mark scribbled down a note to start there. "Next?"

"Okay, so she and her friends have these big gaming parties. They take their stuff and rent an Air BnB. They've gone to the same place the last few times, and I'm pretty sure I found the right one."

"Those things have to use a credit card. Flynne wouldn't."

"I disagree." Tyler tossed an apologetic look but didn't back down. "I think when Flynne has been a good customer for several times, if she showed up and said she was having trouble with her card or something, I bet because of a customer relationship, she could get them to rent with cash. They have experience with her, you know?"

"Maybe... but can you find it?"

He swiped the screen and several houses with small guest bungalows or pool houses appeared. "It's probably one of these places because she's talked about how they get to swim in the pool and can see big house parties sometimes. According to Flynne, the owners of the big house leave the rental stuff to a friend of the family. The friend gets to keep half the income for her trouble, so she is on it." Tyler hesitated before adding, "I checked and almost all of them are empty for the next three weeks — totally the slow season in the St. Louis area for Air BnBs, so another reason the manager girl might do it."

"Or because with cash, she doesn't have to split with

the owners. The owners wouldn't know."

After staring first at the screen, over at Mark, and back at the screen again, Tyler frowned and pushed the Air BnB option to the top. "Flynne would like helping someone. If she thought of that, she'd do it."

She'd think. I'm sure of that.

"Third option might be out there, but Flynne hates camping. I mean *seriously* hates camping. She tries to hide it, because her whole family is really into this camping thing—even their family reunions are huge camping events. So, I wondered if she might not go buy all the stuff and get someone to drop them off at a campground."

"Drop them off? Why?"

"Because she wouldn't stay long if she had a way out. So... enforced... something?"

Three options—equally plausible, in Mark's opinion, but Tyler knew Flynne best. *Then again, it makes him too close, potentially. Then what?*

The screen changed. Surveillance cameras appeared. Seven of them. Tyler tapped each as he spoke. "Okay, so this was the morning she took Erika. This is the last traffic cam I could hack before her neighborhood." A new image formed. "I *think* that's her twenty-five minutes later. That's a few streets over. Then, I found this one..." Flynne— *obviously* Flynne riding a bicycle with a trailer appeared. "And again..." the picture clicked. "If you look at the tires..."

"Something's in the trailer." He leaned closer to be sure. "Right. Okay. So, where does that trailer go?"

Tyler shrugged. "No idea. I drove around that area last night and found three companies advertised with stickers and such—security companies. Three photos cascaded onto the screen. "But that's as far as I've gotten.

HomeSure has the easiest site to hack into, so I'm working with everything I can find there. The problem is..." He zoomed in on one of the company logos. "SmartServe sends all video footage alerts to the owner. The owner has to pass it to the company. So, I'd have to find each owner, find their phone service, then hack all of it."

"What you're saying is finding any footage of Erika and Flynne is almost impossible."

The screen went blank as Tyler moved toward the door. "No... not if any of the other houses have anything facing toward the street. But if they're still *in* that neighborhood, the only way we'd see what house it is, is if they or the neighbors across the street *don't* have SmartServe."

"What's your plan?"

Tyler turned off the screens and moved to the door. "I'm starting with campgrounds and Air BnB. The only way to do the lake house thing is to send someone up there. We can't afford the manpower right now."

"Which..." Mark refrained from throwing his pen across the room—barely. "Flynne would know. Send Claire to Grand Haven. We need to know."

If the look on Tyler's face meant anything, the kid had been about to protest, but that shifted. "Got it. Helo should arrive in about twenty minutes. I'll go make those calls."

Left alone, Mark stared again at the now empty screen. "You're doing better than I expected, Miss Dortmann... now make a mistake, will you? Don't have time for this stuff."

NINE

Langat groused all the way from Fairbury to the Dolman Highway. Muffled words Keith couldn't understand filled the back of the van, but he ignored them. Concentration was everything. Twice, he'd seen vehicles that unsettled him, but both times, they'd turned onto other roads without doing anything odd at all.

However, when a third one appeared ahead of him, Keith let the vehicle go over a small hill without him and pulled over. He jumped into the back of the van and jerked the gag down over the man's jaw. "Where's the tracker?"

"I do not know—"

Keith's hand shot out and gripped the man's throat. "Don't lie to me. You've got two choices before you right now. You either tell me where your tracker is, or I leave you on the side of the road and our contract is canceled. You do *not* get a refund. I'll give you five seconds to decide."

"That's preposterous!"

"Four."

"I don't have to—"

"Three." Langat swallowed hard as Keith followed that with, "Two."

"I—"

"One." Keith ripped open the van door and pulled out his knife. He went to slice the rope free, but Langat shrank back, kicking at him.

"No, no." The man pointed to a gold tooth in the back of his mouth. "There. That is it. It removes for charging."

Keith pulled the thing from the man's mouth and grabbed a Ziplock bag from a bin. He hopped out, tucked it all under a rock, snapped a picture of the rock and of a nearby mile marker, and climbed in. "Just in case," he assured Langat as he climbed back in. "It's just in case." He started to put the van in gear, but the sight of Langat without his gag made him double back.

The man begged. "I won't complain anymore."

"It helps muffle things if there's an accident. It's natural to scream. We do it with cooperatives, too. I'll get you out of this—safe. Just give me a bit of time."

With that, he shot as fast as he could to the same hill the other vehicle had disappeared behind and slowed on his descent. The vehicle had vanished down the road—only a dot. "Looks like I was overly cautious. Sorry. Shouldn't have taken the time—"

A black SUV shot over the hill behind Keith. His mouth went dry. "Um, brace yourself. I think we have to race this one."

Scenarios whizzed through his mind, each pausing long enough to be rejected. The SUV gained on him. If Langat could get buckled somehow, slamming on the brakes might be the best choice, but the man would be flung about like a rag doll right now. No, he'd have to outrace them... somehow.

Only a quarter mile back. Bile inched its way up Keith's throat. He clenched his teeth and punched it. The van whined, wheezed, and strained forward. The SUV grew even closer. A turn signal came on.

Keith lifted his foot off the gas pedal and watched as

the SUV shot around him. He braked enough not to lay down rubber and slowed. The SUV didn't. It zoomed ahead as if on a mission.

I could turn around now… probably out race them back to the Fairbury highway. Or…

He pushed the van back to sixty and kept going. Another two miles passed before he saw the helo with its spinning blades in the field—right where he'd sent it. Another mile passed before he thought he saw something off with it.

At a quarter mile, he couldn't see anything being in a small valley, but as he came back out, there they were. Helo. SUV. Men with AR-15s trained on the helo.

Lord, help us all.

0000 01 000 0000 1 01 110   010 111 110 001 0

A bang and the faint sound of oof! preceded Tyler's entrance into Mark's office. Red-faced and stammering, the kid rushed to him, thrusting a phone out as if it explained everything. "I was trying to hack into the Air BnB website—that thing is ridiculously secure, by the way—when this came in."

"#HASHTAGROGUE. Not unexpected." On the other hand, the second hashtag changed everything. Again. "Does that really say #-does-he-still-come-for-coffee?"

"Yep. Got goosebumps when I saw it.

Mark looked closer. Erikaff2 "Erika's account still, right?"

"Yep."

Before passing back the phone, he gave it one last glance. "Did you pull up Java the Hut's surveillance and

91

see?"

"Not yet—brought it to you first."

"Excellent." Mark typed in the URL to Erika's account before nodding at the door. "Now, go check that out."

A ping told him the helo was landing. Mark moved that satellite monitor to the foreground and, a minute later, watched as the helo touched down. It sat there... all alone in the field, its blades creating waves in the new spring grasses. A black speck formed at the left corner of the screen. It grew until it became obvious that it was a dark-colored SUV—probably black.

Mark reached for his phone, but it rang as his fingers wrapped around the handset. "This better be Keith."

"I'm assuming breach—not sure if the breach was me making a stupid mistake somewhere or if it was back at the cabin, but I just drove past the rendezvous spot to see guns on the helo pilot."

"Client safe?"

"Yes—confused, but safe." He growled something Mark couldn't hear, but the next words came through—each one louder than the last. "Maybe next time he'll *listen* when we tell him something."

Another growl hit. "Aaaargh. All the curse words I can't say or think! They're chasing. Scarecrow protocol. Thursdays."

The line went dead.

In three seconds, he'd disconnected and punched a speed dial for the Rockland Gazette. The automatic system kicked in immediately, but Mark just punched in 4229 for the extension he wanted. "Doe here. Need a classified in the personals put in tonight."

A cough filled the headset before a voice on the other side said, "Go ahead."

"Let's go with... 'Dear John. I never want to see you again. You'll find your stuff at the old house. It'll be gone by Saturday, so get it while you can, you jerk.'"

"That's all?"

Mark grinned. "Yep."

"Harsh."

"John needs help realizing it's over." After choking back a snicker, Mark added, "Payment will hit your account by five." Without waiting for acknowledgment, he disconnected.

That settled, Mark went to fill a duffel bag—listing items one by one. Cash... phones... guns... cartridges... His gut sank. It's just like what Flynne did.

TEN

The car drove straight at them as Flynne turned off Rosewood and onto 42nd Street. Just as it turned back onto Rosewood, she caught a glimpse of the driver. He didn't even look her way, but he didn't need to. The moment his facial features morphed into a profile, she knew she knew him. "Sit up and look at that car. Do you recognize it?"

Too late. It was gone by the time Erika struggled to a seated position. "Didn't see. Why? Should I? Was it Keith? Tyler?"

Flynne froze. She wanted to close her eyes and remember—*needed* to, but they needed to get out of there, too. "I don't think he saw us. Can I, like, stop for a minute?"

"Sure." Flynne might have ignored that, but Erika added, "Just pull into a driveway so you look like you belong there, and he probably won't notice if he comes back. *Is* it Tyler?"

The next empty drive was near Elmhurst. She could go to the nearest parking lot… *No! I've gotta do it while I can still remember.*

Tires squealed as she jerked the wheel hard and shot up the drive and almost to the detached garage in back. Erika's complaints filled the backseat, but Flynne gripped the steering wheel and took a long, slow, deep breath. *Exhale...* She forced the air through her lips and took another long draw of air through her nose.

It worked. Second by second, a sense of peace calmed her racing heart. The slower her heartrate dropped, the more clarity she found. "I know the car. I know I do. I can see it. The guy, too... sort of. Maybe not. But it's not, like, Tyler or any of the agents—except maybe Sol? Could it be Sol? I think this guy was totes too short, but then Sol drives with his seat, like way back—so far back that he looks like he's five-foot nothing."

"You know none of that means anything to me, right?"

No matter what she did, all Flynne knew was that the car, the guy, or both felt familiar. "I'll think about it later. We've gotta get out of here."

"Well, it worked for Scarlett O'Hara."

"What did?"

Erika just snorted.

A mile from the freeway Flynne saw the car again. "Wait. How? How did he *find us?!*"

"What?"

"The *car!*" A moment later, the bumper came into view as Flynne braked hard. "Wait, no. The other one didn't have a 'My kid owns Elmhurst Elementary' bumper sticker." Beads of perspirated relief dotted every surface of her skin. "I'm just being a couple of Brooklyn nerds about it."

Silence followed that. Flynne grinned as she shot onto the loop. *Just gotta wait for it.*

"I give. What are two Brooklyn nerds?"

"A pair of noids." That grin grew as Flynne counted down. *Five... four... three...*

There it was—the groan. Erika stayed silent for a quarter mile and then said, "Remember to send that to me when we're done with this mess. Between saying thanks and beating you up, I'll send it to my dad. He'll like it."

"He gets humor?"

"Yep. Just not emotions."

Flynne couldn't comprehend that. How could you find something funny without emotions? "So… he, like, laughs, but not because he's happy?"

"He laughs because he sees what you did with the words—how you used them differently than expected. And since he's been programmed to laugh when that happens, he laughs."

In that one line, everything she hadn't understood about Erika's emotionless father came together. "Oh, so when he kisses your mom after she says I love you, it's because they coded it into him that it's what you do?"

"No…" Flynne thought that she heard a snicker. "He kisses Mom because he likes the endorphin and dopamine rush that comes with a kiss, and an 'I love you' means she will be happy to get one."

Five miles around the loop—miles that she spent trying to figure out what to do next. Then she saw it—I-64 West. "St. Louis. We're totes going to St. Louis. I know a supes delish place—Air BnB. It's perfecto. No one knows that I go there—not really. Just vagueness. They'd never find it, even if they thought to look."

At that moment, fog cleared from her mind. "The dude! From The Java Hut! *That's* the car! What'sisname?"

"Brent Knupp? And it's Java *the* Hut."

"Whatevs. He's the one! He's the one in the car!"

Erika sounded doubtful as she said, "The one who you stared down in front of that house?"

97

Without bothering to answer, Flynne shot off the exit for I-64 West and down the first offramp. At the bottom, with no cars behind them, she pulled out the phone and signed into Erika's account. It didn't request a verification code. "The gods are with me—or yours is."

"Why do you say that?"

"It didn't ask for a verification code for your account. Signing in from a different device and all..."

Two hashtags. That's all she sent. Two.

0000 01 000 0000 1 01 110   010 111 110 001 0

Just shy of St. Louis, the car slowed. Flynne hadn't spoken for the last hour or two, and though it had been a relief at first, the grunted answers to her recent questions had grown "Totes anoyz." *I can't believe I just thought that.*

"Will you—?"

"Will *you* just *shut up*? I'm going on memory here!"

Erika made it several seconds before she blurted out, "How do you usually get there?"

No response. It took five more minutes, not that Erika counted every second of them or anything, before the car slowed to a rolling stop. She snapped off the engine and turned to face Erika. "GPS. Can't use that now. Obvies."

It took Erika much too long to figure out what "obvies" were, and by the time she did, Flynne had started in on something else. She interrupted. "What?"

"I *said*," Flynne growled. "You need to stay low. I'll go talk to Morgan and be right back. I need to get his okay, first."

"Okay for *what*?"

"Cash." Flynne blinked down at her. "He has to be

willing to take cash."

She'd kick herself later, but Erika couldn't help but suggest, "Maybe tell him you'll pay upfront, but he can run it through a card when we leave if he prefers."

"We can't—oh. Leave..." Flynne grinned at her. "Yeah... that." She scooted out the door and leaned close to the back window with her index finger pressed against her lips.

Ten minutes later, the sounds of shoes slapping against pavement announced Flynne's impending arrival. She hopped in the car with more energy than she'd shown through the whole ordeal—all, what... forty-eight, sixty... or so hours of it?—and started the engine. "He's totes coolio with it. You'll love him. Well..." Dead silence followed. "But you can't see him. I didn't tell him you were here. We've gotta keep you doin' the radar limbo."

Oh, don't go there. Just. Don't.

"Okay, so I'm going to do something weird. I'm, like, going to dig around in the backseat and undo your stuff. Then you scooch down by the floorboard so I can dig out suitcases from the trunk—you know, behind the seat?"

"So it makes sense that you were in the back seat?"

"Right!" As if that solved the issue of the world's lack of peace, Flynne parked the car and began the process. "Don't mess this up. Morgan will freak if he finds out you're here. He thinks I'm hiding out from my abusive boyfriend."

She had to admit—it was a nice move. "Keeping him sympathetic... good one."

They stopped, and Erika rolled to the floor so Flynne didn't have as much to do—just a few seconds at most, but maybe it would help. *Why am I helping her? I could scream. She didn't gag me—should have. Keith usually did.*

It didn't take long for Flynne to jerk the back seat down. "Oof!"

"Sorries," Flynne whispered.

Another voice appeared. "Need help?"

The door slammed shut with Erika curled like a squished pretzel under the seat. Flynne's voice barely drifted in. "No, but that's totes sweets of you!"

She couldn't be sure, but it sounded like Morgan asked if Flynne wanted to play a game of Dragon's Circle. Confirmation came when he said, "I got the new bonus pack."

"Ooooh! Yaaaasss!"

I hate you.

"Just give me, like, two hours to crash. I'm dead. All the driving."

"I'll order pizza." It seemed innocuous enough, but then he added, "You like pastrami and dill pickles, right?"

If you remember that, things just got interesting. What will you do when Flynne mentions her boyfriend?

"Oooh! You're awesomesauce to remember my faves!"

Flirting? I might need a translator most of the time, but I don't need one for tone. That was "all the flirts."

Claustrophobia had never been a part of Erika's infirmity repertoire, but with every passing minute—half of which included actual *giggles* on Flynne's part, no less—the temptation to scream for air shifted from an idea to a need.

I can't actually be oxygen deprived down here, can I? The windows are up...

Her leg cramped. Tears poured down Erika's face as she fought to straighten that calf and tilt her toes forward. Gasping for air, fighting back the screams, stretching with no room to stretch anything. Pain…

What she endured for hours probably lasted a minute at most.

The car door opened, the seat flipped up, and amid Flynne's "Sorries!" Erika's leg shot out and her foot connected perfectly with Flynne's chin.

0000 01 000 0000 1 01 110   010 111 110 001 0

They'd made it through the first quest when the worst thought she'd had hit her. "Oh, noooo."

"What? Is he here? I'll call the police. Hang on."

Flynne snatched Morgan's phone from his hands. "No! No one's here but you and me."

She could have sworn his eyebrows tried to waggle — tried and failed. *Thank goodness, or the lord, or… whatever you're supposed to thank. Morgan and waggles don't work.*

"Just the way I like it. You should come without the gaggle more often."

All thoughts of extraction woes zipped away with that one. "The gaggle?"

"That's what Jim calls you guys. He hears you're here and says, "Well… should we count on the gaggle taking over the pool tomorrow?""

Her heart sank. "He doesn't like us being here?"

"No! It's just his way of saying he knows we've got guests, and he'll leave the pool free for you guys. He does it with everyone — just doesn't give everyone a nickname."

"Not sure how I feel about being called a *goose*, but whatevs."

Morgan excused himself to the bathroom, and Flynne lost herself in panic mode. *What do I do now? I've got her out*

101

safe. Now *what? I don't have anyone back home who has my back—who's trying to catch the bad guy. They think I'm he—she—her—whatevs.*

A buzz sent her fumbling for her phone, but the screen lit up on Morgan's. "Someone's calling you!"

"See who it is?"

The screen said Jim Werner. "The lord and master of the realm!"

"Answer it?"

"Hey! This is head gaggle girl here answering Morgan's phone. Hi, Mr. Werner!"

"Flynne?"

Can't believe he remembers me!

"Hello?"

"Sorry, Mr. Werner. Yeah. Didn't expect you to remember me."

A low chuckle sounded more maniacal than the guy probably intended. "Well, as often as Morgan talks about you, it's not easy to forget."

"Aw... that's totes adorbs!" The bathroom door opened. "Yeah, he's coming. Hang on."

She thrust the phone at Morgan and hopped up to clean up their pizza mess. "He says you talk about me a lot."

Morgan flopped to the couch just as his face flamed. "Jim!"

The "guest cottage" was bigger than Flynne's duplex. Boasting three small bedrooms, a large kitchen-dining combo, and a roomy living area, the place was bright, clean, and furnished like an Ikea catalog photo shoot. *Except this is, like, the stuff Ikea knocks off or something.*

Despite the size and taste of their surroundings, nothing overrode the knowledge that Erika was trapped in a room twenty feet away, and Flynne had no idea of how she'd get them out of there. *What would Keith do?* didn't solve much. Perhaps it would have helped if she'd ever been "protected."

Even if I lose my job, I'm telling Mark that he has to train new office technicians by putting them in protective custody long enough to get the deets on what needs to happen. They'll, like, be so much better in emergies.

"So... want to go swimming?"

Flynne heard the question, but that didn't make it any easier to answer—not with her brain fighting for some idea... any.

"Flynne?"

Coming up with an excuse for being distracted—not easy. And then, as if handed to her, it was. "Sorry... just trying to remember the name of a book I started to read at the doctor's off—"

"Doctor? Are you sick?"

She brushed off the question with a dismissive, "Annual exam."

"Right..." Morgan sank against the back cushion and, if her "spidey senses" could be relied on, watched her. "I should do that, too. I never go."

He'd interrupted her thoughts—again. Flynne tossed him a look that should have quelled his curiosity but only incited it. "Um... no. No, you shouldn't."

"I shouldn't?"

"Guys don't need girlie swipes." Green gills blended with a flushed red and formed a rather grotesque puce. *Yeah, well. You totes deserves that one.*

"Right. No. Um... sorry. Book?" He spat out the word so fast, his desperation was almost cute.

"Can't remember the name..." Flynne turned to him

103

and crossed her legs into a pretzel. "Okay, so this office girl discovers that some gg—uy is in danger, so she, like, kidnaps him."

"Because that doesn't put him in danger—kidnapping."

I could kick you right now. Just one swift jab. You'd totes deserve that one, too—like me with Erika.

"Sorry. Go on."

Okay... he did sound really sorry. Flynne gave him the smile she suspected he liked best and went back to work on her story. "So, she does it, right? She gets the gir...uy out of the picture and off to a safe place where no one should be able to follow them. But someone does."

"It wouldn't be a good book if they didn't. How'd she get away?"

"Stole a car. Anyway," Flynne continued. She'd hooked him, and it was time to get him reeled in. "After that, she got them to this other place. She was all safe. And, like, it wasn't even the middle of the book!"

There it was—that look. No doubt. Morgan had a thing for her. All she had to do was send the right signal or two and he'd help with anything. *Even if I need him to help me hide Erika, I bet.*

"So... oh! Duh. Sure." Morgan hopped up and held out his hand. "Let's go look it up. Come on inside."

Flynne sat there, staring up at him. Her hand reached out to take his, but she didn't stand. "Look what up?"

"The book? So, you can finish it? Just download it to your phone—"

"No!" She winced. *Oops. That was totes ridik.* "Sorry. But, man, all that online stuff is dangerous. No access to the accounts, or anything like that."

He didn't hesitate. Morgan just pulled her to her feet

and almost into his arms. She'd just begun the split-second debate on yes or no when he thought better of it. "Whoa... sorry. Anyway, you can use mine."

"I don't know the title."

"We'll find it. C'mon..."

You're supposed to be helping me, like, you know, figure out the end? Not helping me buy some non-existent book!

"I just can't figure out," Flynne began as he led her, his hand still wrapped around hers, from the bungalow. "—how this office girl is going to get someone to find the bad guy, neutralize the threat, and get word to her that it's all safe, if she's hiding out!"

Morgan squeezed her hand before lacing their fingers together in an even more intimate move than the last. "That's why you read the book. If you could figure it out, it wouldn't be a good book!"

ELEVEN

At the sight of a black speck on his rear horizon, Keith knew the worst. He hung up with Mark and began barking at Langat. "I need you to try something and fast. You need to try to break those restraints."

A muffled "Mmph" was Langat's only response.

"Put your hands as high back as you can get them, and then jerk them down and apart."

The man tumbled, headfirst, into the floor of the van each time.

"Okay, that's not going to work. Pull as far away from that loop as you can and rub your arms up and down. We need to break the ties or the loop. If you see anything else that might wear it down, do that."

Another, "Mmph" preceded shuffling sounds.

A glance in his side mirrors showed the black spot growing larger. "They're gaining. Okay... um..."

The problem wasn't that he didn't have a plan. No, he had one, all right. Keith just didn't like it. Too many risks. Still, they couldn't outrun the Suburbans in a little Mitsubishi mini cargo van.

Langat's arms worked with impressive fervor, but it wouldn't work, and Keith knew it. He shot a prayer heavenward, another, and yet another. Time to act, though. "Okay, this is what's going to happen."

As he talked, Keith pulled a knife from a strap around

his ankle and held it in his hand. "We're nearing the curve. The moment we're out of sight, I'm coming for you. Remember, if I cut you, *squeeze your wrist*. I'll take care of getting you out of here. You take care of your wrist. Got it?"

He shifted his left foot to the gas and twisted sideways. Accelerating *before* a curve was never a good idea—especially not in a top-heavy mini cargo van. Still, he needed every bit of leverage.

Tires squealed, and the left tires did rise off the ground. Keith kept it steady for a hundred feet and then leaped to the side door and threw it open. The van slowed as he dove for Langat and ripped the loop off the seat with one slice.

At the door, Keith threw the knife first and then tossed Langat after it. The man's height and weight made it easier than he'd expected. He jerked a small loop over the top of the door as he jumped and rolled down the embankment.

Langat tried to rise. "Get *down!*"

Keith army crawled toward the man, but only made it three feet or so before the van exploded. *It worked. Cool. Mark'll be glad to know.* With that, he dashed for Langat and shoved the man down.

"Stay here. I'll be right back."

His knife was a hundred feet away. *Throw farther next time. Then again, Langat could have landed on it.*

The SUV would be there—faster now. He had to move. Keith bolted back to Langat, cut the foot and hand restraints, and pushed the man across the highway and toward a boggy creek. "Walk in the middle. Don't make any more noise than you have to, but go fast. When I make a bird call, stop and drop to the bank. Got it?"

Only a nod followed.

The squealing of tires announced the SUV's arrival. Keith made a tremolo and Langat turned, eyes wide. He pointed to a large growth of wild elderberry and they scrambled up to it. "Get as under it as you can and don't move."

The wait began.

0000 01 000 0000 1 01 110   010 111 110 001 0

The door flung open just as an alert hit his computer. "Mark! Did you see?" Tyler's expression flickered between abject panic and delight. "It worked!"

"Do we have eyes on Keith?"

Without a word, the kid fled out the door.

He'd kill me if he knew I just called him a kid. And I'm going to have to trust him. Too much happening right now. Wish I could confirm the God thing.

A ping on his messenger told him to check the satellite monitors. Though grainier than usual, there was no mistaking the burning van and five men half-surrounding the inferno. *Adding those channels of pellet fuel and the cannisters of alcohol was brilliant. I wasn't so sure, but...*

The question rang out from the other room. "Did you get it?"

Feeling much too much like a benevolent and bemused father, Mark smiled to himself. "Got it."

It was probably futile, but seeing that the men began fanning out to check the surrounding area, Mark zipped a message to Keith's phone. ONE HEADING TOWARD THE CREEK. CURSORY GLANCES.

Wait became an unsavory four-letter word as Mark watched for the standard response. Had Keith already disposed of the phone? Left it in the van? It was just the kind of thing he'd do, but…

Another call came through. "Help."

He'd recognize the soft accent of Otto Schmatloch anywhere.

"Agents on the way, Mr. Schmatloch. Do you remember what to do?"

"Ja, I—"

"Don't tell me. Leave everything and do it. Now."

Once the call disconnected, he pinged Tyler. MOBILIZE DOYLE AND SAM.

A moment later, Tyler's, RIGHT-O, followed.

Oh, brother.

The fear in Otto's voice still lingered in Mark's ear. *An eighty-year-old man shouldn't have to fear for his life for something his father did when he was a tiny boy. Hatred's appetite for new victims cannot be satisfied.*

The Langat team's cell went to voicemail. A huffed sigh did nothing to resettle Mark's rumpled nerves. "Probably tied up. They're not going to like admitting that."

He punched a number and waited for Karen to answer. "Raina and Sol need extraction. Looks like Langat's people got one up on them."

"They're not…?"

Some questions one didn't ask in their line of work. *Ball players have lucky socks, the theater folks always say, "The Scottish play" for MacBeth, and agents never say dead.*

Mark hit the rewind on the satellite recording and watched as the Kenyan guard drew close to where he assumed Keith and Langat hid. The man stood at the bank, it seemed. Mark imagined him on tiptoe, peering over at the thicket and… beyond? A moment later, he turned and walked back.

And I don't even know that it is *a man. I just assume.*

Though he could watch the footage all day, Mark had things to do that didn't include obsessive scrolling. *But will Keith come back now that he's had a taste of it again?* One last look at the screen showed another car approaching. Guns disappeared. All would be well.

He disconnected the feed and turned to the next pressing issue. A swivel brought him facing the credenza behind his desk. The WPA-styled painting of Rockland's skyline hovered over it. It had been a joke—the gift of that painting. Rickwood, of the West Coast Agency, had sent it with a teasing note about Mark being the "Batman" of Rockland.

Those words rankled at the memory of Mr. Schmatloch in Chicago waiting for agents to rescue him from a hidden room in his basement. *The irony there... the tragic irony...*

The third drawer from the left boasted half a dozen cellphones with labels to remind him of each. One jumped out at him. *Don French—Rockland Chronicle.*

He first asked Tyler to adjust the newspaper's website to include him, and then he sent a text to his contact at the Chronicle. ACTIVATED.

Time to call Olivienne Todd.

The voice—he'd never forget Lucy's voice, and her sister's couldn't have been more "Lucy" if she'd made a deliberate effort to imitate—ripped at his heart. *We failed Lucy Todd.*

"My name is Don French, from the Rockland Chronicle. Detective Fahrina gave me your name—said you have a story."

"Who?"

"Don French—reporter at the Rockland Chronicle? I was following up on your claim of foul play with your sister? Something about a cover up?"

He could hear it—keys on a keyboard tapping out what would be the URL and then his name in the search bar. "Don French?"

A sick feeling came over him. *If Flynne didn't get the new pictures updated...* He tapped out his own query and waited for the page to load, as he said, "That's me." Beads of perspiration formed above the now-silver eyebrows. Would they match the man on screen or...?

It appeared. *If she hadn't just gone "hashtag-rogue" on me, I'd be surfing the Burberry website tonight. That girl does love her overpriced British accessories.*

"Oookay. So, what do you want from me?"

"I just wondered if I could get some information. I thought I'd look into it—see if there's a story there. I've got contacts and might be able to come up with some information." He waited for excitement to kick in before he added, "It might turn out to be nothing. I don't know. But if you're willing to meet somewhere, I'd like to try."

Her voice changed to the same suspicious tones Lucy had used when he'd entered that room just a year or so ago. "Yeah. That's not going to happen. I'm not stupid."

"Public place, Olivienne—"

"Liv."

Mark grinned to himself. *Gotcha.* "Okay, Liv. I need the public place, too. Gotta protect myself. Fiddleleaf? Four o'clock?"

"I don't get off until five-thirty."

Even better. Mark played it down. "Not sure if I can get there before seven, then. I have a meeting at five."

"Seven o'clock then. Fiddleleaf. I've been craving their

112

Turkish wrap, anyway."

He couldn't help himself. "Liv, if you like their Turkish, you need to go to Bodrum on Winchester. Amazing." It had a fifty-fifty chance of relaxing her. Mark held his breath and waited.

"Cool. Thanks."

It's as good as handled.

Tyler appeared with a printed code. "This just arrived from Keith—by text. I hate Morse code by text."

The modified "binary" Morse just looked like gibberish computer code—ones and zeroes. Mark's Morse—not so good. But Tyler had probably used a translator, so it should be accurate. He read each word, gut churning, and leaned back in his chair. "Are you sure?"

The kid's shoulders slumped. "Yeah."

Mark read it once more. TRACKER TOOTH IN ZIPLOCK UNDER ROCK 1/4 MILE FROM HELO. LANGAT KEPT A PHONE. HOW THEY FOUND US. SHOTS FIRED AT RAINA AND SOL. GO WITH MEDICS. OUT.

"Send Karen and Brian—*now!*"

0000 01 000 0000 1 01 110   010 111 110 001 0

Despite the midday sun outside, darkness shrouded the room. A lone desk-lamp bulb illuminated a fuzzy-edged circle in the middle—a spotlight on the center stage of unfolding plans.

Click—click. The pen served as a diversion more than a writing instrument. *Click—click.*

Sticky notes covered the surface of the desk. Pink, blue, yellow, green, orange. Check boxes with names beside them had been created on the yellow one in the center and read, *Langat. Schmatloch. Todd.*

Click.

A slash formed through the box beside Langat. A moment later, another one appeared in the one beside Schmatloch. The pen touched paper at the top left of the box next to Schmatloch. Hesitation. This time, it moved down to Todd and began creating slow, lazy ellipticals around it.

Plans took time. Haste only meant mistakes—and warnings. Warnings would never do. *Click—click.*

Or would they…?

Index finger and thumb stroked each side of the blue note. It lifted and affixed below the yellow. On it the one name. *Polowski.* The pen scrawled another name below that. *St. Louis.* One more.

Knupp.

The hand grasped the pink paper and set it just below the blue. One finger swiped across the top, affixing it securely. Block letters. Underlined. <u>AUGER?</u>

Once more the pen created lazy circles around the name. A finger flipped the blue note. Back to the pink. *Click—click.*

Lifted. Studied. After an exasperated huff, the paper crumpled into a ball and landed at one end of the desk. Out of the spotlight. A moment later, an index finger flicked it and it landed in the bin. Just as he had after they'd shot him. In the paper graveyard. All dead and gone.

The green note was set aside. *Click—click.*

That left only orange. Paris and Henry. Those two worked together too much. It would be tough to lose them, but maybe worth it…

Click—click.

114

TWELVE

Coherent solitude—the first time in what... two? Three days?

Erika counted. "Four days," she whispered. "Feels like a lifetime."

The little bungalow had no phone, and Flynne had taken hers with her. The duffel with the tranq guns was locked in Flynne's room, and so far Erika hadn't found anything to pick that lock with. Blinds instead of drapes, plastic hangers instead of wire—"Mommie dearest" would approve, anyway—and forks so tough she couldn't bend a tine to save her life.

That was one advantage to "kidnapped-for-her-own-good" round two—or was it three? Anyway, multiple rounds of involuntary extractions had their perks. She knew she wouldn't die—not if Flynne could help it. The problem was whether Flynne *could* help it. *I know more of what she should be doing than she does.*

Considering Flynne now floated in the pool on a lounger that Morgan pushed around like the obedient little lap dog that he was, it was safe to say that this statement was not an exaggeration. Twice, Morgan would have kissed her hooky-playing protector, but Flynne had the coy thing down pat. *Who knew?*

Splashes commenced. Flynne tumbled into the water and what had begun as a game became all-out war. *And*

Flynne will win.

Erika might have been correct but for one thing. *I underestimated the power of a cute guy with abs. He's no Keith, but for a gamer...*

At that moment, Flynne tried to up-end Morgan. It failed. He caught her around the waist and pulled her close enough to kiss. All Flynne had to do was give him half a reason to do it, but would she?

Conscience said it was none of her business. Morbid fascination, combined with utter boredom and more than a little irritation, kept Erika glued to the side of the window where she could see all and Morgan nothing. Their gazes locked—or so it seemed from her position thirty-feet away.

Morgan pushed the curls that Erika hadn't known Flynne had from the girl's eyes and cupped her cheek. "Oh, yeah. A whole lotta kissin' about to be goin' on."

But she was wrong. Flynne leaned her cheek into his hand for exactly three seconds. Erika counted for reasons she couldn't hope to understand, and it was exactly three seconds. Then, as if spurred by some instinct that popular girls at school had always possessed and Erika never had, Flynne pushed him away, swam to the side of the pool and wriggled—seriously, she wriggled—her way up and over the side.

You've got ovaries of steel, girl!

He chased her halfway to the bungalow before Erika forced herself to retreat to the bedroom. *I should munch on chips in here. Would serve her right.*

It could also get them killed if, by some bizarre chance, Morgan was the enemy. If Keith had taught her anything, it was that you couldn't trust anyone. *Probably not even Flynne.*

Giggles reached her as the front door opened and the

flirty couple entered. What Morgan said, she couldn't hear, but Flynne's, "Oh, you are just too supes adorbalicious!" prompted daydreams of waltzing out of the room and introducing herself as Flynne's "ghost of employment past."

Adorbalicious? Erika couldn't help herself. *Gag me with a puffy spoon.*

What happened after that, she could only imagine. Morgan's next words rumbled through the bungalow and barely made it past the door to Erika's room, but she heard it all the same. "I could stay... tonight."

You just made the torment worth it. This I gotta hear. And now I've got leverage. If Tyler knew...

Something deep within her suggested that she probably shouldn't be as delighted by that leverage, but Erika pushed aside the guilt and waited for Flynne's response.

"You could..."

Erika's throat went dry.

"But you won't. I don't work that way."

Well, good for you.

"Then let me take you out for that awesome shawarma we had last time you came." His voice drew nearer, and Erika backed away from the door. The closer he came, the faster her heart raced. "I'll—"

"What're you *doing?* I said *no!*"

"Just getting you a towel. You're shivering!" A few choice words followed, and Flynne threw a few more after it. He backed down. "Right... boyfriend. I forgot. Look, I'm just getting you a towel, okay? I'd never—"

"Get out, Morgan. Okay? I need you to go."

A cabinet banged shut. Seconds later, a low murmur followed, and just before the front door shut with somewhat excess force, Flynne called out, "Sorry. Can we talk later?"

It opened again. Erika didn't hear it, but she knew when Morgan's voice started up again. Indistinct words prompted Erika to crack open the bedroom door and listen. "—get it. Just come get me when you're hungry, okay?"

"Yeah…"

If her ears didn't deceive her, that agreement was followed by a kiss—one he wouldn't complain about. "You really are totes adorbified…"

"Glad you think so. See you later."

Erika stood there, arms folded over her chest, waiting for Flynne to come check on her. It took less than seven seconds. The door pushed open and banged into Erika's folded arms. "Wha—? Were you just standing there doing the evesies on us?"

"I don't even have words for that," Erika retorted. "But what I'd like to know is what Tyler will think of you and Morgan."

"He won't know, so who cares?"

"For a girl with decent morals on not jumping into any old bed, you're cavalier about your dating practices." Flynne shot a glare at her, but Erika wasn't finished. "Do you really think it's no big deal to be flirting with one guy while another guy has a reasonable expectation of loyalty?" Hands on hips and an unreadable smile on lips, Flynne confronted Erika with what seemed to be her best attempt at bravado—the adorable little thing.

"Look, Erika. I'm gonna do whatevs it takes to keep you safe, and if that means I have to, like, totes flirt with a cute guy, then I'm doing it." She blinked at Erika and shook her head like a confused puppy. "Wow. That didn't sound nearly as self-sacrificing as I meant it to…"

"Poor Tyler..."

To Flynne's credit, she blushed. A curl also flopped down over her forehead and plastered itself there. The effect looked like a misplaced flapper curl and was, Erika had to admit, "Totes adorbs" on her. *Again, gag me.*

0000 01 000 0000 1 01 110   010 111 110 001 0

Though Erika may not have appreciated Flynne's self-sacrifice, and Flynne knew it wasn't much of one, going out to dinner with Morgan left her gut swirling with indecision from the moment she met him out front, through a date that superseded any she'd ever had, and only increased as Morgan led her back along the path to where Erika waited. *I sure hope it was the right thing to do. He'd be suspish if I didn't...*

The dark bungalow looked so innocuous, but the signal was there—no porch light. Considering Morgan's continued determination to cement some sort of relationship, it was probably best. All the grandiose ideas of keeping things slow, casual, and maybe just a little fake on her side weren't going to happen. Not without help. Enter unwanted responsibility: Erika.

As they neared the door, Morgan slid an arm around her waist and murmured something about wanting to come in and kick her bum at *Dragon's Circle*. She didn't buy it. "You just think I'll let you stay if I, like, say yes."

The way he shrank back hinted that she'd wounded him. "I'm not just looking for a hook-up, Flynne." He stepped back, fists jammed in his jeans' pockets. "I just like being with you." He eyed her before turning and muttering, "Usually."

That one word shredded her heart with the speed and efficiency of a cat with toilet paper. She jumped after him. "Wait, Morgan. Sorry. Um..." What could she tell him? She'd already lied about—that'd do it.

"I lied to you."

That got his attention. He turned and peered at her through the darkness. "About what?"

"Why I'm here."

Flynne imagined that his eyes lit up as he said, "So... no boyfriend?"

"Sorta boyfriend... maybe. Before I got here, I would have totes said yes, but..." Until she'd spoken the words, Flynne hadn't taken anything either of them had said seriously. Now... now she wasn't so sure. *And I can't even tell Tyler. That's just eptastically icks.*

"I should feel sorry for him, but I can't." He stepped closer, and Flynne didn't even think twice about allowing him to slide his hand through her hair. "I've thought about finding a job in Rockland, but leaving a great place to live and an easy job so I can write games..."

She'd have been certain his words wouldn't mean a thing to her—but they did. The very thought of Morgan coming to Rockland sent shivers of excitement through her. "That's, like, some serious awesome sauce right there! Are you serious?!"

"What would your boyfriend say about it?"

All excitement shorted out and died. "Oh."

He just stared at her, his thumb caressing her cheek, and watched expressions she didn't even know if he could see. "Flynne?"

"Hmmm?"

"Why *are* you here?"

Answering that could get her killed by Erika, Keith,

and Mark—in that order. Not to mention Knupp. "All I can say is that there's, like, a situation at work, and I've got to figure out how to solve it. Can't do that there, so I came here because it's my fave and no one could find me and bug me."

The way he stepped forward and tugged her head with that kind of gentle gesture that melts hearts in every rom-com ever made told her he'd kiss her. The look she could finally see in his eyes told her that, this time, it would be a real one. The swirl in her gut and her swooning heart told her she wouldn't stop him.

The touch of his lips ensured it.

He said goodnight. Flynne was sure of it, but she didn't *hear* him until she'd closed the door behind herself and—yes, she did—leaned against it.

"Glad you've been getting your daily endorphin rush, but meanwhile back at the ranch…"

Flynne's eyes flew open—proof positive they'd been closed. *I'm like supes brill with that one.*

Erika sat on the couch, legs crossed, and arms folded over her chest. "Just clarify for me how making out with the lord and master's flunky is getting me home safe?"

"I was keeping him away from here! He's used to, you know, hanging with us. Can't let him get all suspish!"

"Are you not capable of coherent speech, or do you just like tormenting us with outdated teen-speak?"

Oh, yeah. She's feelin' salty. After a moment's thought, Flynne answered. "Yes."

"To which?"

Flynne grinned, arms folded over her own chest now. "Both."

"And you're—"

The door opened and Morgan rushed in mid-sentence. "—want you to know that if the whole 'fight for you—'" He blinked at the sight of Erika. "Who's that? When did she—?" His eyes bugged out. "*She's* not your boyfriend, is she?"

Flynne's giggle ended in a snort. "No... work problem."

"Flynne!" Erika hopped up and body slammed Morgan into the door, one arm pressed against his neck, her right knee poised for the kills, if it became necessary. "Have you gone insane?"

Morgan grunted and squeaked out, "I'd say you have."

"Like he wasn't going to, like, figure it out," Flynne protested. "Let. Him. Go."

"Not until—"

She bolted from the room and returned with a pistol— one that fit much nicer in her hand than the tranqs. "Back off, Erika."

To her surprise, it worked. Erika took two steps back, never taking her eyes of Morgan.

"What're you doing with a gun?" Morgan stepped close, but Flynne turned it on him. "Sit down, Morgan."

If one more thing could go wrong, Erika couldn't imagine what it was. There she sat next to Flynne's sorta new boyfriend and watched the gun with extra curiosity. *That doesn't look like a tranq. Where'd she get it?*

"Flynne, what's wrong. You look about ready to cry."

Erika shot a glance first at Morgan and then stared at Flynne. He was right. She did look about done in.

"Well, duh! I don't know how to protect someone from—"

"Oh!" Morgan gave Erika a sympathetic glance. "*She's* the one with the abusive boyfriend. Got it. Someone from your work?"

Before Flynne could mess it up even more, Erika nodded. "Yeah. Don't want to talk about it, okay?"

"So, what's with the gun?"

"No one can know I'm here. *No one.*" She shot a look at Flynne. "Right?"

"Right." Flynne moved to tuck her gun into her back waistband and dropped it. She snatched it up and swept the room with it like some seventies cop show girl.

Erika managed to avoid a snicker. Barely. Morgan, however, swallowed hard enough for Erika to hear and promised he wasn't out to get anyone. "I'll do whatever you need me to. I'll help hide her."

Both girls blurted out their objections in near perfect unison. "No!"

"At least we agree on that," Erika muttered. She inched toward the edge of the couch. "But we need to keep my existence here quiet, so the less you learn the better."

Flynne stepped forward, gun hanging at her side, finger off the trigger. "That's true. I mean, if we can think of anything for you to do—"

"I could call your ex-boyfriend and ask him if he's seen you. That you were supposed to come but you never got here. He wouldn't look here then."

That was the *last* thing they needed. Then again, Keith would come just to be sure. He'd check out everything, find them... *I wonder if I can convince Flynne without making her suspicious.*

"That won't work. She wouldn't give you the phone

number of a boyfriend she was running from before she ran."

Drat. She's thinking again.

"But... maybe you could..." Flynne paced, the gun swinging back and forth with each step. "Yeah. Send me a text message and ask where I am. Someone wants to rent the bungalow, so if I'm not coming, you need to know."

Where's the teen-speak, Flynne?

"What good will that do?"

Flynne gave him a pained look. "When *my* boyfriend realizes I'm gone, he's going to come looking for me. He'll start by hacking into my phone account."

This caught Morgan's attention. While Erika tried to guess if he'd be impressed or irritated, Morgan huffed and growled. "That's just—that's not right. You *do* have an abusive boyfriend—just a different kind of abusive."

"He's a totes sweet guy, Morgan. He's just not..."

How adorable. You blush. Who knew? And, yeah... Tyler's lost himself a girlfriend if I read people half as well as I think I do. Still, as cute as you guys were, you were more like competitive kids. This guy treats you like an adult while still—

Morgan hopping up and wrapping his arms around Flynne interrupted those thoughts. "I'll go do that right now. You call me if you want me to sleep out on the porch or something."

That touched a part of her that Erika hadn't expected. The moment the door closed behind him, she turned to Flynne. "Okay... I officially like him. But seriously? You can't *do* this stuff!"

The door popped open. "Don't yell at her. She's trying to help you."

Oy!

THIRTEEN

No one responded to calls. No one. Not even Claire, who was supposedly on her way back from Grand Haven. Claire, who had given every indication of *enjoying* talking to him. Claire, who he needed to be as safe as he felt certain Sol and Raina weren't.

Mark first watched the clock, then the door, in erratic cycles as he waited for word on Sol and Raina. Pacing—up one side of the room, pivot, back to the window. Each minute past the very longest it could have taken Brian and Karen to reach the cabin created a new horrific scenario in his mind.

If some of Langat's men had stayed behind, Mark's agents could need help. If Raina and Sol were injured, it could be a matter of simple medical needs trumping notification. And it could mean that they needed to get the team secure first.

It could mean they're dead.

Waiting wouldn't help. Mark had work to do anyway—starting with figuring out how Langat had been able to hide both a tracker *and* a phone from his agents. He seated himself at the desk and typed a quick message to Tyler. NEED YOU.

The door flew open a minute later. "What's up?"

Mark allowed himself the luxury of a glare.

"Sorry. I was digging through everything we've

125

gotten from Sol and Raina since Langat's extraction to see if I could figure out how he had a phone and a tracker that they missed."

Should have known. Along with a gesture for Tyler to be seated, Mark asked, "What'd you find?"

"Well, the tooth makes the most sense. We don't have many clients who would have something like that, so extractions don't include scans to detect stuff like that. We might need to figure out a protocol for it, though."

"Stuff like that takes time agents can't afford during an extraction. Still…"

Tyler dashed from the room and returned with the iPad. "We can ask, and if they admit to it, then we're good up front. But a two-step extraction with people who have the kind of money it takes for something that high tech—"

Both men froze. Mark cleared his throat and picked up the phone. With a wave of his hand, he sent Tyler from the room. His fingers danced above the keypad. Attorney General or Homeland Security? He chose the latter.

A sailor's dictionary of unsavory words flew at him when Jehnson answered. "—don't tell me you've got more bad news. I'm still trying to find Shin."

"Well, you won't. And I actually have a question that I don't want traced to me. You owe me."

"I owe *you?!*"

Rather than engaging, Mark just waited while Jehnson spewed the filth that could have gotten him brig time in the Navy. *They talk about swearing like sailors… but it's really that sailors make up for lost time the minute they're discharged.*

"Fine. What do you want?"

"I want to know how Langat could have the resources to have a GPS tracker."

"Pocket or semi-permanent?" Before Mark could

answer, Jehnson added, "Should've known you had him."

He might regret it, but without word of his agents, Mark needed reassurance that he'd done the right thing. "Yeah, well, if I didn't, he'd be dead. He may have cost me two agents."

This time, Mark counted to three before interrupting the tirade of expletives. "Okay. That's enough. Answer the question."

"There's no way Kenya would spend the money it takes for more than a pocket tracker—not on a guy like Langat. Maybe for the president, but even then... those things are expensive. Kenya doesn't have the resources for that kind of thing unless it's essential."

"So, this means what I suspected?"

"Yeah. We all got played." This time, Mark relished the simple, one-word curse. Jehnson sighed. "I'm on it, Mark. I'll let you know what I find.

The line went dead.

And at the same moment, Karen burst through the door. One look at her eyes said it all. Mark clenched his jaw and ground out, "Dead?"

She nodded. "Brian's on escort duty."

Another thought slammed into his brain before Mark could react to that. He jerked an envelope from the drawer and scrawled a note. "I've got to go leave this for Keith. Stay here and rest—or go home if you prefer, but I recommend here."

Karen stopped him long enough to say, "It wasn't your fault. Remember that. It wasn't yours."

0000 01 000 0000 1 01 110   010 111 110 001 0

Mark found the assumption of a persona preferable when dealing with difficult cases—especially after the afternoon's news. In this case, the nosy, brash reporter would have to do. The evening rush was winding down as he entered the Fiddleleaf Cafe, and thanks to bribing the hostess, she led him to the corner booth and promised to send Miss Todd to his table.

He knew her the moment she approached. Nothing in Lucy's dossier had said anything about a twin. A younger sister, yes. But anyone who saw the girl would assume... He blinked up at her. "Yes?"

"I'm Liv Todd? The girl up front said you're Dan—"

Standing to greet her might be common courtesy, but it was out of the question. Instead, he continued looking at her and shook his head. "Right, right. I didn't know I was dealing with a kid." He scowled at her. "This is all kinds of illegal. Sorry. Don't know what Fahrina was thinking."

She pulled a driver's license from her wallet and placed it before him with a tap to the photo. "I'm twenty-two, thank-you-very-much."

He picked up the card and memorized the license number before passing it back. "If you say so."

She dumped a purse half her size on the bench opposite him and plopped onto the seat. "So, are you going to research this or not?"

"Depends on what you have."

If he'd expected random theories and vague stories, Liv wouldn't have delivered. She pulled out a notebook with a pen, a mechanical pencil, and a thin stack of mini sticky notes affixed to the inside cover. An elastic band held it all shut, but once she opened it, a dossier his agents would kill for—or to protect, anyway—appeared.

"Okay, so I know she went to work..."

The download began. Dates, times, even the last moment her accounts were accessed—all there. He recognized every single date on her list. After all, Flynne had manufactured half of them.

Liv pointed to the date in question. "So, we were told she fell while hiking that spot above Lake Vienna. She—" a barely choked back sob followed. "Broke her neck. I asked the guy at the mortuary if there was anything inconsistent in what he found versus what we were told, and he said he wasn't an M.E. but not that he could tell."

Bonus to Gregg... Tyler can handle it.

"And then I got ahold of the coroner's report." Liv wrinkled her nose. "Those are nasty things. Ew."

"You should see ones after something gruesome—hit and run, mauled by animals, the—"

"I get it. They're gross." Liv huffed before adding, "Sorry. I get squeamish about stuff like this. Anyway, he says he didn't get a look at the body as it came in, but everything on the paperwork worked with what he found."

"And so, the story is... where?"

Liv tapped that date—the one where Lucy had paid the bill. "She couldn't have paid that bill from that place at that time. I think..."

What she'd say hit him before she found it. *Oh, we blew it big time.*

"Yeah. See... Payment was *after* the time of death. How's that possible?"

Mark had two ways to run with it. He could explain it all away right then, or he could call later and tell her he'd figured out it was an accidental date switch. But which would work best in the long run? He held out his hand for the notebook. "May I?"

She hesitated, searching his face for something she must have found. "Yeah... okay."

He scribbled down a few notes—things he already knew, of course—and passed both her notebook back and his chicken scratches. "Is that right?"

It worked. He didn't care what she said or thought next. It had worked. She trusted him to take it seriously. *And Rickwood, that's why sometimes you get your own hands dirty.*

"Yeah. Thanks. I thought you'd just brush me off like everyone else. Even my parents think I'm nuts. Dad keeps saying..." Liv's voice dropped to a mock bass as she said, "'I've had payments take days to show up after I made them.'" She huffed. "Yeah, well, cellphone logs don't lie. She made it. From her phone. The times correspond!"

Mark pulled a card from his pocket. "Okay, I'll check it all. I've got a contact in the coroner's office. Maybe he can get me some answers."

"It's out of county, so..."

He brushed that off as if nothing. "These guys work together. If my guy asks, the other guy will send copies of what I need. Logbooks and stuff that don't come with the report." He slid the card across the table. "If there's something, I'll find it. Meanwhile, if you think of anything or find anything else that looks suspicious—in journals or..." He'd found her weak spot, and Mark hated himself for it.

"I tried to read them. I did. But..."

"Want me to?" At her glare, he held up his hands. "I know! But I'm not connected to her. It might be easier for me. But if she had them, I need to see them. Also, do you have cellphone printouts? Who else did she call the day before, that day, the day after...?"

"She was dead. She couldn't call."

He gave what he hoped was a sympathetic smile. "But, Liv... that's why you're here, isn't it? Because she did make a call? So, what if she wasn't... gone? Not yet, anyway. I need that information, or I can't help you."

Her eyes narrowed into slits that gave her an Asiatic look. "What's in this for you?"

"Exclusive rights to the story. Well..." He allowed his own features to soften. "And if there is something messed up with this, I want justice for her. Everyone deserves justice."

In slow, precise movements, Liv reassembled her notebook. She paused just as she was about to put the rubber band back on and spread it out again. "Gimme your phone."

Mark complied.

Page by page, she did what he couldn't have hoped for. She snapped a picture of each page and passed back the phone. "Maybe you'll see something I can't if you have it all there." Liv stood and hoisted the purse on her shoulder. It should have sent her listing to starboard, but she stood there ramrod and determined. "Thanks again. Really."

With that, she turned and left... without ordering a thing.

The server arrived. "Ready to order? She said to come back once she left..."

Mark nodded, "Turkish Wrap. To go, please."

Twenty minutes later, he parked on the corner of Winchester and Savant. A slow stroll past Bodrum showed Liv bent over a plate, rereading that notebook. *I wish I could hire you.*

0000 01 000 0000 1 01 110   010 111 110 001 0

The charcoal Lexus slid into an open parking spot exactly opposite of Bodrum. Watching. Waiting.

In precise, thirty-second intervals, the turn signal flipped up, clicked a triple beat, and flipped down again. *Flick-thock... Flick-thock...*

Up from the corner, a waif of a girl strolled with purpose and determination. Four strides past the door at Bodrum, she backtracked and reached for the handle. A couple pushed out and nearly knocked her over. Apologies followed, if sign and body languages could be believed. The man held open the door, and the tiny girl slipped inside, presumably to wait for a table.

Flick-thock... Flick-thock...

A few minutes passed before she was seated in perfect view from the Lexus' windows. Without looking at the menu, she ordered and pulled something from her purse. Seated behind the wheel, the observer waited. Watched. *Flick-thock... Flick-thock...*

Food arrived and the girl hardly moved her... what was it? A book? Whatever it was, she hardly moved it. The plate sat to one side, waiting for her to take a bite. One finger held her place before she picked up a fork and cut into something. Dipped. Ate. After a second bite, the book moved left while the plate took up residence where it belonged.

Flick-thock... Flick-thock...

It might be worth trying the food... later.

The wait continued through each bite. Each page turned. Each person who walked and drove past the restaurant. *Flick-thock... Flick-thock...*

Twenty minutes passed before it happened. A car slowed before the restaurant—appeared to search for a parking place, as if it wasn't obvious that there weren't any on that side—and continued down the street.

Flick-thock... Flick-thock...

A decision swung on a pendulum from now to later. Advantages to both appeared, which only made things more difficult. *Flick-thock... Flick-thock...*

The empty plate did it. When the girl looked down to find nothing there, hunger nudged curiosity and careful planning into action. Keys rattled as a door opened. A car's horn blared.

Fingers itched to flick the blinker, but it wasn't there. Keys swung around a finger as the observer now jogged across the street and opened the door. *Show time.*

0000 01 000 0000 1 01 110   010 111 110 001 0

At midnight, just as Mark had pulled out the bookcase Murphy bed below his large screen monitor, the phone rang—a line they hadn't used in over a year. He hesitated, but with agents everywhere, two dead, Flynne on the run, and Fahrina fielding too-clever girls, he didn't have much choice but to answer it. But how... Cho or Mendina?

Mark snapped up the phone and just answered, "Mark here."

"Hey, Mark. Sorry. I didn't even know if this line was good anymore."

Corey?

"Mark?"

He cleared his throat. "Yes. What can I do for you?"

"You know I wouldn't be calling if it wasn't

133

important, right? And I'm sure Dr. Sorrano has kept you abreast of my progress after the debacle with Erika Polowski, so you know I'm doing much better."

Mark did know. He also knew it had taken her almost a full year to show the slightest progress, but the unrealistic hope of earning his trust back enough to be reconsidered as an agent had finally broken and opened her to real help. "I do. I am glad to hear it, Corey."

"I've done everything I know to do, but I don't have the resources you do."

"Again… what do you need from me?"

Here, her voice wavered. He'd never seen that side of her. "It's my brother. My sister-in-law called four days ago. He never came home. He's just gone—poof! No trace. No accessing of his accounts. Nothing." She swallowed hard enough for him to hear it through the phone line. "You don't have him… do you?"

Mark tossed the pillow he'd been holding onto the bed and moved back to his desk. He set up an email specifically for Corey and calmed her as he worked. "Okay, first… no I don't have him. Next, you've checked hospitals and morgues, right?"

"We've called the police—everything. I know what to do, Mark. No channels make sense. They have no sign of him anywhere. We're moving to places he used to go so we can figure out the last time people saw him—gas stations, restaurants, coffee shops, Walmart…"

"You do that. Meanwhile, send me anything you think I can use—name, license number, license plate, make and model… you know the drill. I want *everything* you can come up with sent to this email. Are you ready?"

Silence followed—silence broken only by soft weeping. "Thanks, Mark. Really. I—"

He assumed his sternest "boss voice" and asked again, "Are you ready, Corey?"

"Let me have it."

The moment he disconnected, Mark turned out the lamp and went to crawl into bed. *Tyler can handle that in the morning. Should take him an hour to find out that her brother has run out on his wife with a younger woman—to some South American or Asian country where they can live like kings on a modest income.*

FOURTEEN

Erika had been deposed as his most difficult client. Next to Langat, she was tractable—easy, even. *And he's not nearly as interesting or cute.*

He'd get blasted for that one—cute. Still, she'd have smiled, and she would have liked being called "cute," despite her protests. *Can't wait to tell her about this.*

Thoughts of where she was and how she fared only made Langat's indignant reaction to putting on coveralls and climbing into a tow truck even more irritating. "You have to do it. So, do it yourself or I'll knock you out and do it for you."

"I'm not a—"

Keith interrupted. "Right now, you're part of a tow truck team—as am I. I'm a highly trained security specialist, but to keep you safe, I have to pretend to know what I'm doing with this truck. We're *both* out of our elements. So, stop whining and get. The coveralls. On."

The Agency hadn't used the garage-turned-safe house yet, but since they needed to stay close to the city, Keith opted to do it. Opening the door would alert Mark, and him alone, to where they'd gone unless he punched in the right code. Keith deliberated on the use of that code. Just how necessary was total silence at this juncture?

They rolled down streets that always seemed to miss a chance on the repair dockets, and Rockland's worst area loomed closer with each block. Every few streets or so, he'd tell Langat to put his head down, make a few roundabout turns, and let the man up again. Just five blocks outside what locals called "The Crypt," Keith pulled into a ramshackle auto yard with enough locks and security measures to keep Castro safe.

Langat lifted his head just as the bay doors opened. "Where have you taken me? This does not look safe."

"You're safer here than almost anywhere."

The irony of rolling into a bay and having the door closed just as Langat protested, "There are gangs. I can see them," wasn't wasted on Keith.

"We can put all kinds of security measures here because of the area. No one thinks anything of it. And no one in your detail will imagine we've brought you to the middle of Rockland to hide you."

Langat's next protest began just as a few pops filled the air in quick succession. Langat dove for cover, but Keith jerked him back up again. "It's just a car backfiring." He nudged the man toward the stairwell and wished like anything he could have some wacky front for it. *Like that movie where they step into a phone box and it sucks them through a toilet into headquarters.* Another thought hit him halfway down the stairs. *Or better yet, an elevator. You go in, close the doors, and another door opens to the stairwell. What I wouldn't give to see his reaction to* that.

The apartment Mark had created—complete with state-of-the-art security measures, no less—gave every appearance of a luxury penthouse—below ground. With all the natural light spectrum bulbs inserted about the place, guests almost wouldn't miss windows... almost. Langat visibly relaxed.

"This is a very nice place. I understand now. It is a

disguise. Very clever."

And you'll hate it the first time I have to use restraints.

In about twelve hours, he could buy a newspaper and discover where Mark had left supplies. *This isn't supposed to be my job anymore. I should be out there looking for Erika. Instead, I have to babysit an egotistical diplomat.*

"When will we have a meal? I missed lunch and did not eat enough for breakfast for the worry."

"Well, since you held back a tracking device *and* a cellphone..." He couldn't help but focus on that one for a moment. "Just *where* did you manage to hide a cellphone?"

Langat stared at him, unspeaking.

Note to tell Mark that agents must now pat down every bit of a client's person. If he could have, Keith would have shuddered. *So glad I'm no longer an agent.*

"As I was saying," he continued. "Since I had to be pulled in last second, you'll get whatever is frozen or canned or boxed. I'll see what we have."

Something deep within him hinted that he could show more understanding to a man who was, after all, on the run for his life. *Yeah, and he could be understanding that it's not my job anymore.*

That Langat had no reason to know or understand that did not, in Keith's not-so-humble opinion, have any bearing on the case. None. Whatsoever. Not today. Not with Erika missing.

The freezer boasted several frozen meals that were, unfortunately, several steps up from the ninety-nine cent pot pies and burritos he'd hoped for. A few plain-labeled things hinted that maybe there he'd find the generic food he ached to serve—a means of venting all his frustrations and feeding the client in one move. Quite efficient, in Keith's estimation.

Cabinets offered more familiar fare—cold cereal, powdered milk with which to eat said cereal, canned soups and... ravioli. A smile formed. Erika would have pummeled him for it, but catharsis won out over fear of his girlfriend's opinion. "We'll start with this. It's fast and filling."

Disgust warred with relief when Langat polished off the entire can and asked if there was another. "Such a tasty treat. It's my favorite."

That's what you get for trying to stick it to a client, Auger— um, Shafter.

0000 01 000 0000 1 01 110   010 111 110 001 0

The morning edition would hit the local mini marts by four o'clock. Keith's alarm woke him at ten till. Rise... stretch... yawn... A yowl pierced the silent darkness—*his* yowl. Courtesy of Langat, of course. The man hadn't been able to land a punch when it came time for nighttime restraints, but he had managed a nice kick to the jaw.

It better not be broken.

All evidence pointed otherwise. Usually, he'd be pulled for an injury like that. It made him vulnerable. Still, he should only be there for a day or two more—just until he could pass off Langat to other agents and get back to finding Erika.

A quick peek showed the man sleeping soundly— snoring, even. The temptation to wake the man and make him go sit in the living room with lights on should have shamed him. Another yawn removed all shame. *It would serve you right.*

Locking a prisoner in a house was always a risk—

especially if leaving for longer than five minutes. Fire, robbery—anything could happen. But without backup, Keith had little choice. He couldn't have Langat wandering around with him, and he needed the money and communication supplies, if nothing else.

The relative quiet of early morning near the crypt offered a pleasant contrast to the midday and late-night pulse of rap and hip-hop music, threats, curses, and the occasional backfires and gunshots. A taxi shot past, obviously ready to call it a night and *not* looking for another fare. A cat yowled somewhere, and another took up the cry. Several moments later, dueling yowls and screeches pierced the air.

Keith strode with confidence—speed but not even close to running. He kept his eyes forward, except when the rare car approached. Then he watched, reaching one hand into his pocket until the car slipped past. The closest 7-Eleven took ten times longer to get to than it should have—in his mind, at least. He'd only seen five cars in the whole time he'd been gone. Perfect.

The man behind the counter greeted him. "Gas?"

"Paper."

He nodded at stacks beside the door. "One dollar." An accent, one Keith couldn't place, laced the words.

Middle Eastern, I think. Or maybe Pakistani.

Only spending a dollar on a paper didn't suit Keith. The store owner wouldn't get any of that—or if he did, not enough. A glance around him showed a few bananas and a few apples. He set two of each on the counter with the paper and went to grab a half-gallon of milk and a quart of orange juice.

Premade salads tempted him, but Keith reminded himself that it wasn't Erika. Langat probably would inhale

141

the rest of the canned raviolis. Still, the man might need some vegetables... Guilt piled on him as he forked over ten dollars and forty-two cents. *You wouldn't have hesitated for anyone else. You'd have done it because it was right—was kind.*

If only kindness was enough to ensure safety.

Outside, Keith strode away from the parking lot to the nearest garbage dumpster and ripped out three random pages—and the one he needed. He folded that one up and stuffed it in his pocket. The other three he wadded up and tossed as he made his way back. One in the backseat of a cluttered car, another in a trash can just outside the subway station a few blocks away. Overkill? Probably, but unnecessary caution rarely hurt.

Once on the train, he pulled the folded page from his pocket and read the ad. Twice.

DEAR JOHN. I NEVER WANT TO SEE YOU AGAIN. YOU'LL FIND YOUR STUFF AT THE OLD HOUSE. IT'LL BE GONE BY SATURDAY, SO GET IT WHILE YOU CAN, YOU JERK.

"Don't come back." Great. That's not good. And did he have to take the stuff all the way to the house on the other side of town? To the one I had to take Erika to? Below the belt, Mark. That thought shifted as he tossed it in a recycle bin on his way to the next train. *Or, are you saying Erika is safe? I took Erika there to be safe... is that it?*

Hope welled in him. If Flynne was a threat, there'd be more—the warning of someone coming after him if he didn't accept that it was over... or something. *I'll check that hashtag when I've got phones.*

Forty minutes—it took him forty minutes to get to that house and retrieve the bag. Fifty-two minutes to make it back to the station closest to the tow yard. He paused by the lockers and unloaded half the cash and a phone. As much as he ached to leave a gun as well, it wasn't wise.

People broke into those lockers. Sometimes, you just had to deal with what you were given. This was one of those times.

The temptation to take the time to call in an ad asking to go back to that house with Langat almost overrode prudence. The man couldn't escape and probably couldn't hurt himself, but he'd proven incapable of forethought. If he tried...

Keith booked it out of the station double-time and tried to act as nonchalant as possible as he neared the yard. A loose shoelace taunted him. Take a moment to tie it—usually a smart idea—or rush home first? He opted for tying. Tripping over a shoelace while fleeing anyone was a stupid way to get oneself killed.

Three thugs rounded the corner of the alleyway just as Keith stood. The biggest, a tow-headed giant who should have been named "Thor" spoke first. "What's in the bag?"

Aaand... here we go. Keith shrugged. If he gave it up too soon, they'd suspect he had more. Then they'd beat him until he gave that up, too—well, if they had any sense, they would.

"I *said* what's in the bag?"

"My stuff." Keith kept walking—advancing. It really was the best option, but his gut told him what his head had already deduced. It wouldn't work. Not this time.

"Give over."

This time, the scrawny kid beside him jutted his chin out. "Yeah. Give over."

Keith kept walking. "None of your business. Now get out of my way."

The other kid—they were all just kids, really—picked up the taunt. It couldn't have resembled a school-yard bullying more if they'd read from a script. "OOOh... listen to the big man." His voice rose in a cracked falsetto.

Yep, a kid.

"'Now, get out of my way!'"

The other two snickered.

Keith pushed past and entered the alley. Nothing. He took another step—two—four. Nothing. *Thank you, Lor—*

The prayer ended with a face-plant to the asphalt. A foot connected with his side, missing a rib—somehow. Keith didn't have time to figure that one out. Another one followed. *Bullseye! Oof...*

Despite every effort, he groaned. He also tasted blood. *Bit my tongue?*

An attempt to move his jaw failed—and sent shooting pains of agony down his neck. *How is that even possible?*

Thor must have unzipped the bag, because he squealed like a girl at Christmas. A stream of curses that no little girl should hear, much less say, followed. "Check it *out*! This guy is loaded. Wow."

He jumped to his feet, ready to grab the kid nearest him, when something hit him over the head. *Baseball bat? Stick? Langat's ego?*

"That's at least a grand!"

Make that four, and at least I haven't completely lost it. Deep breath. Gotta get one up on them.

"Guns? That is a weird-lookin' gun!"

Please don't aim it. Keith tried to plead with them to let it drop, but his mouth refused to work.

The two thinner boys jerked him up. "What's that?" They shook him so hard his face hit the barrel. "Paint ball? You goin' ballin' later, big guy?"

He'd just filled his lungs again and managed to get his bearings when the next blow came. A head butt—right to his nose. Blood spurted. No longer stunned, he dove for Thor.

And underestimated the guy. Lighter on his feet than a ballet dancer, Thor dodged the attack and kicked Keith into a fence. *I think that just displaced the fracture. Great.*

Only two real options remained. Get up and hope to overtake one—possible, but difficult the way he kept seeing black spots—or pretend to be out. Langat needed him to make it. Keith struggled to rise and let himself fall. *Lord, please don't let them see I didn't let my face hit the ground.*

Even without seeing or hearing, Keith knew. Thor squeezed that trigger. A moment later, he figured the safety was now off. One of the other boys pointed. "Look. It's air soft—like they do in those things on YouTube."

Oh, do not...

The other kid piped up. "I think you need these containers. BBs in there?" Silence followed.

And now you shook it...

"No, to push the BBs out. You need..." Rifling sounds followed. A low whistle. "Whoa... these are like—you know, for animals."

The other scrawny one started shuffling away from him. "He's probably a cop!"

Thor scoffed. "Cops carry real guns, stupid."

"Not if they're animal control. They use those for, like, rabies and big game. We gotta get outta here!"

Scuffles. A kick to his shin. Keith did everything he could to flop and ignore the next wave of nausea that followed his chin hitting the ground. Again.

"Hold 'im, Skeez."

What kind of nickname is Skeez?

The sounds—Keith knew them well. He had to try. More than one tranq... "If you shoot him more than once, he could die."

His words came out garbled. *Probably that jawbone not moving like it should.*

It earned him another kick, another scrape of his face across the asphalt, and likely a shot of his own. *At least I can take two—maybe three.*

The first one hit his ankle. *Not too bad.*

The second hit the kid, if the yowling and cursing meant what he thought. Keith tried to rise and found his head crushed to the ground by an oversized shoe. *Probably a Nike. He "just did it."*

When the second tranq hit his thigh, the other boy protested. "I'm not gettin' caught for killing someone. Let's go!"

"What about Talon?"

Thor snickered. "He knows what's good for him."

A thud followed—likely "Talon" hitting the ground. "Gonna search his pockets—see if he's a cop."

They took his cash—what was left of it, anyway—and tossed the crumpled newspaper page on the ground beside him. Crunches followed. Keith grew groggier and groggier. One eyeball pried open and saw the last wadded up newspaper page lay in the gutter, wet, dirty, soaking up blood.

His blood.

FIFTEEN

Saltshaker to the left and peppershaker a few inches above it, Flynne's hand hovered over both, clutching the napkin holder and waving it about as if some housekeeper's magic wand. She sighed and set it left of the saltshaker. "That'll have to be Minneapolis."

"What are you talking about?"

Flynne jumped and sent the napkins flying across the table and onto the floor. "Don't. *Do*. That!" She turned to glare at Erika. "It's supes annoyzballs."

"That's a new level of cheese, even for you"

"Well, I'm *trying* to figure out how to get you somewhere safe. And it's not easy when you don't know what you're doing! I'm going cray-cray!"

"Stop!"

Erika had the grace to look chagrined at Flynne's second glare of the night... or was it morning? Flynne didn't know anymore.

"Sorry. But seriously. How does someone as intelligent as you are decide to dumb it all down into teen-speak... that no one uses anymore?" She dropped to a chair next to Flynne and moved napkin Minneapolis over to Fargo, North Dakota. "You know that, right? No one says 'awesalicious'—which sounds like something salacious, by the way—or 'totes adorbs' or most of that stuff anymore?"

Flynne moved Minneapolis back to where it belonged.

"I don't know anything about Fargo."

"Huh?" Erika reached for St. Louis the saltshaker, but Flynne swatted her hand away. "What?"

She pointed. "That's Chicago. We're pepper here in St. Louis, and the napkin holder is Minneapolis." She tapped the spot where Erika had moved the napkin holder. "That would be Fargo or something over there. I don't know anything about Fargo—just where it is."

"Oh."

"And as for how I talk…" She shot her best frustrated look at Erika and said, "I worked *hard* to learn all the totes cool stuff so people would quit saying how I'm 'so ooold for such a young person.' They don't do it anymore, so it worked."

"Yeah, well they don't 'do' your 'supes last year' teen-speak anymore, either."

As if she didn't know it. Still, habits die hard, and the memory of Mark's smile and shaking head when he thought she wasn't looking… "So what? I learned it. Spent *foreves* learning it. Got it all wrong at first. Totes newbie. Now it's me."

She pulled a water glass down and to the left of the pepper shaker. "Tulsa. We could go to Tulsa."

"Why?"

It was a fair question. "I don't know! That's what they do, though. They move you guys all over the place."

"Not always, Flynne." In a tornado of epic proportions, Erika swept the cities and their markers into the center of the table. "Look, I lived here." She put the peppershaker on the left of the table. The salt went right next to it. "One street over is where Keith took me. We immediately went in a van…" She dragged the napkin holder off to the right. "Up to this cabin over here. Probably up by Lake Vienna, but not sure where, actually."

"And you stayed there the whole time?"

Erika shook her head and reached for the water glass. "No. Then, they got word for us to get out of there. So..." She dragged it down from the napkin holder cabin. "We went really close and were there for quite a while. But, usually, we only moved if they thought Helen was getting close—although, we didn't know it was Helen."

That caught her attention. "Who's Helen?"

Erika tapped the peppershaker. "That was her house. I was a house sitter for her. Lived there most of the time because she was down in Australia. Turns out, she was into human trafficking. She was being protected *by* the Agency... hired them to protect *me!* And then tried to take me out."

"So, she's, like, totes jailie?" Flynne winked at Erika's wince. "C'mon. You asked for that one."

"As far as I know, she's locked up for good and won't ever get out again."

Those words didn't set well with Flynne. "What do you mean, 'as far as you know?'"

Erika toyed with the house—was it the safe house or Helen's?—and avoided her question until Flynne pressed again. After shoving the shaker away, Erika folded her arms over her chest and huffed. "Look, I know it's stupid and everything, but I just didn't want to know if they found some technicality that got her a reduced sentence. I like to think of her sharing a cell with someone tough enough to keep her in her place."

It made sense—it did. But Flynne knew she never could do it. Still, something told her that saying as much to a "client" was probably not the right thing to do. Besides, Erika had given her more to think about. "So... does

Morgan knowing about you here mean we have to move?"

0000 01 000 0000 1 01 110   010 111 110 001 0

"...*does Morgan knowing about you here mean we have to move?*"

The question looped itself through Erika's mind until she thought she'd go crazy. *I shouldn't have to wonder. I should be able to trust that she knows. And why am I still here? She doesn't seem to know that Keith locked me in or actually used chains on me to keep me there. I could get out of here, walk to a gas station or something, and call Keith. He'd be here in just a few hours at worst.*

Why she wasn't leaving... that question nagged and badgered her until Erika faced facts. She sat up in bed and muttered, "I'm seriously still here because I don't want to make the girl who *kidnapped—*" the word came out in a hiss. "—me feel bad? Really?"

Off went the covers. In less than a minute, she'd donned fresh yoga pants, t-shirt, and hoodie. Nothing else mattered—not now. With such a short drive, there was no reason she couldn't be home in a matter of half a day.

A soft snore from the couch told her Flynne had at least had the sense to *try* to prevent escape. *Maybe she has decent instincts that just need a bit of training.* The idea of paying to listen to Flynne's chatter, however, nearly drove Erika nuts. *Nope. She needs to stay where she is.*

Blankets rustled as Erika inched the door open and slipped out. She hesitated, deliberating between running like mad and stealth. Stealth won—barely. The half-moon and clouds colluded with her and provided enough shadows to creep between until she made it to what she thought was the end of the drive. The street, however, turned out to be an alleyway. Still, escape was escape.

Erika made it three steps before a familiar voice said, "I have her gun. Don't make me figure out how to use it."

Furious, both at him and herself, Erika whirled and stormed over to rip it from his hands. "Seriously, Morgan? What are you *thinking*? If you don't know how to use a gun... *Don't point it at people!*"

"Give that back."

If God gave bonus points, Erika wanted them for not laughing. "You're kidding me, right?"

"Do *you* know how to shoot?"

"I've shot a gun before." *Okay, I shot myself, but he doesn't need to know that.* "That makes me the one with experience. Now..." she fumbled with the chamber and then frowned. "Seriously? Is this a BB gun?"

He shrugged. "How should I know? Flynne's the one with the cool moves. I'm just trying to keep her from losing her job."

You have no idea that doing *this probably lost it for her.*

"Smoke Gets in Your Eyes" began playing from Morgan's pocket. She couldn't see his expression, or his skin tone, but Erika decided he blushed as he fumbled and answered. "Flynne?"

Erika took two steps back, still holding the gun on Morgan—just in case he'd forgotten that air soft wouldn't kill him. *Or seriously maim him—dddrraat it all.* Something in her spirit poked. *Sorry, Lord.*

Flynne's voice filled their little spot in the alley. "She's, like, vannie!"

"She's what?"

"Poofs! Gone. Vannie!"

Before she could consider the wisdom of the

movement, Erika snatched the phone from Morgan and demanded to know just what "vannie" meant. "Seriously, Flynne?"

"Are you out there like... *with my boyfriend—sorta?*"

If the grin on Morgan's face—anyone could have seen it in the middle of a black hole if they wanted to—meant anything, she'd just made the night's hassles worth it for him. Erika tossed him a bone. "He's out here trying to stop me from leaving. To *help* you, you twit. Now what does 'vannie' mean?"

"You know... vanished. Vamoosed. Vannie. Everyone says it."

"No, Flynne. No one says it. No one has ever said it, and neither should you."

"Toodles de-la tough. I'll say what I want. Gimme Morgan."

She passed him the phone and took a few steps back. "You can have him."

It was a risk—a big one, but Erika took it. The moment Morgan half-turned away to talk to Flynne, she bolted. Three feet, five. Ten.

"Hey!"

Footsteps behind her. *Oh, man. It's déjà vu... but on asphalt! And Morgan doesn't know how to tackle without hurting me.*

They grew closer. A glance back showed him just a few feet behind her. *Step aside before he tackles...*

"I'm takin' you down, Erika. You'd better stop."

The déjà vu moment ended. Erika slowed and jerked out of his path. Morgan landed, arms outstretched to grab her. His scream rent the night air. From behind, more footsteps followed—Flynne pounding her way to him.

"What'd you do?"

"Avoided getting tackled?"

Morgan just laid there, shaking. Fighting back... pain? Tears? She wouldn't blame him. He'd probably left half his skin behind.

Flynne shot daggers at Erika as she passed. "He's *hurt!*"

"He was going to *hurt* me," Erika shot back.

"Well, *you* left!"

"Because *you*..." Part of her didn't have the heart to say it. The other ninety-eight percent outvoted that part. "—don't know what you're doing. I was going to call a *professional.*"

As if they hadn't been having a perfectly lovely argument, Flynne beckoned her. "Help me get him up."

Like an idiot, Erika complied. *This Christianity thing is going to be the death of me.*

From somewhere deep within came the memory of Keith reading a verse about dying with Christ. *Didn't know it was supposed to be literal...*

The moment they settled Morgan at the kitchen table, Flynne turned on Erika and snatched the gun from her hand. "Give. Me. That. What is *wrong* with you? Are you trying to get us all killed?"

"I'd say you've got that covered."

Morgan's pain-filled voice interrupted the burgeoning argument. "Can you hate on each other later? I think I need to go to the ER."

Both women scoffed. "We just need to clean it out," Flynne insisted. "Erika—find the hydrogen peroxide."

Poor Morgan whimpered. "Don't think," he gasped. "—we have any."

"Oscar performance." Erika turned to Flynne. "So, where would I find this medical wonder?"

"Be nice." The problem was, Flynne didn't know the answer to that question. "Um… Bathroom?"

While Erika went to retrieve basic medical supplies, Flynne filled a bowl of warm water and grabbed a washcloth from the linen closet. They met back at the table with Erika looking disappointed. "Nothing." She pulled a bottle of rubbing alcohol from behind her back. "It'd sting more, but at least he'd—"

"First aid kit behind the pantry door!" Morgan dropped his head. "Please, *God*, let there be something with lidocaine in it."

When Erika set both hydrogen peroxide and lidocaine spray in front of Flynne, she said, "I didn't know you believed in God."

"I don't."

She snatched back the lidocaine. "Then stop asking Him for stuff."

Despite her giggles, Flynne held out her hand for the can. "I'm, like, sursies that Jesus would want you to be nice."

"And I'm like…" Erika stuck quoting fingers in the air. "Sursies that I'll smack you if you ever say that again."

"Do I have to turn the other cheek if I don't believe Jesus was God?"

Erika shrugged. "No."

"Good." Flynne tried to hide the grin spreading. "Do you?"

"Probably." Before Flynne could gloat, Erika added, "But I doubt I will."

Morgan muttered something about her not needing to repent at least. So, while Flynne tried to squeeze a washcloth of warm water over the arm to clean it out, she asked what repenting actually did. "I've heard Claire say that, but…"

"It's just deciding you won't do something again and asking forgiveness for doing it in the first place." Morgan hissed the words between each squeeze of water over his arm.

"So, you don't believe now, but you did?"

Flynne's gaze swung from Morgan to Erika and back to Morgan again as both women waited for his answer. When he wasn't forthcoming, she threatened to add a bit of the alcohol to the water.

"My parents were Christians, all right? I just didn't get the Jesus gene."

A "discussion" began. Erika informed him that even she, as a new Christian, knew that you didn't inherit Jesus like you did crossed eyes. Morgan interrupted and tried to talk over her, insisting she knew what he meant. Flynne told him to shut up. "*I* don't know what she means. What's with the inheriting Jesus? So, if I want to be a Jesus freak, my parents have to be? What about grandparents?"

"You can be one without anyone in your bloodline believing all the way back to Pentecost!"

Both Flynne and Erika asked, "What's Pentecost?" Erika added, "Again" to it like she thought she should know but wasn't sure. Morgan just pointed to his arm. "Unless you've got some gift of healing that'll take care of the pain and burgeoning infection going on here, either clean it up or get out of my way so I can get to the ER."

"I think he should go, actually."

Flynne shot Erika a look that was intended to say,

"Are you totes cray cray?"

She got the memo, too. Before Flynne knew what hit her, Erika had dragged her down the hall. "We can take him to the ER, get him all cleaned up, and give him Uber money to go home Then we can drive around and find an escape plan in case we need to get out of there fast."

"So... that's what you were doing this morning? Just..." Flynne hooked her fingers on each side of her head. "—checking out alternate things?"

"Nope. I was calling Keith to get me out of here. We need someone who knows what they're doing. I barely know more than you... and *you're* the so-called agent in this scenario."

The worst of it all was Erika was right. Flynne peered around the corner and stared at Morgan, shot a glance back at Erika, and went to inspect the wound again. The water in the bowl was bright pink from all the blood. Rocks were embedded in raw flesh.

"That's it. Get him in the car. We're going."

Both Erika and Morgan pumped their right arms. Erika's was accompanied by a, "Yassss!"

Morgan's victory shout ended in, "Noooo..." however.

SIXTEEN

Consciousness approached with the subtlety of a marching band in the Rose Bowl Parade. With each footstep, pain pierced deeper, throbbed harder, begged for a whimper. Even in a semiconscious, pain-induced stupor, Keith suspected it was a bad idea to indulge. He just couldn't gather his muddle-headed thoughts enough to figure out why.

Metallic and thick, he spat out the saliva congealing in his mouth and gagged at the pain it caused. *Blood. Pain. I should know this.*

When baby steps proved too much, he tried for minuscule steps. One eye open—asphalt. Another eye. More asphalt. Deduction? *Okay, so I'm lying on the ground... in the street...*

Trying to move his arms felt like he imagined moving through mud might be. *I can imagine and it's mud. Second deduction. I'm not dead. Heaven doesn't have mud bogs on asphalt. Hell doesn't either. I think. Fire and mud don't mix, right?*

Each semi-coherent thought prompted a bit more coherency, until Keith dropped his forehead to his hands and nearly screamed with the pain. *Jaw broken. Shot.* He sucked in air and winced at that, too. *Cracked rib...* Another attempt. *Or two.*

That's when the memory of seeing the asphalt

connected a few important synapses. *Gotta get off the ground.*

His head spun as he pushed through pain and got himself seated upright. His vision swam and blurred. *Focus.*

The throbbing shifted to the right side of his head. Reaching up? Bad idea. Pain stabbed through one side and out his left ear. Sticky, semi-congealed blood covered that hand.

That's when Keith saw him—the skinny kid. Another memory flashed—the kids turning on each other. *And me.*

Standing wasn't a good idea—not yet. Instead, Keith crawled to the boy's side. Three tranq darts. *No way he could survive that.* Checking the kid's pulse confirmed. Dead. *Kids are cruel.* His conscience pricked him at that. *People are cruel… we just hope kids will be the innocent creatures we want them to be and then are revolted when they aren't.*

They'd gotten Keith in the thigh, right? He patted himself until he found the dart. Instinct took over. Break the needle, find dirt, press it deep into the dirt, hide evidence of disturbance. Stuff dart in pocket.

There was another one—my ankle.

Quick movements meant more blur, more swimming. He found it, though, and repeated the needle disposal process. That's when it hit him. *For me to be this messed up, they had to have gotten me again.*

He found it as consciousness continued to be a thing. Right there… bobbing out of his neck. It took more self-discipline to pull it out than Keith could have expected. *Just the after effects of the drugs. No biggie. Pull.* If only his psyche listened to his brain. *Stupid TV shows.*

By the time he'd disposed of his final needle and pocketed the tranq, his head felt clear enough to allow him to process even more pain. *Lucky me.*

A nearby chain-link fence, one he suspected he should recognize, gave him the support he needed to try to stand. Knees tried to buckle. Mouth filled with gunk again. Keith tried *not* to vomit. *That'll hurt with a broken jaw.*

Clutching the fence, he scooted down a few feet, paused, and scooted some more. Broken-down cars in the yard triggered another thought. *The tow yard.* And finally, the one that sucked the strength from him. *Langat.*

Releasing one hand from the fence, Keith made his way as quickly as he could manage to where the gate stood locked. Combination. A glance up at razor wire told him he couldn't go over. He'd *have* to remember.

If I get it wrong more than twice, they'll know where I am.

A scan of the sky blinded him until Keith forced one arm over his head to shade his eyes from the glare of the morning sun. It had to be after ten o'clock. Langat would be a mess.

C'mon, think. *Combination.*

The seconds ticked in his mind with the relentless pressure of a bomb counting down to explosion. A minute followed. Two. *Not words spelled as numbers. Not anything related to the Agency. Not personal like a birthday...*

A smile tried to form — and failed as pain shot through his jaw. *Who knew?* Keith thought as he punched in 1776 — Independence Year. *Who knew that smiling requires your jaw to function properly?*

Every bit of him wanted to race inside, get down, free Langat, and get them out of there. He just couldn't. He needed a trip to Dr. Brecham, the Agency's private doctor, and a new vehicle.

The memory of the boy in the alley added another item to that list. *And a clean-up crew.*

Something didn't add up. The threat to Schmatloch came from a woman who had just posted pictures on Instagram of the family at the Dachau Memorial. The caption read: *Met this man whose great grandfather was a guard here on liberation day. Like our grandfather, his didn't survive.*

The image captured a young man holding one half of a sign and the woman who had built a hate-filled case against Schmatloch holding the other half. The sign read: *Never Again. #nomorehate.*

The time stamp was just about the time that the call from Schmatloch came through.

Mark captured a screenshot and zipped it to Tyler with a message saying he'd be right there. In the office, Tyler sat at Flynne's desk scanning a bank of screens. Centered in front of him, Flynne's Newton's cradle plinked back and forth in a rhythmic cadence. "Do you see it?"

Tyler stopped the swinging balls and looked up at him. "Flynne checked their online history, right? All of it?"

"Yes." Mark's gut churned at the images Flynne had shown him. "They have a public persona and a dark web presence that redefines vile."

"I'll dig but…"

He hated to do it. Poor Mr. Schmatloch would be frightened, but there wasn't any way to avoid it. "Move Doyle and Sam off-grid. Motor home. Southwest area. No cliffs. And tell them to change the license plates every thirty-six hours."

"That bad?"

Answering that one was tougher than he'd expected.

"More like, that confusing."

"Could the IG thing be a cover for what's coming?"

No matter how many times he recalculated, the numbers were impossible. "No. So, either the threat to personally and physically destroy Walther Schmatloch's son was bogus or…"

Tyler grabbed the end ball on the right side of the cradle, lifted, and released. The steady, *plink, splink, plink, splink* of the so-called "perpetual motion machine" started up again. "I get why Flynne loves this thing. It does help you think." He sighed. "Someone's being set up, aren't they?"

"Probably."

"Why?"

One finger at a time, Mark unclenched each fist and forced his shoulders to relax. "Haven't a clue."

"Should you bunker?"

"No." In the most honest corner of his mind, Mark amended that answer. *Definitely.*

Silenced reigned. Silence marred only by the continuing *plink, splink, plink, splink* of Flynne's bouncing metal balls. A short huff preceded Tyler squaring his shoulders and pulling the keyboard toward him.

"I'll find it."

And if Flynne was here, she'd have it done in half the time.

That prompted a rue-filled inner snicker. Who was he kidding? If Flynne walked in the door that moment, he'd fire her sorry backside before he could reconsider. *And this just called that Cayman account into question. Might have to call the IRS Commissioner.*

In Mark's office, a phone rang. The two men stared at one another before bolting, one after the other, to answer it. Mark snatched it up. "The Bark Inn, your doggy daycare specialists, Bernard speaking."

"Need help, Mark."

He gripped the back of his chair. "Keith?"

"Yeah, sorry. Gimme the shortest protocol you've got. Jaw's broken."

Covering the handset, he barked orders at Tyler. "Get Dr. Brecham on the phone. See if he can make a house call for a broken jaw or if we need to come in."

"Ribs." The word came through with a wheezed cough followed by a groan.

Mark considered before asking, "Punctured lung?"

"Not. Sure."

It had been six—no, seven—years since he'd done it, but Mark grabbed keys to a minivan and passed the phone to Tyler. "Tell him I'm on my way. Get whatever info I need and text it to me. Then get Karen, Claire, and Brian over to the tow yard."

"That's where he is?"

Mark didn't bother to answer that one.

0000 01 000 0000 1 01 110   010 111 110 001 0

"Keith."

Pain sliced through him as Keith jumped to his feet, knife at the ready. The sight of Mark standing there proved a theory he'd always had about hidden entrances to key locations. His arm dropped. The knife clattered to the floor.

Langat spoke from the doorway behind him. "How did they find us?"

Mark would want to know, too, so Keith said it again. "They didn't. Random mugging."

With a dismissive wave, Langat scoffed, "You let a

mugger get you?"

He'd have ignored the man's opinions if the insult hadn't crushed the injury to his jaw—if Langat hadn't been responsible for it in the first place. "Hard to fight with a broken jaw."

"How'd they break your jaw, Keith?"

He turned to Mark and tried to enunciate without moving his mouth too much. *"They* didn't." His glare indicated the real culprit. *"He* did."

Protests filled the room. Langat ranted, raved, wailed about the injustice of a man of his importance being chained up like a common criminal. Keith just waited. He hadn't expected to be privy to this moment.

"You're in breach of contract, Mr. Langat." Mark stepped closer. He could be an intimidating man in a casual conversation. Ticked off and worried about an agent made him almost terrifying to Keith. He could only imagine what Langat thought of it.

"You *agreed* to it. Page four, paragraph six, line three. You initialed. Would you like to see a copy?"

A short shake of the head. Downcast eyes. For a moment, Keith actually thought the man would capitulate. A moment later, that thought died.

Langat rushed Mark, ready to fight his way out.

Survival. That's good. He's still fighting.

Mark had him against the back of the couch in a cop's hold in five seconds flat. "I should drop you off at your embassy."

"No!" The barked order shifted to pleading. "I am sorry. I did not think you would actually do it."

Why did people always assume those possibilities were for everyone but themselves? Keith shot the question at Mark who somehow managed to roll his eyes without moving them. Keith couldn't hear what Mark said to the man, but when Langat stepped away from the couch, he adopted an air of deference and apologized. "I did not mean to hurt you."

A small smile played about the corners of the man's mouth. Despite feigned respect, Langat liked thinking he'd bested an agent. *Maybe I should have clocked him one. It's so hard to know sometimes.*

"If Keith wasn't the nice guy he is, *you'd* be the one sporting the broken jaw. If I know my man, he let you get the punch—"

Both men blurted out, "Kick."

"Fine, get the *kick* in because he didn't want to have to hurt you."

Whatever else was said, Keith missed. Mark relegated him to the secure room while dealing with Langat and joined him there a few minutes later. The moment he stepped into the room and saw Keith's face, his expression changed from grim to concerned.

"Are you really okay?"

"Dr. Brecham would be a better one to ask. I think so, though. Then again, it's getting harder to breathe. Can't decide if that's me not wanting to because of the pain or because of a punctured lung."

"Claire is going to get him. I sent her here first and then decided he could look at you and choose where to treat. Faster that way in the long run."

If he could have sagged with relief, he would have. Instead, Keith nodded and leaned against the table. "We need cleanup out there. I left blood in the alley. Couldn't take care of that and get back to Langat. I did take care of the tranq needles."

Understanding darkened Mark's face. "They got the

guns?"

It hurt more to admit that than any attempt to move his jaw. "Sorry, Mark. I tried." He took as deep a breath as he could without losing his cool and filled Mark in on the rest."

"Skeez? That's good. Talon?"

Keith nodded.

"Okay, we can work with that. I'll send Tyler in skinny jeans and Converse this afternoon. Someone around here will know all their names."

"Gotta call the police soon. Talon shouldn't be left out there alone."

Mark's response was interrupted by Claire bursting in with a hooded Dr. Brecham in tow. "He was only a few blocks from where I was when you called!"

Translation: He was in his office near the Mayflower building and you were on the way to the office.

Within five minutes, they were on their way to St. Joseph's in Westbury.

SEVENTEEN

Four photos lay in a large rectangle on the desk. Lucy Todd leaving Thornton-Weinbach Research Labs—time stamped at 9:04. Lucy Todd leaving a deli down the street at 9:17—in braids and missing a jacket. Lucy Todd entering a synagogue at 10:22. Lucy Todd going through the subway turnstile at 11:01.

All just days before Lucy died in a "hiking accident." The photo on the screen showed the logbook from Lucy Todd's arrival at the morgue—another few days after she supposedly died. Where had she been all that time?

A click sent the printer whirring, and the picture of the logbook dropped into the tray.

Hesitation mounted with each click of the mouse, each shifting image on screen. Such a fine line between pressure and resistance. Then again, there were always other ways to push back again. Plans B, C, D, M, Q, and Z if necessary. Always alternates…

One finger stroked a metal frame.

Before the hand could reach to start things in motion, an email chime filled the room. The subject line prompted a smile. IP addresses for RG&E.

It took several minutes to find the number and paste it in for confirmation, but there it came. Buffalo Point, Manitoba. "Gotcha."

A slide, a click, and *whirr…* the printer spat out

another page. This time, that finger slid down columns of numbers until the IP address appeared. A highlighter, pink, in honor of Lucy, swiped across the numbers. A screen shot of the IP lookup website followed. Trim out any identifying peripherals and… another click. Print.

Each piece of proof was stacked and slid into an envelope. Speakerphone—dial. The voice. "Send Knupp to St. Louis. The address I gave you. Then take the girl."

"That it?"

The left index finger stroked the edge of the envelope. "I have a package for Todd. Meet with her tonight."

"Usual drop place?"

"Yes."

The call went dead. Everything was ready. A thumb caressed the polished ball of a Newton's cradle. Swing to the right. Release. *Snap-plink-snap-plink.*

The thrumming beat of music was accompanied by blush-inducing lyrics. Though not exactly a prude, Tyler found himself fighting to drown them out as he leaned against a minimart wall and waited for the first wave of boxer-baring, penguin-walking banger wannabes. *Otherwise known as teen boys. I never knew how good I had it as a kid in rural Indiana.*

A pack of girls, five in all, sashayed past with laughter, giggles, and more than a few glances thrown over their shoulders—presumably at boys who followed. He shoved off the wall, fists jammed in his pockets and his hoodie pulled back just enough that he didn't look creepy. One girl winked at him as he neared.

168

"Hey, seen Skeez or Talon?"

She shrugged. "Don't know them."

A girl to her right shot him a dirty look. "We don't hang around Kyle and his loser friends."

"They took something of mine," he said. "Gotta get it back."

"Good luck with that. Kyle doesn't do take backs unless he's the one taking back."

The first girl offered him a shy smile. Something about the way she was dressed reminded him of pictures of his mom from the eighties—shirt with a wide neck sliding off her shoulder and hanging baggy over leggings and boots. Scrunchie. That's what his mom called those poofy things to hold up ponytails. Scrunchies. This girl had one of them, too.

"You wanna come with us? We're going to see the new Dylan Dunston movie."

"Cool…" Tyler gave every hint he could of wanting to go and then drooped his shoulders. "Wish I could. Gotta get my stuff back, though."

The friend jerked the girl away. "He's probably a druggie. Stay away. Let's go."

Scrunchie girl shook off her grip and eyed him. "You after drugs?"

"My dad's air soft guns. He's gonna kill me if I don't get them back."

The group of guys they'd been smiling at had slowed as Tyler chatted, but now as they passed, one heard him. "You talkin' about those weird guns Kyle was showin' off?"

Scrunchie pounced on that for him. "Yeah. Know where Kyle is? My friend is lookin' for him."

"Kyle'll dust you, man. Stay away. Your dad's a safer

bet."

Tyler shook his head and turned to go. "You don't know my dad."

He'd made it ten steps before the guy called out again. "I heard he was going into the Crypt to score some ice. Good luck."

As he called out his thanks, Tyler shuddered. "I'm gonna need it."

Each step into Rockland's worst area emphasized exactly why it had been dubbed, "The Crypt." Every bit of Tyler's gang training became a vital part of moment-by-moment survival. Move to this side of the street when those gang colors appeared. Shift to that. Ask the old lady who looked ready to beat him with her handbag if he stepped too close, stop a little kid who had probably messed himself just at the contact.

Keith should be doing this. They're gonna see right through me. Then I'll die.

But he kept going. Those tranqs in the hands of a kid were as or more lethal than a Glock. People didn't respect or understand how tranqs worked. Mark kept refining his combinations all the time. Protocol for weight and slowing time had changed twice in his short term as an Agent. Keith said it had been seven for him.

Three kids swaggered toward him, and Tyler prepared himself. This would be it. *I'd recognize that bag any day. I packed it just last month.*

The size of the ringleader gave away just how a couple of teenagers had been able to flatten Keith. This kid was huge and had the most expressionless eyes Tyler had ever seen. He sneered and elbowed his friend. "Look who thinks he can walk through our turf."

You've got to be kidding me. Been watching The Outsiders

lately? Are you ready to rumble?

Tyler backed away, toward an alley. As expected, they followed, taunting. Laughing. Oh, so stupidly cocky. *It's almost not fair.*

They'd just gotten out of sight, when Tyler lashed out and kicked the closest one in the groin. That left the other two. While the smaller one lunged, Kyle went for the bag — presumably for a gun. Tyler braced for impact and then stepped aside at the last second. The kid crashed into the wall, stunning him just enough to make him stumble a few feet away.

Tyler drew his gun and leveled it on Kyle. "Back. Away from. That. Bag."

The stupid kid kept fumbling. A sound to his right sent Tyler spinning. With a sweep of his leg, and a crack of the gun on the kid's head, number two punk dropped. Groin boy hobbled away despite Kyle's orders to charge.

That's when Tyler racked the slide and held it out, ready to fire. "Shove the bag over. Now."

When Kyle laughed, Tyler shot the ground next to his foot.

"Now."

The duffel slid his direction.

"Get out of here." At Kyle's hesitation, Tyler shifted aim from the ground to the boy's head. "I said, *go.*"

It was probably the first time since kindergarten that the boy had moved any swifter than a swagger. As Tyler slung the bag over one shoulder, he watched. *You run like a girl.*

Her new faith warred with self-preservation. Was it wrong to manipulate the situation in order to create the opportunity to contact Keith? Manipulation had to be some kind of sin, and if it wasn't, it should be. Still… what about self-preservation? Wasn't that okay?

Erika glared at the duo playing their stupid video game and flirting with subtext. She might not understand the meaning, but no one could miss the point. *If I brought Tyler into it, she'd capitulate.*

And that's all it took. "Get me out of here, Flynne."

"We're in the middle of a game."

"And you're going to be in the middle of full-blown psychosis if you do not get me out of here."

That got her a paused game. Flynne turned and really looked at her. "What're you talking about?"

"Ever heard of cabin fever?" Flynne's expression turned skeptical, so Erika turned up the drama a few decibels. "*The Shining*? I'm about to go all, 'Heeerrre's Johnny!' on your butt. Keith at least cared about the mental health of his—" She'd almost blown it and used the word client. "Prisoners."

Change came slowly, but the skepticism eventually morphed into understanding and then into concern. "What can I do? This is, like, a neighborhood, not a cabin in the woods! We can't do the cats and mousers thing just to keep you all, like, mentally sharp and stuff."

Thank you, Jesus, that she didn't say "stufsies." However, it wouldn't do to show that relief to Flynne, so she just glared.

"What? Just *tell* me."

"Get me out of here." The memory of a trip to the Mall of America parking lot gave her all the truth she needed and a boatload of deception she might have to repent of.

Desperation drove her to leap. "Keith took me to the Mall of America. The least you could do is get me to a Target or something."

This caught Morgan's attention. "Gives new meaning to a 'target on your back,' don't you think?"

Come on... come on... bait! Take the bait!

"I don't know..."

If she'd had something in her hand, Erika would have thrown it. Then it happened. Morgan stepped in again. "We could take her to the Galleria. You were wanting St. Louis Bread Company, anyway. What could someone do in a giant mall full of people? Worst case scenario, you run up to a security guard and say you're being stalked."

Flynne didn't even seem to hear that last bit. The moment Morgan mentioned that bread company, the girl was sold. *So, the way to your heart is through your breadbasket. Got it.*

They left the house at four o'clock. All three of them. By the time they reached the mall it was after five — oh, the joys of rush hour traffic. Then, of course, Flynne spent forty minutes moving them from space to space, trying to decide which was the best and changing her mind with every decision.

Desperation, rather than mercy, drove Erika to tell her what Keith had said. "Trying to do the opposite thing is just as obvious as doing the obvious thing. Small changes. If you usually park near the entrance, go for the middle, not the outskirts. If you usually park far away for your daily exercise, then park in the middle. If you usually—"

"Got it. Parking up front because I only do that when there's a spot. And I can't park in the middle."

After another fifteen minutes of circling the area around Dillard's, they found a spot up close to

Nordstrom—by the sheer grace of God, Erika decided. Flynne made them stay in the car and scanned the area twice before demanding they race from the car to inside.

Erika refused. "There's no way I'm drawing attention to myself that way. Not. Happening."

God's mercy continued as Morgan agreed. "Let's just stroll in. Casual."

There wasn't anything casual about the way they moved. Flynne bounced around them like an over-eager shepherd, determined to keep them all corralled where she could, what? Glare someone to death? She hadn't brought a tranq or the air soft gun. She didn't have a knife. She didn't even have martial arts skills. *She's got nothing. Zippo, nada, nuttin'.*

After months at HearthLand, with its minimalistic, eco-conscious lifestyle, the sheer volume of future archaeological landfill treasures nearly smothered her. Store after store, packed to the gills with… *stuff*. A pause by the mall map brought a smile. "Too bad there's not a Burberry store."

Flynne huffed. "Yeah… Mall of America has one. So not fair." She perked up a moment later. "Let's get bread first. Then we can, like, walk it off."

"It's probably on the other end of the mall." Erika put every bit of annoyance she could into those words. "We'll walk it off *before* we even get there."

"Nope!" Flynne dragged her to the right. "It's right next to Nordstrom. Ha!"

A muttered, "Don't get in the way of Flynne and her bread," from behind her told Erika she'd seriously underestimated the magnetic pull of St. Louis' bread.

She hadn't expected to find a menu board full of amazing-looking sandwiches and soups waiting for her. It only took one look to see the Mediterranean veggie and Erika was sold. "I'll get drinks. What do you guys want?"

They hadn't had a chance to tell her when Erika froze. "Um, guys…"

0000 01 000 0000 1 01 110   010 111 110 001 0

Flynne, still salivating over the forthcoming Pepperblue steak sandwich, hardly glanced at Erika. "What?"

The answer came in a hiss. "Slide those eyes to the left, would you? Gray shirt. Sunglasses. Drink cup in his hand."

The words flustered her just as she reached for money. The bills fluttered to the floor before Flynne could grab them again. The man stood fifteen feet away, his profile to her. Nothing about him looked familiar or threatening. "Yeah? So?"

"Knupp."

She dropped the bills again. "Ugh!" In her peripheral vision, Flynne saw the man look their way. "I'm—I'm so hungry I can't hold onto my money! It's totes annoys sauce!" Something in the way Erika relaxed hinted that maybe she'd done the right thing. "I've been waiting for this *all* day."

"Should we get these to go?" Erika pointed to a clock. "What time does the movie start again?"

"Mo—"

Morgan broke in before Flynne could continue. "Good idea. Let's get it all to go."

Every instinct said to run away, to tackle Erika and body-shield her—anything. But Morgan took over again, for which she'd kiss him the first chance she got. "Erika,

175

can you get me a Dr. Pepper? Flynne probably wants lemonade, right? I'll get napkins and straws and stuff."

He's going with her. I so puffy heart that guy. The memory of Tyler's face tried to invade her thoughts, but she shoved him aside. *Later.*

Knupp left the restaurant first, heading toward Dillard's. Flynne ached to try to slip into the elevators there, but it wouldn't work. What if he waited for them when the doors opened? Trapped. *Better stick to the escalators... right?*

"Do we follow *him*?" Morgan kept stepping a few inches in front of them as if he could dive if Knupp whipped out an AK-47 hidden somewhere under the gray polo. "Or do we try to book it out of here?"

She couldn't help herself. Flynne glanced at Erika to get a feel for what would work and what wouldn't. The look on Erika's face belied the nerve-wracking situation. "What's wrong?"

"That jerk *followed* us here, let us think we made it, and then just *shows himself*? What do you think? I'm ticked!" A few seconds later, she added, "Great cover with dropping the money, by the way. You were smooth."

They'd made it to the escalators before Flynne managed to answer. "Um... I, um..."

"It wasn't an accident. Flynne got flustered." Morgan took her hand. "But it worked, and we've got this."

Once on the escalators, Flynne could scan the area. Women in business attire strode past stores, clearly on a mission. Moms—you could tell them by their practical clothes with just a nod to fashion, well and the stream of ducklings masquerading as children streaming in front and behind them. Teens clumped like hydrangea bushes in front of cool stores, and Flynne tried not to envy several girls with varying shades of hair pointing upstairs. She knew where they'd go. *Hot Topic. Can I come, too? I'll, like be your new bestie and buy everyone something. Just let me out of this nightmare!*

Just as they neared bottom, she saw Knupp. He stood right by the movie poster for the new superhero blockbuster and sipped that same cup. *Bet it's empty.*

"Three o'clock."

Flynne looked around for a clock and didn't see it. "It's got to be closer to six-thirty. We left after... oooh... Yeah. Saw him."

"I think we should get tickets, go into three different movies, slip out when he doesn't show up—or after he does, for that lucky dog, and then meet up at the car at eight." Morgan leaned closer and whispered, "We play that evasion game all the time. I'm good. I'll try to get him to follow me while you guys escape. If I'm not at the car by eight, don't worry. I'll Uber it outta here."

She started to protest. Letting Erika out of her sight wasn't in the plan. Not at all. Just as she opened her mouth to say as much, Erika agreed. "That's a great idea. I'll try to find someone to let me use their phone. That way it's not traceable to any of us. I'll leave a note with Ralph at HearthLand to get to Keith."

"You can't—!"

Erika slowed as they neared the ticket counter. "I don't care what you say, Flynne. Keith knowing where we are is safer than Knupp! I don't know what he's doing here, but this is no coincidence. You were *right*. Okay? I get it. But now I know what to do. And I call Keith. You divert Knupp with Morgan. He won't hurt you because he knows you'll be meeting with me. So, go divert and let me do the only thing I know we need to do."

She had a point. As much as Flynne hated to admit it, Erika had a really good point. The problem was if she could do it. Morgan took off to buy his ticket, leaving them standing there in the wide open. *If he wanted to go all mall shooter on us, we'd be dead, and everyone would think it was just a random shooting.*

That's all it took. Being out in the open could be as dangerous as trapped in a theater. "Okay. Let's try it."

Erika squeezed her arm and turned to go to the ticket booth. "You owe me a movie, Flynne. Pay up."

I'll pay up, all right. She forked over a twenty. *And then I'll follow him following you. I'm not letting you out of my sight.* A rephrase presented itself, and Flynne almost spoke it aloud. *Basically, I'm keepin' my peepers on my peeps.*

EIGHTEEN

They stood in one corner of the ER waiting area. Claire fidgeted until Mark laced his fingers through hers and squeezed. That's all it took for her to curl into him. He felt the tears rather than heard them. "He'll be fine. I promise."

"I know, but he's all mangled. He's *hurting*, and Erika isn't even here."

Translation, you need comfort, so you assume he does, too. That was all the invitation he needed. Mark wrapped his arms around her and held her fast. "Dr. Brecham will be here to tell us how bad things are soon. Just give it a few more minutes."

"I'm scared."

Public displays of affection had never been easy, but what about relationships were easy? Claire needed him to step up. After a kiss to her head, he pressed his cheek over it and held fast. "You know he'll be fine. He's a kicker—a fighter. And he has God on his side."

She stiffened for a moment. Large eyes gazed up at him a moment later. "I thought you didn't know what you thought about God."

"Been reading like you asked." The memory of throwing the Bible prompted him to add, "Not that I always like what I read…"

Before Claire could process that, Brecham entered and scanned the area. "Hey, he's here."

"Keith?" At the sight of the doctor, she sagged. "Oh."

Brecham pulled them outside before he spoke. "Okay, this is what I've done. He definitely has a pneumothorax—the left lung is greatly affected. They could deal with it with needles and tubes, but I pressed for immediate surgery. I need medical records to back up a history of those procedures not working."

Mark passed Claire his phone and continued to listen while she called Tyler. "What about his jaw?"

"Definitely broken. They'll have to wire it. I told them only four wires, though—easy to snip quickly if necessary."

The way Brecham stood, his demeanor, all of it hinted at there being more. "And…?"

"Concussion. It's complicated by the drugs in his system. Until those are gone, we can't be certain of the impact it's having. Right now, there is some cognitive impairment—nothing too severe, if it's the tranquilizers in his system. If it's the head injury, it could be more serious."

What Brecham said next, Mark didn't hear. Claire's eyes had gone wide. She looked his way, questioning… beseeching. "Sorry. Another emergency."

"Keep him here through tomorrow afternoon at the least, okay?"

Mark nodded and moved to Claire's side. "What is it?"

"Erika called."

Without a word, Mark held out his hand for his phone and gave her as much of a reassuring smile as he could before he turned his attention to the call. "What is it, Tyler?"

"She's in St. Louis," Tyler began. "The guy Flynne was worried about?"

Knupp. The churning foreboding of bad news stirred in Mark's gut. "Yeah?"

"He found them. Erika knows who he is."

All the evidence — valid. Tyler's figured out Knupp, which means he'll know that Flynne was right. And I didn't listen.

" — there's more. The guy?"

"I don't have time for this. What's wrong?"

Tyler apologized, wasting more precious seconds, and blurted it all out. "He's got the same last name as Corey. His name is Brent Knupp. Oh, and there's another hash tag out there. #HASHTAGROGUE #SENDKEITH."

"That's not going to happen. Okay, check out the others. I want to know how Langat and Schmatloch are. ASAP. Oh, and find someone to go to St. Louis. Get a call into Rickwood, and have him put a team on a plane just in case."

Tyler promised and disconnected. As he pondered, Mark's thumb slid along the edge of the phone, tracing the curves, the lines. Something unsettled him, but what? Langat? The cleanup crew? St. Louis? Knupp? The hashtag?

The obvious answer was everything. Everything bothered him. But it wasn't just that. It was more. Much, much more.

But what?

All angst dissipated at the touch of Claire's fingers. "Can I call Aunt Kathi — tell her the truth? Keith was mugged and his boss called me? He'll have those wires for six weeks. She'll know."

"If she comes, can you go with me?"

The hesitation almost killed him. Her words, however, soothed. "You want me?"

You've no idea. All Mark trusted himself to do was nod.

181

A smile bright enough to power a toy oven told him he'd said the right thing. Claire kissed his cheek and plucked his phone from his fingers. "Be right back."

As he watched her walk away, one side of him protested. *She's too young for you.* It wasn't an exaggeration, and yet *he* was. His entire appearance exaggerated everything. *She may be too young for me, but* I'm *too young for me. Does age even matter when you look twenty years older than you really are?*

Twenty years... they represented his false identity and the span of a life lived almost before Claire was even born. If he had any consideration for her, he'd get her a job with Rickwood's organization and walk away from her life. He could do it without her knowing... at first.

Claire rounded the corner, and at the sight of her, everything changed. *Yeah, it might be the right thing to do, but it would hurt her, too. I can't do it... to either of us.*

0000 01 000 0000 1 01 110   010 111 110 001 0

He'd once heard Mark say that Flynne had revolutionized the office. It hadn't been a joke. Though Tyler had created quite a few of the systems that still seemed in use, he did see that she'd refined them, improved them, and scrapped every single thing that could be made simpler—more efficient.

And it stung.

After every minute he spent on her computers, a new notification popped up. Due to the offline aspects of most of The Agency's protocols, Flynne had written her own calendar/reminder/scheduling program that kept everything running smoothly. Well, everything except the ones that told him to schedule the next thing. He didn't know what that next thing was supposed to be.

His phone played an Imagine Dragons album on a repeating loop as he struggled to keep up with work that sometimes he didn't even understand anymore. *Why are we monitoring Bennington, Vermont?*

A call came through—brief, succinct. "Keith needs his medical history altered. Look up pneumothorax and create a history that shows surgical repair as the only thing that worked. Give him at least three instances. Now."

"Great. Medical. Not my strong suit." That word "now" hinted that Mark needed it an hour ago, so he pulled out his phone and went online—author groups on Facebook. Inside ten minutes, he had four people who had medical histories close enough to give Tyler the search terms he needed. Five minutes after that, and after hacking into a rural Wisconsin hospital's database, he managed to add everything into Keith's records. Once they uploaded, any medical facility would see the updated information.

"Aaand... done."

Another notification to schedule out future work appeared on one of the monitors. Tyler tapped in a date eighteen months out and typed in, "*Remove pneumothorax references not connected with St. Joseph's from Keith Shafter's medical records.*"

"Fine. It's convenient. I'd have forgotten."

An email pinged the moment Tyler finished with the records order—a notification from Dan French's phone. Missed call from Liv Todd. He called Mark. Nothing. A call to Claire got him a frustrated agent.

"What? We're kind of—"

"Tell Mark he has a voice message from Liv Todd on the French account."

Silence. "The what account?"

"It's kind of urgent, Claire. Tell him. Todd and French. He'll get it."

He'd made it to Mark's office door before he heard Mark say, "What do you have for me?"

"Can I access—?"

"Get it. Play it on speaker."

Ouch. Someone's testy.

The message came through half a minute later. "Hey, Dan. It's Liv Todd. Look, I had some guy contact me. He said he had photo proof that my sister did not die the day they said she did. We met at the Fiddleleaf. I kind of thought he was you, but he wasn't. Anyway, he just walked up, dropped a manila envelope on the table, and said, 'Just watch yourself. That's all I'm saying. Watch yourself.' Then he took off! So, I opened the packet. We've gotta meet. This is weird stuff here. Call me."

That's when Tyler received verbal confirmation that Mark wasn't in Keith's room.

0000 01 000 0000 1 01 110   010 111 110 001 0

The artificial hush of the hospital sent Mark's nerves on hyperdrive. Each time the double doors opened and the harsh *whoosh* of the fans that tried to blow any bugs *out* sounded, he jumped inside. Standing just to one side of the doorway, Claire twirled her hair around a finger, released, and twirled again—a sure sign of nerves. *Just hers, or is she sensing mine?*

Their eyes met. An uncertain smile answered his attempt at a reassuring one. Too public—too soon. Her aunt would arrive any moment. Keith's mother.

Still, when she began to wrap hair around her finger again, Mark couldn't take it. He held out one hand, ready to take hers, and the moment her gaze met his, he mouthed, *Come here.*

Claire didn't even hesitate. She was at his side, arms wrapped around his waist, head burrowed in his shoulder, fighting back tears. "I'm so scared."

"He'll be fine."

"But it shouldn't have happened. This is *Keith*. Are we sure he's telling us everything? That he *remembers* everything?"

The words stabbed deep wounds within him. Mark held her tighter, made a note to talk to her about honesty, and spoke the words he needed to say—the ones *she* needed him to say. "I'll grant you that Langat got in a lucky kick. *That* was unusual."

"Right? I don't see how that happened?"

It would be harder than he'd expected. "Claire, until Keith tells us how, everything is pure conjecture. Still, he's the best. So, if Langat got in a kick, it's because something was off somewhere, and probably before he even stepped in." To himself he added, *I just hope that something wasn't Erika.*

There it was... that slow, steady relaxation that assured him he'd said all the right things. *But how many of them are lies?*

"True..."

For just a moment, he thought they were in the clear. *At least until we can talk.*

"Mark?"

He stood there, eyes closed, arms wrapped around her, tension slowly fading. "Hmmm?"

"Isn't this a lot all at once?"

She'd said it—the thing he'd been trying to force himself to acknowledge. Still, her input might be insightful. "What do you mean?"

"Last month we nearly lost someone, this month we lost two, got a bunch of cases all at once…"

And one of them appears to be bogus.

"…Flynne takes off on some rogue mission, kidnapping Erika in the process…" She gazed up at him, and he knew exactly what she'd say next. It took every ounce of self-control not to kiss the next words away. "Hey, how did she manage that, anyway? Erika has way more skills than Flynne does."

"Don't know." That was the problem, of course. He didn't know. He didn't know how they'd missed that the Schmatloch case was probably bogus—but on whose part? With one arm still around her, Mark thumb-typed a text to Tyler. CHECK OUT SCHMATLOCH. SEE IF HE HAS ANY GAMBLING, LOAN, OR OTHER CONCERNING ACTIVITY. Before he sent it, Mark showed her. It would keep her mind focused there.

"Oooh… good thought. Maybe he set up that other gal. What about Langat?"

"Accident." It had to be. The guy would be dead if Keith hadn't acted, acted fast, and acted well. Then again, the safe house. Did Langat's pursuers do that, or someone else? And Brent Knupp? Where'd he fit into anything? How? Why?

The lack of answers proved the problem and provided the most unwelcome solution. A glance at her showed Claire watching the door. When a woman appeared, she stiffened and relaxed again. Obviously not Aunt Kathi.

But when she looked up at him, all sense and reason fled. "I have to bunker. Come with me?"

"What?"

"I have a place I can go—work from. Safe." So public, so exposed... but Mark couldn't resist brushing her hair from her face and kissing her forehead. His lips moved across the skin as he murmured again, "Come with me."

"I..."

Selfish words welled up—ones warning her that being connected with him put her in danger. Words that demanded she come where he could keep her safe. But that, of course, was a lie. He couldn't keep her safe. He knew that now. *Safer, though.*

"Where—?"

"Can't tell you. You just have to come. Once I get there, I can't come out until we know what's going on." He could insist. As her boss, and as a necessity to keeping his agent alive, he could insist. But alone, locked in together for what could be weeks... "It could be a long time, Claire. But I can keep you safe there—as safe as possible, anyway."

Of all the answers or questions she could have given him, "When?" wouldn't have made the list.

"Maybe not today, but soon. *Very* soon. Tomorrow... no later than the next day."

"But Keith—"

Truth time—hard, fast, truths. "Keith would be yelling at me for not being gone already—if he could. I should have gone instead of coming here, but..."

Claire started to kiss him. Just as she stood on her toes and leaned in, she bounced away, dashing for the door. "Aunt Kathi!"

Mark slipped around the corner and into the men's room. *Time to go.* He shot her a text message. BE AT THE HARBINGER PLACE BY 9:00 P.M. IF YOU'RE COMING. GIVE MY

187

0000 01 000 0000 1 01 110   010 111 110 001 0

The sun set over Rockland in a blaze of glory Mark rarely got to see. He'd paced the length of the window wall of his living room until a furrow should have formed. Just at the golden moment, he paused, his forearm leaning against one of the frames and watched the sun cast its golden glow across the towers of glass and steel that made up the familiar Rockland skyline.

An idea formed, but he waited, watching. Absorbing. Drinking in the moment. *It could only be better if Claire had come.*

That wasn't true, of course. Many things could make it better—clients out of danger, Keith whole and free. *Sol and Raina alive.*

It wasn't the first time he'd thought of them, of course, but the dying day, the moment of peace, and the realization that he faced similar danger for reasons he still didn't understand, combined to press on him. An ache formed and swelled in his throat. It grew, forming roots and growing deep inside until it reached his chest. Each root wrapped itself around his heart and squeezed until he gasped at the pain of it.

The first sob ripped through him before he could prepare for it. Mark slid down the length of that frame and drew his knees to his chest. With arms slung over his knees and his chin dropped to his chest, he shook, choked, gasped through each wracking sob.

It wasn't supposed to be this way. He'd used his trust fund to form The Agency to *prevent* this kind of pain. He'd expected people to be saved from danger—from fear. Instead, even his own people were going home to their loved ones… in caskets.

Keith would turn to his God—the Being that, if Mark were honest with himself, he believed in but didn't trust. But what did one *do* when turning to God? What did that even mean?

"Why do religions have all this jargon, anyway?" The question was followed by a hiccough and a huge sniff that sent him searching for Kleenex. Beside his chair, and next to the Kleenex box, sat the Bible he'd been reading when he stayed at the Harbinger apartment. At the sight of it, a thought formed.

"Works in movies," he muttered. And with that, Mark picked up the book, closed his eyes, fanned the floppy pages a few times, and jabbed his finger onto the page. I Chronicles 4:27 *"Now Shimei had sixteen sons and six daughters; but his brothers did not have many sons, nor did all their family multiply like the sons of Judah."*

"I would get something like that—something that makes no sense." He started to close the book but stopped. "Unless it's a code. Does God work in code?"

As silly as he felt, Mark couldn't stop himself from looking at Shimei to see if he could find any other meaning in it. Sixteen and six. That made twenty-two. Claire's age? Even if it meant anything, what? Confirmation for or against a relationship? A reminder that she was legally an adult? A reminder of how much younger?

Then again, it could be 166. But that number meant nothing to him. 1606? By the time he'd tried to work out Judah, Mark gave up. Once more, he went to shut the book when another idea hit him. "Okay, God. Did I hit the wrong verse? Maybe that's the problem?"

Just in case, he read every verse on both pages. All about the descendants of this guy or that—and how many warriors were included in those numbers. If it had *anything* to do with him, and Mark doubted that very much, he had no idea how to figure out what. "Keith would know, but..."

He tried once more, feeling every moment like the fool he knew himself to be. This time, his finger landed on Daniel chapter eleven. Verse thirty-three. Mark read it aloud. "'Those who have insight among the people will give understanding to the many; yet they will fall by sword and by flame, by captivity and by plunder for many days. Now when they fall, they will be granted a little help, and many will join with them in hypocrisy.'"

At thirty-five, he stared at the words, shaking. "'Some of those who have insight will fall, in order to refine, purge and make them pure until the end time; because it is still to come at the appointed time.'"

Mark didn't know what any of that meant, but it sounded ominous. He pulled out his phone and zipped a text message to Claire, asking her to leave the reference with Keith to see what he had to say about it. It wasn't fair of him. She'd want to know why, and when he told her, she'd have hope. He couldn't give her that hope yet. Not yet. Not now.

A sigh escaped. "Maybe not ever."

Once more, he read the words. "'Some of those who have insight will fall, in order to refine, purge and make them pure until the end time; because it is still to come at the appointed time.'"

It sounded like Keith. He had insight into the whole God thing—and into Agency business. He'd taken a big hit. One might say he'd fallen but... why? So, he'd be forced to take the time to see clearly? Is that what God was saying—was doing? Or was it just some stupid, random verse about… whatever it was about.

The secure landline rang in the other room. Mark groaned and dashed for it. Landline probably meant… "Hello?"

Tyler's voice held a note of confusion as he said, "Got a call from Corey."

Figured out that your brother is up to something, did you?

"—says that her niece has gone missing now. Her sister-in-law is frantic."

As much as he hated to do it, Mark had to call. "I'll take care of it. Thanks, Tyler."

"Have you heard anything about Keith?"

"Not yet. I'll call. I promise." Silence hung there, as if asking permission for Tyler to say something more. "What is it?"

"I just wondered… should we be at the hospital at all? If someone suspected Keith wasn't dead, wouldn't our people being there be confirmation…"

All alone in his apartment, without any chance of offending Keith or Claire, Mark disconnected the call and shouted every foul word he'd ever heard at the top of his lungs. Once finished, he waited for Cosmic punishment, and when it didn't arrive, he grabbed the phone handset again and dialed. "Brecham. Get Keith out of there— somehow. Send family home. Keep everyone far away."

"Is Rockland Memorial okay, or do we fly him to Louisville?"

Mark gripped the handset with more force than could ever be necessary, took a steadying breath, and said, "RM is fine. Just move him. Now."

NINETEEN

Erika snored on the couch. Morgan watched from a chair, both arms wrapped in gauze and hopped up on a Tylenol/ibuprofen regime. Only the rumble of the ice maker and Erika's olfactory symphony kept the house from being graveyard silent.

Three sticky notes lay on the table, spread out in a perfect line of uncertainty. The green one read *Stay*. A pink one read *Go*. And the yellow read *Stay but go to hostel*. Flynne stared at each one, wishing she had an answer for even one of those.

Leaving the area seemed risky. Tulsa was a possibility. She sort of knew the area and vaguely remembered a cabin her family kept near Skiatook. Surely, her cousin wouldn't care if she took it over for a few days. Hands on her shoulders made her jump, but as Morgan kneaded the muscles, she relaxed. "Thanks."

"Where would you go?"

Flynne almost told him—further proof that she wasn't cut out for this agent thing. While she considered how to answer, she pulled "go" closer to her, flicking the bottom of the note with one finger. "Can't tell you."

"What's the point in going?"

"To get away from Knupp?"

It happened again. Every time she said or heard someone say that name, hairs rose on the back of her neck.

"I feel like I should know him. I just can't figure out why."

Morgan's arms slid around her as he slid into the chair beside her. It nearly pushed her off. "Leaving puts you in likely wide-open places where you're vulnerable. The city offers easier places to hide."

"But if he saw the car, he could, like, find us again. I don't have dupsie plates like—" she choked back what she'd started to say and finished with, "—they do in spy movies and other coolio stuff."

Without a word, Morgan lifted the "go" sticky and set it aside. He placed the hostel one on top. Under stay, he filled out two more notes. One read, *Move into main house,* and the other, *Morgan drives your car to lure him away.*

"Um... that's a problem."

"Why?"

She winced as she said, "It's not my car. I borrowed it from the people I housesit for." Even as she spoke, Flynne's mind churned. "But you could... yeah... maybe..."

"Is this where I tell you that I know you have to be working for some special ops group or something?"

A giggle escaped. "You're so wrong it isn't even funny."

"I know what I see. This is your first detail?"

Ouch... so wrong and so right at the same time.

"Look, I don't want you to tell me and then have to kill me or anything. I just want you to know that I get that you have to protect her. I don't know why, and I don't need to. It's just—"

She stopped him as a new idea hit her. "Wait." Turning to look at him put their faces so close it seemed almost criminal not to kiss him, but she didn't. *The movies would make this a moment, and if it, like, didn't mean I could get Erika dead, I'd do it just to avoid having to think about it.*

"Too tempting, Dortmann. Back away. We need our wits about us."

"You have no idea," she began, "how tempting you just made everything."

He dragged a chair to her side and tapped his notes. "Tell me what idea you got and get your mind off more interesting ideas."

"So not cool." But she did. "You could take the car back to Rockland—and cash. I have gobstoppers of cash. You could buy a good used car for cash and drive it back. It'd be in your name. No one would even, like, know!"

As if ripped from a movie in the fifties, he took her hand, squeezed, and kissed the back of it. "I was getting concerned until you threw that 'like' in there. Whew!"

"Not cool."

He winked at her. "You already said that."

The wink did her in. All the fears and frustrations of the past week... had it been a whole week? Almost. They culminated in an unwelcome torrent of tears. Morgan's apologies only made it worse.

"Hey, Flynne. I'm sorry. It was just a joke. I didn't mean—"

She tried to explain, but something about his tenderness—the way her game buddy became a source of comfort— turned everything into a soggy emotional release fest. "I—"

"Let her cry. I've been waiting for it."

Flynne turned to the couch, and saw a blurred Erika sitting up. "Sorries."

"Don't be. You needed it. Forget that. I need it, but the tears aren't there."

"I just don't know what I'm doing! Every time I try to figure out how to keep you safe, I think, 'What would Keith do?' But I don't *know!* Why didn't Mark *listen* to me! I could *do* something from the office, but here I'm just, like, *guessing!*

Morgan squeezed her. "Again, whew! Finally got a like in there."

She'd have kicked him if he hadn't been hugging her so tight. Erika pulled out a chair and leaned against the table as she sat. "You're doing great, actually. Yeah, I was ticked at you, but Flynne…"

"Don't even try to go all patzies on me."

"Patzies?"

Morgan translated. "Patronize her."

"Oh, brother. Look. I think you know I wouldn't bother saying it if I didn't mean it. You got me *out* of there. You got me here. You even got Morgie dorgs here…" She winked at both of them before continuing, "And you so deserved that. You got Morgan so loyal that he kept me from escaping for you. This was good work."

A sniffle escaped before she could say, "Keith wouldn't—"

"Okay! So, you're not as good as the *best* the Agency has. So what? You've done as well as Karen did! *Infinitely* better than Corey. And I like you more than—"

"Corey." Flynne jumped up. "Corey…"

"You probably didn't meet her," Erika said. "I mean, I think she was gone before you worked there."

But Flynne worked to tune her out. She could see the agent file in the drawer. Corey…

"She never told me her—"

"Shut up! I can almost see it…"

When she did, Flynne went cold. Without a word, she dashed to her bedroom and pulled out the backpack. "Five… one. Five… two. Five…" She counted out six thousand dollars and hovered over the other bundles. Snatching two more up, she shoved everything else back in the backpack and locked the door behind her as she left the room.

Morgan's eyes bugged as she dumped it all on the table. Flynne went to retrieve the St. Louis Bread Company bag she'd saved and dumped it in with the order, "There's seven thousand. Make sure you don't buy something so expensive that you can't pay the taxes and registration."

"Go now?"

She nodded.

Erika, however, had lost all patience with her. "Go why, and what happened here?"

"Knupp, Erika. Corey's last name is Knupp."

A flickering reel of emotions flitted over Erika's face before an indecipherable one settled there. "Hashtag scared."

A small weekender sat on the bench in his bathroom. Mark had already put a few things in it—a favorite sweatshirt, a couple of books, and a bit of cash. From the hook on the bathroom door, he retrieved his favorite bathrobe, sniffed, and folded. Of course, the bunker had a perfectly good robe, but favorites were favorites.

As he passed through the bedroom, the Bible he'd been trying to work through beckoned him. He'd almost decided against it when the memory of throwing it and the mental image of what Claire would think if he confessed beat down his resistance. *If she comes, she'll see I'm making an effort, too.*

If she came. That would be the sticking point. Could he convince her?

Mark hefted the bag—all five pounds of the thing—and set it by the front door. He pulled out his phone and sent Will Rickwood of the West Coast Agency a text message. WEATHER'S AWFUL. MIGHT BE A BAD TIME FOR YOUR FRIENDS TO VISIT. WHAT DO YOU THINK?

The instinctual temptation to plead, "Please let them come, please let them come, please let them come" both made him feel like a teenaged girl *and* prompted a new thought about how even people without faith in anything still pray. *I'll have to ask Claire about that.*

His perpetual motion clock chimed the three-quarter hour. After staring at it, almost willing the hands to slide back to the half-hour position, Mark moved to the couch, plopped down with the floppiness of a teenager, and began sending messages.

Dr. Brecham—when could Keith leave?

Tyler—figure out where and how to make the Todd family safe.

Doyle—status on Schmatloch.

Before he could send a request for an update on Langat, Karen called. "Just put Langat on a plane to Nairobi via Qatar. He's out of our hands."

"And he'll be dead inside a week."

Her voice went soft—like it always did when they knew they couldn't prevent a death. "You did what you could. If they won't hire the South African Agency, there's nothing we can do for him. You aren't God."

That truth rarely provided comfort. A soft ding rang out through the apartment—notification that the elevator button for his floor had been pushed. "Hey, I have something to monitor. I won't see you for a while, but you know how to get messages to me. Stay safe, Karen."

"You, too. Without you, there *is* no Agency, and people need us."

No one knew that better than Karen. He sighed. "Wish I could have known about your parents, Karen. Talk to you soon." And before she could try to reassure him, Mark disconnected. He folded back a panel and looked at the monitor. A grin formed, despite his studied nonchalance.

She came.

Claire stood there, smoothing her hair, checking her teeth for particles, adjusting her skirt. None of it necessary, of course. Only knowing that someone could step onto the elevator on any floor kept him watching. Then, as if it read his thoughts, the car slowed. Ten floors down.

A man got on—Jadon Parker. A player of a guy, if Mark had ever met one. Since he was going up, Mark guessed the floor below—Madylin Morrison's. Claire smiled at something he said. "Bad idea, Claire."

He'd been right. That's all it took for Jadon to step closer, lean his forearm over her head and say... something. Claire frowned and stepped back.

Mark's hand hovered over the volume control. He preferred not to listen but...

Claire looked up at the guy and laughed in his face. What she said Mark might never know, but he'd never forget the man's poorly concealed embarrassment. "Good girl."

That would have gotten him kicked if she'd heard it— and rightly so. The fact that he'd have said it to a granny or a toddler as well wouldn't have mattered. *I guess I can see how it could sound patronizing. Even if it wasn't meant to be.*

It was proof, he supposed, that even a dog as old as he looked could learn new tricks with sufficient inducement.

And I bet she wouldn't like being considered "inducement" any more than a "good girl." I make her sound like a lap dog.

By the time the man exited and the other ding announcing she'd arrived at his floor sounded, Mark had decided it was time. If he only knew what that even meant. *But it is. She's coming. It's time.*

He opened the door even before she rang the bell. "What'd Parker want?" It was the simplest way to let Claire know he'd watched—to remind her that he could.

"Parker? He said his name was Jadon!"

"It is. Jadon Parker."

She kissed his cheek as she passed. "Well, I know you can listen. Why don't you tell *me* what he wanted?"

"Because, while I have to protect myself and my people..." Mark reached out and pulled her close. "*Especially* my people."

A slow smile formed as she gazed up at him. "Yeah?"

"Yeah. I don't listen if I don't need to. I don't like being invasive if I can avoid it. If you looked distressed at all, I'd have done it without a second thought, but..."

"Thanks. Every time I think who you are and what you do will choke me, you prove it won't."

You've got no idea that's exactly what I needed to hear. He caught her hand in his, kissed it, closed his eyes as her arms slid around his neck. Half a second before his lips would have touched hers, he froze.

"Mark?"

Still holding her hand, he turned and scanned the area by the door. "Where's your bag?" The unspoken answer echoed in his mind as she refused to look at him. "Claire?"

"I can't go."

"Why?"

She buried her face in his chest, clinging to his sleeves

200

and struggling—against tears, he suspected. "I can't spend days, weeks… maybe even longer with you. Not alone like that."

Of course, she couldn't. He shouldn't have even considered it, but the idea of leaving her behind, vulnerable… it choked him. "How will you stay safe?"

Claire gazed at him for a moment before moving to the window and staring out over the city. "I was going to ask if I could use your Wexfield place. I thought maybe…"

"The security is best there."

"And I could contact you—keep you updated on stuff."

That wouldn't work. The point of the bunker was no contact. "It doesn't work—"

"But it does! I'll just talk to you in the house. You can listen to the recordings. We'll create a code. Movies and stuff maybe. I'll tell you how I watched *You've Got Mail* and just noticed that Tom Hanks moved out of his apartment instead of kicking out the girl. How sweet and cool that was of him when she was the jerk."

"I'd rather move you into the apartment and take my chances on the boat, too." Her smile told him he'd translated correctly.

In a voice so soft he could barely hear it, Claire whispered, "If I talk about Gilbert Blythe on the horse… when he says, 'Hello, Anne…'"

If he could only tell her—admit what he didn't dare say. Not now. Not yet. Instead, he said, "Better watch it with that one. I've seen that movie."

She shot a look at him. "You have not!"

"Detail on one of my first cases. An eleven-year-old incurable romantic. We watched it a dozen times in three days." Mark moved to hold her, and in his bid to maintain a bit of self-control reiterated his original words. "So, like I said. Watch it with that one. I'm liable to call you 'Carrots.'"

The first tears fell. "When do you go?"

"As soon as I hear Keith is safe to leave the hospital."

"Then we've got time for a movie." She pulled away and turned toward the kitchen. "I'll make popcorn."

0000 01 000 0000 1 01 110   010 111 110 001 0

His phone buzzed—the message app. Tyler sat up and punched on the overhead lights and blinked against the brightness. Flynne's app—genius. He was almost jealous of it. Honesty drove him to confess that there was no "almost" about it.

The message from Doyle chilled him. MOVING OS. SOMEONE AT RV PARK IS TOO FRIENDLY. IS THREAT STILL IN GERMANY?

It took three minutes to see the latest picture of breakfast in a town between Munich and Dachau. Still... what if the pictures had been scheduled? Certain apps did that. Tyler forced himself up and to the desk. The blank monitors stared at him. *Message or call?*

He snatched up the landline and punched the numbers for the Deutsch Agency. "*Sprechen Sie Englisch?*"

The unexpectedly melodic voice on the other end assured him she did. *I thought the Germans all sounded like they hocked up a loogie.*

"Sir? You're looking for travel information? Is that correct?"

And so began protocols he hadn't had to do in over a year. Twice, he guessed. Only the grace of the God Keith insisted was real could have gotten him through it. He'd light a candle somewhere. Wasn't that what you did when you wanted to say thanks? Movies did that.

"What can we do for you?"

He spelled out the story of Otto Schmatloch and the woman who had been threatening him online. "I don't have the information source. Our tech girl is on personal leave—very sudden."

"Is Flynne well?"

Great. She knows Flynne. A smile formed. *Yeah! Great! Maybe she knows about me.* He tried again. "Okay, if you know Flynne, you might have heard about her boyfriend?"

"Tyler, yes. He sounds like a nice boy, but Flynne needs a man, don't you think?"

Boy!

"I am just teasing you, Tyler. I recognize your voice from when I trained. *Is* Flynne well, though?"

"She's actually on detail right now. And I can't tell you where she found this information, but it was damning enough to ensure we extracted Schmatloch when he got the latest threat." Tyler went on to explain his concern. "Do you have access to CCTV cameras in the area near this restaurant... Cotidiano." As he said it, Tyler paused. "Wait, isn't that Spanish?"

"Yes. For daily or everyday. Common. Habit."

"In Munich?"

He could hear her fingers clacking against a keyboard as she worked to bring up what he needed. "They're a cosmopolitan city." She paused. "This could take a while. They've increased encryption protocols. I'll call you back."

And just like that, she was gone.

Tyler began a sweep of everything in play. The status of Langat—arrived in Qatar safely. Keith's current status—

sleeping. He even checked out Erika's Twitter account. Two new #HASHTAGROGUE tweets appeared. The first was followed by #CHACHING

"Going to spend a lot of that money? Better tell Mark just in case." The second one sent shivers down his spine. #SITTINGDUCKS

He'd just sent the first message to Mark when the call from Germany came through. "I found someone willing to help. Your photograph was taken this morning at nine-seventeen. I saw the woman take and upload it before she even took a bite of her food. Why do Americans do that?"

"We're afraid we'll forget we ate and eat again."

"People do that?"

It wasn't nice, but she sounded so sincere that he couldn't resist. "Why do you think Americans are so fat? We're too busy to pay attention to if we ate or not, so…"

"If you did not sound as if you were trying not to laugh, I would have believed you. It was nice to talk to you, Tyler. You may tell Flynne that I approve of her taste in men."

The line went dead before he could think of a reply.

Mark called a moment later. "Hospital called. Keith left. Has he checked in?"

"No. There are new hashtags—was just about to call you with them."

"Let me have them." At the "cha-ching," Mark snickered. "Spending that cash, huh?"

"But on what?"

"Not Burberry. That's for sure."

Even Tyler had to smile at that. "She loves her Burberry."

"I bet she's buying a car. Check registrations."

It was time to ask. "Why are we doing this? We know

204

she's in St. Louis. Why aren't we just going to get them?"

"That would be what Keith is doing. And since they're alive and keeping us informed, with everything going on, they're probably safer there than here."

"Except if she's buying a car..." Understanding exploded in his mind. Tyler scrambled to compare the number with information he'd been collecting. It wasn't there. He tried again as Mark asked what he was up to. "That hashtag. With the numbers. I feel stupid, but it's a license plate."

"It's Brent Knupp's license plate. I looked it up."

Anger replaced understanding as Tyler's blasting agent. "And you didn't think to say something? It's obvious he's been there this whole time—freaking them out and everything!"

"I doubt it. I suspect Flynne hacked into surveillance cameras from other sides of the building and caught the license plate that way—after talking to Erika or something. If they'd seen Knupp that early, they wouldn't have been so discreet. They'd have called."

That was true enough. "Do you think Keith can handle it after surgery and everything?"

"He'll have to."

TWENTY

The evening air held a bite to it, even in late April. Each step away from the hospital wore Keith down faster than any physical training session ever had. People moved around corners, and he jumped with each one. *They had me on a drip then. She said it was just saline, but...*

Until whatever it was left his system, he'd have to be on his guard to be cautious without overreacting. Not easily done or said. Especially as the painkillers wore off. *So much for handling it so well.*

By the time he reached the nearest subway station, the hospital bag he carried growing heavier with each step, he'd spent every bit of energy he'd stored up. Keith sat in one corner of the car, watching, wary. The looks people sent his way only served to add paranoia to his list of ailments—right up to the moment he caught his reflection in the window. Swollen jaw—purple. Thick lips.

He glanced down at the buttoned-down shirt he'd worn to the hospital and saw a spot of blood on it. He'd soaked through the bandage he'd used to cover the chest tube incision site. *Should have left the stupid tube in.*

Of course, he couldn't do that and travel. He'd have to get more bandages as soon as he made it to the lockers and got the rest of the money. *And a phone.*

A kid not much older than "Thor" had been eyed him. "You okay?"

"Been better. Car accident. Got sick of the hospital." At least, that's what he tried to say. Speaking distinctly with a jaw wired shut proved harder than he'd expected. *That's what you get for refusing to speak the whole time you were in the hospital.* Then again, considering they'd been drugging him up, it was probably best that he hadn't.

"Yeah... I broke ribs with a seatbelt once."

He nodded and tried to look as tired as he felt. "Just want to get home."

Questions followed. How would he drink and eat with the wires? How long did he have to keep them on? Was the other guy insured? As exhausted as he was, and since he was trying to conserve energy, Keith answered each one as it came without consideration for remembering what he said.

At his station, he mumbled something no one could have understood and shuffled from the train. Near the exits, close to the lockers, he paused, resting... watching. Each passenger from his car passed. Several offered reassuring smiles. The kid either stayed on the train or went another way.

That thought did little to stop him from surveying the area the entire time he loaded all but a couple hundred dollars of the cash into the towel he'd stolen from the hospital and stuffed it all in the bag. The cellphone and remaining cash he shoved in his pocket. With one last glance around him, he took off for the train to the transportation hub—and the bus station.

In just over two hours he found himself on the road to St. Louis, half asleep, lost in thought. *"Find the threat. Neutralize, or whatever you call it... don't get dead."*

He'd almost forgotten Annie's admonition. *She'd consider me a fail on that second one. Overreaction.*

Despite his dismissal, the pain radiating through his chest didn't *feel* like an overreaction. *And a double failure since I haven't neutralized that threat.* The fact that originally Flynne was the threat had no bearing on the case. Maybe.

The phone didn't have internet, but his seatmate bolted down the aisle to the restrooms and left a smartphone laying in the seat. It took Keith half a minute to find Erika's Twitter feed, read the hashtags, and clear the search history from the app. He set it on the floor and hoped the guy would think it fell at some point.

The tweets told an interesting story, but he focused on the latest. Cha-ching hinted at them getting a car. Leaving. Would they come home, or would they move on? Flynne would move. It's how she thought. But what about Erika? Would she encourage her to work their way back toward Rockland, or would she try to keep them put?

His seatmate returned, almost frantic in an obvious search for the "missing" phone, and sank into the seat at the sight of it. "Thought I lost it." the guy muttered as he snatched it off the floor.

Keith nodded and pretended to fall asleep. A hundred miles later, his phone buzzed. It would be Mark. No one else had the number. Well, except maybe Tyler.

You DIDN'T EVEN BOTHER TO SIGN THE AMA FORM.

Leaving without telling anyone meant that he didn't have to listen to the "against medical advice" spiel. Keith shot back a quick, I THINK THEY GOT THE MESSAGE.

You OKAY?

A truthful answer was too complicated. The abbreviated version meant enough evasion to be deceptive. He tried for middle ground. I WILL BE. The memory of a text he'd gotten before he left the hospital prompted him to add, IF YOU WANT TO KNOW WHAT GOD SAYS ABOUT

SOMETHING, LOOK IT UP IN THE BIBLE. RANDOM VERSES TAKEN OUT OF CONTEXT ARE ALMOST MEANINGLESS.

Several minutes passed before the next text arrived, telling him to try not to get himself injured anymore, reminding him to purchase tiny wire cutters, and thanking him for not making something up to go with the verse. It ended with, SO WHAT DOES THAT VERSE MEAN?

Exhaustion slammed into him and bowled him over as he read those words. He shot back a reply about how it talked about the persecution of the church before saying goodnight. NEED TO SLEEP IF I'M GOING TO BE ANY GOOD TO ERIKA AND FLYNNE.

0000 01 000 0000 1 01 110   010 111 110 001 0

People could say what they wanted but putting his bunker in Texas had been a no-brainer. For one thing, being the only state on its own power grid made it essential. Using solar and wind power for most of his needs meant he rarely needed to access that grid. The dilapidated farmhouse surrounded by dirt and flatlands wouldn't attract anyone—not with three German shepherds ready to take off a hand or half a face if someone came too close.

The downstairs—looked like it had only had a lick and a promise in the housekeeping department over the past... fifty or sixty years. However, go upstairs or down into the secure basement, and everything shifted into luxury and high tech respectively. Mark would sleep where he could hear what was going on and work where he could watch.

Dust flew up behind him as Mark rattled into the yard in a pickup that had seen better days... and years. He snatched his weekender from the seat beside him and climbed down. It never failed to amuse him to see the rickety, rusty windmill turning in the breeze.

A glance at the modern setup across the road— showed the place people would look if they came calling. There they'd find the computer setups, the solar and wind generators—everything that got rerouted to him in safe, storable bursts.

Thirty miles from the nearest town meant no one bothered him or the men who ran his cattle ranch. Just the way he liked it.

He wanted a bath—a long, hot, couldn't-get-girlier-if-he-tried bath. The papers waiting for him in the printer tray when he keyed into the basement meant he wouldn't. Ones and zeroes. Each double space cut off a word. Sure, anyone with half a brain could figure it out, but it would take time—time that the ones watching monitors needed to get in and neutralize the problem.

Not that they'd ever had to.

Deciphering took time, but the message was clear. Call Jehnson. Charles Jehnson, the Secretary of Homeland Security. He never knew what kind of news to expect from the man. It took ten minutes to set up the routing to make it look like it came from a cellphone in Rockland. The fact that it technically did helped.

"Cho?"

"I'm sorry, Mr. Cho has left The Agency. Marco Mendina at your service."

"Couldn't you use a more original name than 'Marco'?"

The complaint was a common one. "My parents named me what they did for a reason. I honor that."

"Gotta say… you don't even sound yourself. You're good."

It wouldn't work. Why Jehnson thought it might made no sense to him. "You had something to discuss, I believe."

"If you can get down to business, so can I. I've got three things for you. First. I looked into Langat's tracker. It and the detail were paid for by an anonymous donor to the Somalian refugee relief work."

Mark was too tired not to play the game. "And where does the money track to?"

"That's the second thing. So far, it dead ends with a group that has ties to Anastas."

His gut churned at the thought of what a trafficker would want with Somalian refugees. "You've got to find out who it is."

The snarky, crass retort Jehnson threw at him rankled more than the implied stupidity of the statement. Jehnson laughed at his own joke before shifting to serious with the ease of a race car engine. "There's rumblings in D.C. I don't know why, but fingers are pointing in your direction. Watch yourself."

The line went dead.

0000 01 000 0000 1 01 110   010 111 110 001 0

Shhhttt… chith. Shhhttt… chith. The Tic-Tac container shook with each slow pull back and each jerk forward. *Shhhttt… chith. Shhhttt… chith.*

With one elbow propped on the desk, and a hand shaking the container at regular, rhythmic intervals, the other hand scrolled and clicked from screen to screen, reading… watching… searching. Nothing anywhere. It was as if Shin Kim, the North Korean agent, had disappeared into the back hills of nowhere. If all evidence didn't point to someone else looking too, it might be presumed that he, and maybe his whole family, had died.

The US Marshal Service wasn't nearly as brilliant at keeping their witnesses alive and hidden as they liked to hope. That meant someone else had to be hiding him. Did Mark Cho do it before he gave up The Agency, or was it Mendina's doing?

Shhhttt… chith.

Marco Mendina—was it his real name, or was Mark a name like "the dread pirate Roberts" in that princess movie? Just passed along from one person to the next? *And will he be as eager to turn it over to someone?*

Casualties spoke loudest. No one liked the idea of losing people, but one had to do what one had to do. Decision made. *Shhhttt… chith.*

A punched button or two made the call. "Do you have Erika?"

"I did. They got away at the mall."

The box of Tic-Tacs flew across the room, and tiny orange candies sprinkled down on carpeting as the top popped off. "I want her dead."

"How?"

"I don't care. Kill Erika but leave Flynne."

The hesitation prompted a search for another box of Tic-Tacs. Green this time. *Shhhttt… chith. Shhhttt… chith.*

"Okay."

TWENTY-ONE

Guilt wrapped tentacles around his neck—choking until Mark bolted upright in bed. No sounds, no alarms, no shadows lingered where there shouldn't be any. Only guilt squeezing until he couldn't breathe.

Time to get up.

Gray and greenish yellow streaked across the sky, hinting of impending dawn. Mark stood there, soaking up every bit of light as it inched closer to the horizon. Something deep within nudged him, pressed him to pray.

There was a problem with that. Several, actually. He didn't know if he believed that prayer was anything other than private venting, he didn't know how to pray even if he did think it would do some good, and he didn't know what or whom to pray *for*.

"Could we start with the basics? Could You show me what prayer is and what it does?"

It seemed a bit brief... abrupt. Mark tried again. And again. After the third reattempt, he realized he'd just said the same thing in three or four different ways. "I think an amen is in order, because I don't even know what I'm doing."

Never had Mark felt more ridiculous than standing there waiting for some inspiration that never came. The sun glowed golden and shot pink streaks across the sky as it rose above the horizon. Still, nothing.

Time to work.

He stopped in the kitchen to grab a frozen breakfast burrito from the fridge before opening the basement door. A string on a chain overhead lit the raw-wood steps that led down into the dank, dusty, cobweb-laden basement. At the bottom, he opened a pair of doors, shoved aside several leisure suits from the seventies, stepped through an old wardrobe, slid the back panel aside, and keyed in his access code.

Stepping through the wardrobe as if into Narnia never got old—even for someone who looked as old as Mark did. The basement annex held everything he could need—food, recycled oxygen supply, and batteries to keep the place powered for weeks, all wrapped in a sleek, modern design that couldn't have been more incongruous with the house it connected to.

His printer tray held three sheets of computerized Morse code. First up—the Todds. Liv Todd needed protection. For that matter, her parents probably did, too. Splitting them up in his mind was all it took to come up with a plan. He started a phone relay. It would take up to fifteen minutes for Tyler to pick up, but he could get it in motion before turning his attention to the next.

Otto Schmatloch.

The man wasn't in danger. According to the message, Tyler had gotten their intel scrubbed by a professional. All of it had been fabricated—apparently for their benefit. Mona Detweiler wasn't a threat to anyone or anything—except, perhaps, Bavarian pastries. That meant a threat existed, but they didn't know where it originated. Schmatloch still needed protection, but from whom? And why the elaborate scheme to terrify an old man who hadn't done anything worse than pummel a man for speaking

216

crass to a lady back in '62? He'd married that girl, too.

A smile formed. They'd honeymooned at Niagara Falls, Ontario. He could send Otto, Karen, and Brian there—or better yet, Paris and Henry. They were probably ready to get back to the west coast. This would keep them close. That message typed, he instigated another relay—a dozen messengers all over the world, back to home, and over to a designated server just for email coming from the bunker. Tyler had better check it and soon.

That left the last message. Longer than the others, it included a personal note from Corey. *I can't expect Mari to leave now—with a daughter and a husband missing. The things people are saying are vile, Mark! On the other hand, I don't know how else to protect them but to get them out of there. Where is Brent? Where's Alyssa? I don't know how to find them. Help!*

He knew where Brent was. It galled him to even think it, but he could thank Flynne for that. As far as he knew, it wasn't possible for Brent to have taken his daughter without driving back from St. Louis and then returning again. Highly unlikely.

Just as the call to Tyler finally came through, the internet connected. As he typed in a search for any information on the missing Knupp girl, he greeted the kid and said, "Okay, the Todds."

"I had an idea on that."

Mark waited, but Tyler didn't elaborate. "And that idea?"

"Oh, sorry. I thought maybe if they all went on a cruise or something—just far enough away that it gives one of the government agencies time to evaluate the threat and work out a plan to stop whoever it is. My aunt won a cruise once and didn't know it until she got a call saying if she didn't book and sail in the next week, she'd lose it. So, maybe..."

The idea worked with his—and didn't. "Good idea—about the cruise. Put them on an Alaskan cruise ASAP. But not Liv. We need to go full detail on her. We will *not* fail her. So, Dan French has to die. Get an article in the paper about his suspicious death."

Tyler's low whistle filled his ears. "That'll cost."

"It's worth it." Considering the cost of a life, it was a bargain. "Get Karen and Brian on detail. We don't have a job to worry about, but someone will have to do her finals and papers for the last couple of weeks of school."

"She only has two in-person classes—large ones. So that should help."

After considering a moment or two, Mark quadrupled the cost of the operation. "Get Suresh on the project. Have him find out who gave Liv Todd that information."

"Ouch."

Without waiting for further commentary, Mark moved onto his ideas about Otto Schmatloch and then moved to Corey. "Okay, this is what I want Corey to do. Give her access to the Wisconsin cabin and tell her to get the sister there. She'll have to scare Mari Knupp into fearing for her other children's lives, but it's what it is."

"I've been searching for any sign of the girl. Not one thing in her life points to runaway."

"I didn't think so. Something about this Brent Knupp thing is really weird. The daughter took it to new heights of weirdness that I almost wish I could hear Flynne's description of."

A strangled sound reminded Mark that he'd been insensitive. "She's doing well, Tyler. I was angry with her, but she's kept Erika alive and kept us in the loop. That's not easy."

"True..." Tyler sighed. "Okay, better get off. I'll take care of this."

He couldn't resist a bit of teasing. "Want me to order you a Burberry tie?"

Only the trace of a chuckle reached him before the line went dead. Mark smiled—or rather, he tried to. His lips just wouldn't cooperate.

0000 01 000 0000 1 01 110   010 111 110 001 0

The ridged edge of the cellphone case provided a satisfying *zthwit!* with each pass of a thumbnail over the ridges. *Zthwit!*

"—caught an anomaly at Callum Motors. A guy from St. Louis came in and bought a 2004 Echo. Cash. Thirty-two hundred."

Zthwit! "How did you get this information?"

"Monitoring the motor vehicles site. I've been watching every sale that could possibly be connected to your names or to St. Louis from there. Then I go check the dealerships. The salesman was chatty."

"Send me everything you know about it. I want license plate, color, make, model, average MPG— everything." *Zthwit!*

"There's something interesting about this guy—it's why I called. I looked him up on social media."

Seconds passed with the *Zthwit! Zthwit! Zthwit!* of impatience.

"He's posted a lot of pictures and talked about Air BnB a lot. So, I did some digging. He lives at this house as kind of a manager or something. There's a cottage out back that they rent..."

"Have an addy for me?"

The street address and a picture of the place appeared on the monitor to the right. A smile formed. "What would I do without a dag like you?"

"I'm not delusional. You'd find someone else to do your tech work, and I'd be hacking for ransom again."

"I'll wire the funds to your account when we're off."

When the phone nestled in its cradle again, fingers flew across a keyboard and five thousand US dollars dropped into a Canadian account. *Zthwit!*

A few more calls followed before a controller appeared. A few clicks and the search began. *Dragon's Circle.* A hack of her home firewall in previous weeks had shown a tendency to choose that one most.

It offered live streaming of games in progress, and the scrolling began. Some names made sense, but none stood out. *That* they hadn't been able to crack—the username. Without social media as the guide, it left a hole in understanding someone good at keeping herself hidden.

An hour passed. Two. A game with LordFly proved futile. Dorpleganger also futile. Comparing the names to what little they did know about Flynne Dortmann—time consuming.

Computer whiz, dating an agent—maybe. That hadn't been confirmed, but there had been a guy... Teen emoji-speak. Annoying. Semi-earth conscious...

CircDLife proved incorrect.

A weakness for bread, pasta, and Burberry—not necessarily in that order.

Zthwit! Zthwit! Zthwit!

Why did that feel familiar? Back, forward, in and out of games so fast it required changing accounts almost as quickly to avoid annoying the other players. They'd forgive an internet drop, but not a repeat performance. Gamers talked.

Zthwit!

The name appeared again. PuffBerryDragon. *Zthwit!* One click and in.

Let the games begin. Zthwit!

"Level up!"

Erika looked up from a stuffy-looking book and said in a flat, unenthusiastic monotone, "Yay."

"I've never gotten this fa— Oooh! Cool. Look at *that*. That's supes awesome sauce!"

"Please, Lord. Make it stop. Maybe I should find Brent Knupp and beg him to off me now."

Flynne paused the game and eyed Erika with as malevolent a glare as she could manufacture while still awed by the new scenes on the screen. "I probably threw away like the most awesomesauce job for you. So, like, stop being totes annoyzballs!"

"Aaak! My ears bleed!" Erika stood and said, "But I appreciate that you tried not to let someone else kill me."

"Whatevs."

A huff followed that. At the door, Erika added, "I'm going to take a bath."

Without taking her eyes from the screen, Flynne shot back, "Don't drop that book in the tub. It's probably priceless."

"It's an Easton reprint of *The Turn of the Screw*. There's probably fifty of them on eBay."

That's all Flynne needed to know. With a car wheezing

its way to St. Louis from Rockland, and an uncertain future ahead of her, Flynne had promised herself a day of gaming to relax her before the strain began again. Having Erika on her side made the whole protection detail so much easier.

Just as she raised the next iron gate, another player joined her. ReaperKeeper. "Hey, Reaps-keeps. How's it going…?"

"Keep getting stuck here. Haven't seen you in this level before, so I thought I'd step in and see if you know how to get past that cockatrice."

And there it was—the classic rooster-headed dragon. "You're getting too close. It can breathe on you."

"Their breath kills?"

How'd you get, like, this far and not know that? Flynne didn't ask, though. Instead, she suggested a mirror. "If you don't have one, we'll have to go find a rooster first."

"There was that farm just a bit back before we hit the castle. I'll run back for one."

While Reaps dashed off, Flynne searched for something reflective. A silver tray would have worked well, but she couldn't find anything large enough to ensure the nasty creature would see its own reflection. *We'll just have to hope that rooster crows.*

Two hours later, with the cockatrice dead in the keep, and the two of them standing in the oratory, Flynne jumped when she heard Morgan say, "Make sure you have your sword ready."

"Wha—? Oh! You're back!" Flynne held up one finger and turned back to the game. "Sorry, Reaps. My boyfriend just got in from a trip out of town. He said to have your sword ready. I'm going to go. TTYL!"

"Later gator. Thanks for the help."

With the game on pause, Flynne hopped up to greet

Morgan and frowned at the expression he wore. "What's wrong?"

"What'd that car look like? The one that made you decide to help Erika.

She blinked and backed away. "How do you know that?"

"Flynne..."

A vase that looked nice and expensive caught her attention. Flynne snatched it up and might have prayed it was worth thousands if she thought it would do any good. "I said, *how do you know that?*"

"You guys think you're so clandestine about it all, but you forget I'm here half the time."

As Flynne replaced the vase, she sighed. "Mark is so going to kill me. I'm out of a job for suresies."

"Then move here with me."

That stopped her in her tracks. "I thought you were moving to Rockland."

"Only because you're there."

It was exactly what she wanted to hear, but it didn't sound scripted. It sounded real. If the heat in her face meant anything, he'd know she liked it, too. "Oh."

"What color, Flynne?"

"Why?"

She'd expected him to argue—to resist telling her about it. He didn't. Instead, he launched into a story about seeing a car several times on his way back. "I saw a few, actually—but mostly minivans. This car, though... it was a sedan—a Mazda. I thought the driver was similar enough to be your guy. Not for sure, but close enough, you know?"

A chill rippled over her. "Did you make sure no one followed you off the interstate?"

"No one followed me here. I got off at the exit, grabbed

a drink, got back on and drove all the way to Ferguson, came back to the mall, and then here. Didn't see the car again after that minimart."

His words should have reassured her. "Coolio." They didn't.

TWENTY-TWO

Perfect temperatures greeted Keith as he stepped off the bus in St. Louis. The backpack he'd bought at the Rockland station pulled just enough to aggravate his wound, but after being cramped up on the bus, moving around felt wonderful. All the way up 14th Street to Market. By that time, he could have taken a nap.

Still, he trudged along the sidewalks, hardly noticing the changes in buildings as he pushed toward where he thought the Gateway Arch would be. *Walking's good—prevents pneumonia.*

It also delayed the moment he'd have to call for information. Had they found where Erika and Flynne were yet? Detective work wasn't Keith's strong suit. He was a protector, not an investigator. Tyler's experience there meant that, with a few years in the field, he'd probably be the best agent they had.

Each block became harder to move than the last. A bus stop bench called to him, and the feeling that he'd started bleeding again prompted him to answer that call. He dropped to the seat, and a man on the opposite side told him when to expect the next bus.

"Just resting. I remember there being a few parks along here. I wanted to just sit for a bit, but I couldn't make it."

"You're almost there. Just down another block and a

half or so."

A bus rumbled up and a few people jumped off. Keith just stared at a Sprint wireless ad. Prepaid with data. That would work. He'd have access… and no one expected him here anyway. As the bus rolled away, he turned to his bench mate. "How far is Washington?"

"Need a phone?" He must have shown surprise, because the guy grinned. "Saw you starin'. Yeah, you just go over a coupla streets and up a ways and there's a Sprint store up there."

Keith dug for his flip phone and wriggled it in the air. "I think it might be time to give this up and get in the twenty-first century."

"Never had one of them things. Don't trust 'em. Seems like all the TV shows use 'em to find people what don't want to be found."

And that was just his problem. Still, who would be looking for him? He was relatively unknown except by relatives who weren't supposed to mention him much. Habit and instinct rebelled, though. *I have to. I can't afford the time to find libraries to communicate with Erika's Twitter.*

When a patrol car swept past for the second time, his bench mate pulled himself up and reached for his scruffy backpack. "That's my signal to mosey on."

Maybe it was foolish, but Keith couldn't help but ask, "How are you fixed for money?"

"Got some. Not much, but some. People are good to me. I think it's 'cause I don't ask. That's just pride, a-course. Still, I think folks like that I don't badger them none."

Worked on me. Keith dug his fist into his pocket, felt for a couple of bills, and prayed they'd be twenties. As he fished them out and passed them over, he saw a one on one of them and stifled a sigh. It wouldn't do to dig again. As okay as the man seemed, you never knew. "I don't usually carry much cash, but I have some today. You take care."

The man had made it three steps before he turned back and thrust one of the bills back at him. "Can't take this, man. It's too much. Don't think you knew you gave it to me."

In his fist was a hundred-dollar bill. Keith rose as well, hefted his own backpack, and turned toward the Sprint store. "You keep it. I'm fine."

Two steps away, he found himself crushed by stronger arms than he'd have predicted. His chest protested the hug, pain shooting daggers through him over and over. "Thanks, man. I'll pass it along—forward, like they say. You can count on that."

Any doubts he had disappeared as he walked away. *Now, to a phone and a new Twitter account*

Tagged in a tweet. It was the first time that had happened since she left HearthLand. @Erikaff2 #GOTYOURBACK.

The name wasn't familiar, but no one could doubt who "@ErikaFanBoy" was. "Hey, Flynne. Check it out."

Flynne hardly looked up from the screen where she, Morgan, and their new friend "ReaperKeeper" were battling some dragon with more than one head—the Medusa of dragons, Morgan had called it. "What am I looking at?"

"Not looking at is more like it. I think Keith just left me a message. I think he's *here*."

Never had she seen Flynne move faster. The controller

and headset lay abandoned on the couch at almost the same moment she flung herself at the window. "For realsies? He's good!" After scanning the street, she frowned. "Where?"

Erika coughed. "The monitor?"

"Oh." She wasn't certain, but Erika thought she heard Flynne mutter, "I'm so embarrified."

A silent cry went out to the Lord, begging for puff-filled brownie points for not bopping the girl for it. "Look. Says he has our back. That's got to mean he's here, right?"

"You'd know better than me, but coolio. Maybe I'm totes fired and stuffs."

Most people didn't sound so gleeful when speaking of losing their jobs. Erika couldn't blame her, though. Evading and protecting others from would-be nefarious dudes wasn't exactly in her performance plan.

"That handle is adorbilicious."

As much as she hated to admit it, she agreed. In her peripheral vision, Erika watched Morgan fumble with his phone. A moment later, he passed it to Flynne with truly the most adorable, sheepish smile she'd ever seen. Flynne almost flung the phone at her and turned to focus all attention on the new love of her life.

May the spit-swapping commence. Erika wrinkled her nose and began to ponder when she'd become her father when she saw the screen. A reply had been added to Keith's tweet. A reply from @FallingForFlynne. It read simply, #NOMOREROGUE.

Desperate to get on track for solving the problem of protection and off the burgeoning make out session, Erika asked, "Can we post a place to meet? Say something like 'hungry for St. Louis Bread Company' and hope he finds where we're going or something?"

Morgan protested. "Too public. You'd be better off just sending a direct message. Keep it minimal. Something like, 'Sorry, can't make it to your party. Forgot I had to be at the courthouse at five.'"

Both girls stared at him for a moment before Erika gave a low whistle and said, "You're not bad at this."

"You're kidding, right?" Of all the responses he could have offered, an argument wouldn't have occurred to her. "It's pretty obvious. Anyone with hacker skills will find this stuff. Flynne could inside half an hour if she had her equipment."

Flynne's wince hinted he wasn't wrong.

"But you're still thinking right. Your idea at least requires more work than a public hashtag."

An argument regarding where they should hint at a meet commenced. Flynne voted for the mall, certain Knupp wouldn't expect them to go back. Erika refused. "We can't be sure of that."

While they bickered, Morgan took the phone and, as far as Erika could tell, made the choice for them. *It's kind of a relief, but who does he think he is?*

"Looks like he might be near the arch."

"Why do you say that?"

She and Flynne nearly conked heads as he held the phone up for them to see. "Because he took a picture of it—from awfully close?"

"So, what's near there?"

Morgan considered for a moment and typed something into the phone. He passed it back to Flynne, who nodded and shared with Erika. *Sorry we can't make it to the picnic at Malcolm Martin Park tonight. Really wanted to see that fountain, but we have a minor emergency that needs medical attention. Maybe next time.*

She grinned and hit send, but that grin faded a moment later. "Um, guys?"

Flynne tore her adoring eyes from Morgan. "Yeah?"

"Maybe we should scope out that fountain early."

"Why?"

Her heart raced as Erika tried to gather her wits. "Just saw Brent Knupp drive by."

0000 01 000 0000 1 01 110   010 111 110 001 0

"Come on, come on, come on..." Tyler would have thrown the monitor if somehow it would have made the relay go faster. Despite every effort to ignore it, the Twitter handle drew his gaze. @FallingForFlynne.

"It's just Erika reassuring me that things are okay. Pretty smart."

His gut told him otherwise. With every second that passed, his hand pushed the mouse closer to the name. Just a few clicks would verify it—when the account was created, old names... Conversational reversal would tell all in seconds if an old name had kept old tweets.

And he was too chicken to do it.

For testing purposes only, of course, Tyler worked on hacking into Keith's account. At least he'd used password protocol. That made things so much easier. Seeing a direct message from EriKaff2 didn't.

"Come on!"

The first blip of a ring sounded the moment Tyler clicked on @FallingForFlynne. As he answered, his gut twisted at the picture that appeared. Flynne's gaming group all surrounding one guy. "Morgan."

"Haven't changed to that name yet, why?"

"It's a he."

Mark's voice sounded as confused as Tyler felt. "I bought a list of recently purchased cars. One was from a guy from St. Louis. Morgan Garnett."

"Morgan—a guy? I thought it was a girl."

"That makes two of us. He's got a new handle on Twitter." Tyler swallowed a gulp of water before spitting out, "FallingForFlynne."

"Feel sorry for him."

That was unexpected. "Why's that?"

"She'd have to do what she had to do to protect Erika, and if it means making up to a friend, she'd do it. This is Flynne. You know she would."

And he'll be a casualty. Poor guy.

"So, what do you have for me?"

Business first, heart resuscitation later. "Well, this is what I know. Morgan, the gaming house guy, came to Rockland and bought a Toyota Echo. I suspect he's back in St. Louis by now. He also changed his name from Morgan underscore Garnett underscore 1990 to FallingForFlynne— all one word, of course—likely since then."

"And?"

Tyler continued as if he hadn't been interrupted. "Keith has arrived in St. Louis. When I saw him post on Twitter, I went and checked his credit history. He opened an account with Sprint today—at the store closest to Gateway Arch, according to Google. Since then, he's opened a Twitter account as ErikaFanBoy and posted a hashtag of 'got your back.'"

"Good… don't suppose he hinted how he's doing?"

"Nope. But he got a message from Erika's account that says they can't meet at some park… hang on, forgot to check…" The park came up and Tyler nodded to no one in

231

particular. "Okay, it's directly across from the Gateway Arch on the Illinois side. Anyway, some medical emergency."

"Think it's a meet time?"

After reading it a time or two more, Tyler set the Newton's cradle in motion and gave his verdict. "Yeah."

"What time?"

Before he answered, Tyler put the phone on speaker to protect his ears. "No time mentioned—just 'tonight.'"

The move proved unnecessary. As irritated as Mark sounded, he didn't yell. "If that was Keith, I'd dock his pay. Instead, I'm impressed Flynne thought of it."

"Bet it was Erika." Just saying the words felt disloyal, but Tyler trudged on. "She's done this before, you know? Even from the other side of the job, it's more than Flynne has."

"Get ahold of Keith. Tell him to have a van waiting—cargo. He'll extract them. Then tell him to get them to Cape Girardeau. Have a helo there waiting. They can go to the Oregon house."

"What about Liv Todd? Should we get her there, too?"

The silence hinted at a no, but Mark started making murmuring sounds. "Yeah… yeah. Good thought. Send Karen and Brian with Liv to Cape Girardeau. They can all do Oregon. And get Flynne back in the office. I think the Todds might need a new life."

Tyler winced but had to ask. "Can we afford it? Way more money going out than in right now."

"This one's my fault. I have to. While you're at it all, make sure the Shins have nothing to report. That'll give us a good idea if Flynne's covered our tracks well enough." After another few seconds, Mark added, "And check Flynne's Cayman account."

"To see if it's been accessed?"

"Yes."

He sat almost mesmerized by the bouncing metal balls, but his instincts asked the next obvious question. "Anything else?"

"Get me an update on Schmatloch. Go through Rickwood. Traffic light protocol should be sufficient."

With that, the phone went dead, and Tyler went to work.

TWENTY-THREE

In a family room the size of Erika's parents' house, or so it seemed, she stood there and watched as Flynne made a dozen decisions and rescinded each one almost as soon as she'd made it. "What if we head toward that park, and at the last minute, don't get on the bridge? We leave a message about meeting at the water tower in Chicago in like an hour or so?"

Morgan argued that she'd overcomplicated things, something Erika agreed with. Flynne countered with a scheme so elaborate it would be impossible for her to remember what sequence to do what in. Only the soft, muffled wail of, "I just want Mark to see that I did my best to save her," kept Erika from losing what little patience she had left.

"I know what Keith would do."

That got their attention.

"Morgan will bring your new car to the side entrance. I'll get in the back and sneak out the other side when Morgan opens the door to throw in luggage. Then, I'll sneak around back, and we'll drive off in his car. He'll go toward the mall. We'll go to the park."

As much as Flynne seemed to want to do it, she also seemed skeptical. Erika sent a glare Morgan's way, and he caught the point. "I think that sounds smart. I'll just come back this way in an hour or so, and you guys can go back to Rockland."

Discomfort followed. Morgan shuffled. Flynne made a strangled sound which could have been anything from a repressed cough to a stifled sob. Once again, it was up to Erika to make the decision. "Do you want to prove yourself to Mark or not?"

Once more, Flynne perked up. "Yeah. Okay, so we'll · just drive off in Morgan's car?"

"If we're meeting Keith, you'll have to tie me up—gag me. But yeah." Even as she spoke, Erika blasted herself. *What kind of idiot* asks *to be bound and gagged. It's insanity!*

"But why?"

While she explained the reasons Keith had given, Erika began picking up the mess they'd made in Mr. Werner's house. "It's not even for an hour. You don't have to even really gag me. Just put a sock ball in my mouth, so if I scream accidentally, it's muffled. That'll be enough."

If only that had calmed Flynne's jitters. Morgan gave her a look—one Erika translated to mean, "Give us a minute."

"I'm just going to run and use the restroom before we go. We should hurry, though."

The guest bathroom, with its Carrara marble and automatic faucets, still did little to keep her wanting to hang around. *You can only drool over stuff you'll never own while your friends drool over themselves for so—* That thought stopped her short. Friends. Odd that the person who had shot her in the butt—twice, even—could ever be called a friend.

A grin stared back at her in the mirror. "I'm gonna claim Stockholm and get her all messed up. It's what *friends* do."

"Are you done in there? We've got to *go!* I just saw

236

him pass again. Now's the time!"

The irony of her complaining about Flynne delaying departure and Flynne telling her to get a move on didn't escape Erika's notice. She presented herself at the front door and shook her head at the zip ties. "I know how to get out of duct tape better. Those videos we watched should be easy enough if we both have to run. Let's go with that—but we'll do it when we get me in the car. Easier."

"Ooooh! Supes smarticle."

Oh, please.

Morgan led her to the new car, opened the door for her, and pointed for her to lie down. As planned, she slipped out the other side when he made a show of putting duffel bags inside. Erika wove through bushes and behind a small tree and came around to the side-yard entrance where Flynne waited with Morgan's car already running. "Let's get this taping done and this show on the road. I'm about to get fired, and life is oh, so good!"

That's the most normal thing I think I've ever heard you say.

Flynne settled into her seat, snapped the seatbelt in place, blasted the AC, cracked windows for "fresh air"—an exercise in how to make an AC less effective—and checked every mirror. "We're good for take offs!"

By the third turn, Erika was lost already. Flynne spent every second muttering in Flynne-speak about the "obvies" way Brent would do this, or the "supes stupes" thing she just did. Had Erika's mouth not been stuffed with a clean sock, she would have screamed and begged for it all to stop. Instead, she squeezed her eyes as tight as possible and tried to make her ears plug.

Fifteen minutes passed before Flynne spoke directly to her. "I see the Eads Bridge! We're almost there. I think we did it!"

Half a minute passed before she added, "It's supes congestie down here! The hour got all rushed."

Did you really just—?

A scream—*Flynne's scream*—killed that question. "What?" It came out, "Wwmmwph" but Erika tried again.

"Hang on! He's coming for us!"

Who?

The car swerved and jolted as it hit something. Erika tried to sit up, but Flynne floored it, and the backseat seemed to take on a mind of its own as it bounced her around like a rubber ball before landing her on the floor. *What is going on?*

"He's here!"

Who?

"Brace yourself!"

Instead of impact from the rear, Erika felt the front of the car jolt a bit as it shot forward. *Did you just hit—?*

"Noooooooo!"

Another jolt. A shudder. Silence.

Impact came hard and jarring. Erika landed on the inside roof of the car, battered, disoriented, confused. Her body refused to do anything. Panic welled up in her throat, her eyes, her pounding chest. But Erika only stared out in horror as water trickled in through the cracks in the window.

0000 01 000 0000 1 01 110   010 111 110 001 0

The water stared back at her—challenging her. Panic held Flynne captive. Tears blurred her vision, and she squeezed her eyes shut, trying to block out the image of muddy water pushing its way in. *God, I'll be one of your peeps if you just make it all go away.*

She pried one eye open, and water still streamed over the crack in the window. *I'm not speaking to you again.*

A noise behind her reminded Flynne that she wasn't alone. *Erika! She's, like, all tied up and stuffs.*

Flynne fumbled for the seatbelt and managed to disengage. Her head connected with the soggy roof the moment she realized she should have held out her hand to soften impact. "Ooof!"

Instinct said to try to roll the windows down before the electronic mechanism short-circuited. Panic said she'd electrocute them both. *Kick out the window. That's what you're supposed to do. Kick it. Break it.*

Kicking, however, didn't work. She tried again... and again. Hands shaking, heart racing, Flynne grabbed the keys and tried stabbing at the window with them. Failure.

Glove compartment. Breathing became nearly impossible as she fought to work the latch on the compartment from a listing upside down. That's when Flynne noticed that the car had shifted to its right. *Starboard? I don't know.*

Water poured in, more and more with each second, it seemed. She swept everything out of the glove compartment in one swift movement and pounced on the satisfying thunk... of something. The muddy water obscured what it was, but the moment Flynne's fingers wrapped around it, she nearly sobbed in relief. "Got a tire gauge! Gonna bust some moves and get us out. Hang on, Erika!"

Her first whacks at the side window failed. Didn't even cause a spiderweb of a crack. An upward thrust to the corner, however, got her first hope.

And the water was up to her chest. "I'm trying!"

From beside her, all she could hear were Erika's muffled pleas for help. Flynne worked double-time to crack open that window. The car listed backward, and Erika half-tumbled, half-bobbed out of sight. *Noooo! Stay where I can see that you're okay!* Taking the time to check to see that Erika's head remained above water would kill precious seconds. She couldn't allow herself that luxury.

Flynne pounded harder. With each jab of the gauge, she grunted and huffed. "I'd—" *Splink!* "Better get..." *Splink!* "Stock—" *Splink!* "In. The. Bur. Berry—" *Splink! Splink! Splink!* "Company. After. This."

The window gave way. A kick knocked half of it out and sliced her leg. The cold water sent a shock to her system as it filled the car. She kicked, fought, pushed until it was free. The car filled so fast, Flynne became disoriented as she fumbled for Erika.

Erika's eyes were wide, and she fought to say something. Flynne ripped the sock from her mouth and sobbed out an apology. "I tried—"

"No time. Help me break the duct tape. I can't do it in here and under water."

At that moment, the water hit Flynne's chin. A glance up showed the entire interior almost full. With a huge gulp of air, she dove down, ripped the duct tape off Erika's feet and fumbled to find the girl's hands.

Floating. Every movement felt as though she floated through it. With what was left of her air, Flynne shoved Erika toward the front window and pushed until the girl got free. An attempt to grab another gulp of air failed. There wasn't any left. The car had fully submerged.

Can I do take backs? I'll talk to you again. I'm sorry. Not gonna make it. Can't see. Can't swim... Can't breathe.

Erika broke the surface of the water and gulped in almost as much of the nasty stuff as she did air. Coughing, sputtering, she scanned the surface for Flynne. Nothing. The current tugged her further and further away from the car, but she kicked toward it.

The memory of ships sinking and sucking people down with it demanded she should get away. Not seeing Flynne meant she had to try to get back. Against the current. Of course.

Two steps forward and one step back never held truer than swimming against the river current and the constant assault on her by some kind of Kamikaze fish. Her arms ached and burned almost immediately. And she'd only advanced a few yards.

By the time she got close, Erika was ready to give up — on both of them. Twice she lunged for the car and got swept back away. The third time proved to work, however. She dove under and fumbled for the window.

Flynne floated at the top by the roof. That kicked some sense of self and other preservation into gear. *Oh, no you don't!*

It took more tries than she could count, but Erika finally managed to grab a shock of Flynne's hair. She tugged and pulled until she managed to hook an arm under Flynne's neck. Dark streaks followed as she jerked the girl through the window. *Blood, I guess.*

At the surface, déjà vu took over as Erika gasped, sputtered, and fought for a lungful of air that didn't include muddy Mississippi water.

Flynne hung limp.

Attempting to keep her above water—almost impossible.

That's when it occurred to Erika that this might be a good time for prayer. If only her brain would cooperate. Instead, a rather ineloquent and redundant stream of, *Oh, God. Help!* repeated on auto-loop.

And her grip on Flynne slipped with each bump of what felt like torpedo-like fish.

A voice bellowed at her, telling her to hold on. *God?*

Closer... The voice drew closer... Erika looked behind her to find a motorboat headed her way. *I couldn't have heard him!*

Then he did it—pulled out a megaphone and told her again. *"Hang on!"*

Strength left her, despite every effort to do just that. Hang on. *Sorry, Flynne.*

A steady, mechanical, rumbling whine and a steady, yet irregular thrumming in her head pulled Erika into semi-consciousness. A moment later, she vomited up the contents of her stomach onto the bottom of a boat.

Consciousness regained.

Pushing up and away from the mess, she scanned the area and saw Flynne lying on her side against the side of the boat. Erika scrambled, slipped, and scrambled again to reach her. A muffled voice from behind her called, "She hasn't moved."

CPR. It probably wouldn't work, but she'd want someone to do it for her. Taking a deep breath, Erika pleaded for forgiveness and offered the first five rescue breaths. Compressions. Breaths. Compressions. Breaths.

Her body wouldn't cooperate. Erika collapsed against the bottom of the boat, struggling. It slowed and she heard sirens in the distance. *Too late.*

Tears fell.

Coughing, sputtering—vomited river water spewed over the side of her head and face. Erika sat bolt upright and almost didn't mind as she watched Flynne struggle to draw in air. "Breathe!" A few choice words followed, and somewhere in recesses of her mind, Erika knew she'd have to repent of those.

Is it a sin if I don't care?

TWENTY-FOUR

The call came through just as Keith neared Eads Bridge. Only the fact that no one should know his number made him answer. "Yeah?"

"It's Tyler. Go south of the Eads down by the Poplar Street Bridge. Follow the sirens and emergency vehicles."

His gut twisted. "Why?"

"I think Erika and Flynne are in the water. Dispatch has called out for emergency teams. A 9-1-1 came through from a bass boat saying he was picking up two passengers—one might be dead."

Lord, please no…

"Keith?"

He'd just reached Eads and saw it blocked off by police cars. "Trying to get turned around, but congestion…"

"If you weren't hurt, I'd say run it, but…"

As he irritated every other driver on the road, showing them exactly what he'd do to reach his team—his girl—Keith barked out questions. "How'd you find out? What makes you think it's them? Is it the car she bought?"

"Not sure. Can't tell. I was following St. Louis news and dispatch when I saw your tweet. A couple of drivers blocked off another car and wrestled the driver to the ground. Someone called in a license plate."

It's gonna be Knupp.

"It's Knupp's. They got him, though. He's already been arrested." Silence. When Keith asked if the call had dropped, Tyler snapped at him to shut up. A moment later, he spoke again. "Sorry. Was listening in on the ambulance frequency. I think it's our girls for sure." The kid's voice broke. "Sounds like Flynne is unresponsive. EMT 'Noah' is working on her. If he saves her, hug him for me."

That ain't gonna happen.

"How far are you?

"Maybe halfway." Keith shot over the double yellow and passed a car. An oncoming line forced him back in, but not without a few dozen horn blares.

"It's less than a mile!"

"And there are five hundred cars being rerouted away from Eads!" His yelling-through-enforced-clenched-teeth skills had obviously wavered. It took three more tries for Tyler to understand him.

"Still, hurry!"

Keith swerved to miss a car trying to pull into his lane and briefly reconsidered his stance on foul language. Instead, he barked, "Give me a break!"

One squeaked word ripped at his heart. "Flynne!"

"I'll get her. I'll get there. I can't help them if I die or kill a bunch of people on the way, so just gimme—oh, I see it. Um…"

It would get him in more trouble than Mark probably wanted to deal with, and it wasn't fair asking Tyler to make the call, but he did it anyway. "I can abandon the van and get there—"

"Go!"

Keith slammed on the brakes, threw the van in park, and jumped from it. Horns blared, fingers gestured, and the poisoned darts of obscenities flew at his back, but Keith

246

jogged as far and fast as he could. A cordoned-off section just south of Poplar Street told him where to go.

A line from a movie struck him as one officer tried to push him back. "That girl—" It wasn't fair how easy it was to conjure tears at a moment like that. "I was going to marry her."

"What girl?"

"Erika." At the cop's suspicious look, he repeated himself with slow, deliberate enunciation. "Over there on the gurney." Keith milked it for everything he could and ignored the fact that both women were on gurneys. "The other one that the guy is working on is Flynne—Flynne Dortmann. Please!" A bald-faced lie he'd have to repent of came next. "She's allergic to penicillin—all the cillins. They need to know."

That did it. The officer let him through, and he rushed past Flynne to Erika. One look at him and she bolted off the gurney and into his arms. "Flynne!"

"I know. I know…"

"That guy's been working on her for so long…"

"I'll go ask—tell him about her allergy to penicillin." He winked to hint that it wasn't true, helped ease her back onto the gurney, and went to talk to the EMT.

One EMT worked at constant CPR while another worked to set up a bag-valve mask, and a third, likely a paramedic, finished up with an IV and went to help get the BVM going. "Noah?"

The one doing chest compressions tossed a look his way. "We're doing everything we can. I need you to step back, sir."

Keith started to ask if Flynne would be all right and changed his mind. He didn't want to have to lie to Erika if… "What hospital?"

Two puffs followed. "Barnes."

"Can I ride with Erika?"

"Ask Ben."

Keith didn't bother to hide his frustration. Still, the man never quit working to keep Flynne's heart pumping, and Tyler would appreciate knowing it. As Keith started to back away, he said, "By the way. Her boyfriend wanted me to hug you. Consider it done."

"Considered."

One of the others called for help pushing Flynne into the ambulance. With two handling the flow of air and Noah racing alongside to keep her heart going inside the ambulance, everything shifted. In less time than he could have imagined, the doors began to close.

Ben, the paramedic for Erika's ambulance "bus," started to refuse before Keith could get the question out. Frustrated, he dug into his wallet and produced his own EMT license card and shifted from the concerned, pleading boyfriend to authority mode. "I know what to do. I know to stay out of the way. I'm just not leaving them."

That's all it took. Ben pointed to a small corner of the ambulance and told him not to interfere. Keith agreed. *It shouldn't be so easy to manipulate people.*

The moment the ambulance doors closed, Erika told him to message Morgan on Twitter. "No, wait." To Ben, she asked, "Did you say they got the guy?"

Ben didn't have a chance to answer. Keith answered for him. "They got him, Erika. Tyler called me with it."

"Then we're good. Message Morgan and tell him where we are—that Flynne needs him."

Keith's gut twisted. "Needs *him*? Morgan?"

"It's been a long... what? Week? Ten days? I can't even remember right now."

What'm I going to tell Tyler?

Before he could try to get more information, Erika vomited everywhere.

0000 01 000 0000 1 01 110   010 111 110 001 0

Bluebonnets sprinkled the meadow behind the old place. Mark leaned against the back-porch railing, taking in the sight of the sunset over that field. Some verse he'd read—several times, in fact—said something about how the "heavens" proclaimed God's glory and craftsmanship. He'd asked Claire about it—about what the "heavens" were. He'd been right. She said it was all the things you saw in the sky—in the universe.

If bluebonnets kissed by a dying sun aren't proof of a magnificent God being a phenomenal painter, then what is?

In that moment, Mark realized that he'd gone from a nebulous acceptance of a "Supreme Being" of sorts, to a defined acknowledgment of an Almighty Creator. A slow inhale, followed by an even slower exhale, calmed his unsettled nerves— for a moment. When it didn't last, he turned to go inside. Intuition might be a "women's" thing, but he had it. Something was wrong.

The French press, with its dark nectar, called to him as Mark passed through the kitchen to the basement steps. There was no need to let the caffeinated perfection go to waste. So, with a steaming mug in hand, he descended into his "lair" as he'd begun to refer to it and arrived in time to hear the phone ringing.

"They've got him—Brent Knupp. St. Louis police. Keith is there. And Flynne—"

Mark almost expected a burst of weeping from the

crack in Tyler's voice, but it didn't happen. Silence followed. "Tyler?"

"Sorry. Just…"

"Is Flynne all right?"

"They were really working on her according to the dispatch I heard. They went over a bridge…"

It took a full three seconds for Mark to make a decision. "I'm coming back. Have a plane for me in Wichita Falls. I'll be in St. Louis by midnight."

"Thank you." Again, Tyler's voice cracked. "Keith will call soon, won't he?"

"If he can."

He'd disconnected and made it upstairs before Mark decided to take one of the good vehicles. He dashed back downstairs, through the wardrobe, and across to a bookshelf of mystery and suspense novels on the back wall. It only took the flip of a latch, and the whole bookshelf rolled left without much effort. Another keypad, another sliding wall, and a flashlight that awaited him.

With everything back in place, he bolted through the tunnel that ran between the two houses on either side of the old dirt road and keyed in the code to get him inside. A pantry wall slid sideways, the home-canned jars rattling, and Mark stepped into a reasonably bright basement.

Once he'd finally set everything back in place, he began whistling "The Yellow Rose of Texas" and jogged up the steps as loudly as he could. Ruthanne met him at the basement door, a skillet of still-sizzling hash browns in hand. At the sight of him, she froze. "You're not—" She took a defensive stance.

"Ruthanne, it's me. Aged about thirty years, maybe, but me. I go by Mendina now, which I know you'll keep to yourself." He braced himself for what he knew would come next.

"What's my baby's name?"

Oh, Ruthanne... I'm sorry to do it to you. He closed his eyes and asked, "Which one?"

The answer came in a choked, "The one who will *always* be a baby."

"Sarah Jo—after your mother and Garrett's." When her arm wobbled and a giant tear rolled down her cheek, Mark reached for the pan, wrapping as much of his hand around the hot pad as possible, and took it from her. *When twenty years doesn't dull the pain, should I ever risk parenthood?*

Ruthanne wiped the tear away with the corner of her apron and wiped a few more that followed. "See," she joked between sniffles. "You can make fun of my old-fashioned aprons all you like, but they're handy."

Mark just hugged her. "Good to see you, Ruthie."

"Why'd you go old this time?"

"Doc said it's easier to do—hide scars inside wrinkles and things."

She nodded and reached for the spatula as he set the skillet back down. "Hungry?"

"Don't have time. Need to take a vehicle. Which one can you spare until I come back?"

"Take anything but the tractor. Garrett's needing that these days."

As much as he'd like to stay and lose himself in a long chat full of Ruthemisms and Texas wisdom, St. Louis beckoned. Mark kissed her cheek and promised to eat a meal with them when he returned. "Have to go now."

"I'll be prayin'."

For the first time, Mark turned and looked at her— really looked. Their gazes met. He nodded. "Thank you, Ruthanne. That means a lot."

TWENTY-FIVE

The familiar, hushed sounds of every hospital she'd ever been in encroached on her sleep. Each muted beep, each buzzer, each moan from nearby rooms served as an alarm clock, growing louder with each step toward consciousness. The buzz and squeeze of a blood pressure cuff, however, won the prize for jerking her awake.

She jumped, and as her eyes opened, Erika saw Keith there, holding her hand and watching her. A smile formed. "Hey, you."

It came out a bit muffled, too.

"How long've you been there?" Before he could answer, her eyes focused better. "Whoa… what happened to you?" Her own words caused a pounding in her head she hadn't noticed to thrum harder.

Keith's smile morphed into a grin—a metallic one. "Got in a fight with a couple of punks… and lost."

That took a moment to process. "Wait, you *lost*?"

"My client had already broken my jaw when I went to restrain him. Didn't have my gun on him."

Translating the muffled words proved more than a little difficult. "Why not? You did me!"

"He was a paying client. I stupidly didn't think I needed to coerce him to do what he'd agreed to. I just blew it. Probably distracted by a missing-persons issue I got ripped away from."

She tried to sit up and nearly screamed with the pain. Beeps and blips grew louder. A nurse entered. "What's going on? I told you not—"

"She just woke up and tried to sit up."

Erika just nodded her confirmation of Keith's assertion.

"This should be family only. I don't know how you managed to get anyone—"

Head pounding even harder at the woman's sharp tones, Erika couldn't take more than a few words before she interrupted. "If you try to get him out of here, I'll leave."

"That's not happening. We're not going to have you with a pneumothorax, too."

That's when Erika saw it—a drain tube coming out of Keith's buttoned-down shirt and leading down beside him. "Wha—?"

"I had to find you, and you can't carry one of these things around. Your doctor obliged and reinserted it for me."

"Dr. Harrez has lost his mind, if you ask me."

This time Erika heard what she'd missed before—concern. The woman's acerbic responses and disapproval stemmed from concern. That she could work from. "What's your name?"

"Molly."

"Molly, thanks for taking care of both of us." When the woman met her gaze, Erika added, "I mean it. Thanks."

Everything shifted with those words. "Well, you just rest. If he keeps you from sleeping, I'll kick him out myself and deal with Dr. Harrez later."

"He won't. *I'd* kick him, and he knows it." At the woman's smile, Erika forced herself to add, "Besides. For

254

reasons I can't fathom, the guy loves me."

The woman plopped hands on ample hips and peered at Keith. "Well, aside from the colorful face and bad braces, he's not bad to look at. He'll be like my Rodney, too—look better in about twenty years. Guys are jerks—the lot of them. The best ones look better with age, while we languish under wrinkles, laugh lines, and saddlebags." As she said that, Molly slapped her hip and gave Erika a pointed look.

"I bet your Rod loves every inch of that face, too." Keith winced as he shifted and added, "Once you steal a guy's heart, he's usually too blind to see those so-called flaws."

Molly-the-nurse just stared at him until even Erika squirmed. Then a smile lit her whole face—made every one of those wretched laugh lines shine. "Keep this one. He actually means it."

After a few adjustments to dials and buttons, Molly left. Erika asked a few more questions about Keith's injuries before turning the conversation to what she feared most. "Okay, so Flynne…"

"She's going to be okay." At her pointed look, Keith sighed. "Look, they aren't telling me much. Tyler says Mark is on the way, and we'll know more then. The guy, Morgan, is down in a waiting room and refuses to leave until he gets an update." He watched her in an apparent attempt to read her thoughts before asking, "What's up there?"

"Seems Morgan has been interested for a long time. She flirted with him—I think to keep him away from our rental—but then it became real."

Exhaustion hit hard and fast. "Hey, I've got to close my eyes for a few."

"Go ahead," Keith insisted. "The police have Knupp, and I'm not going anywhere."

"Can you go tell Morgan that Flynne saved me. I'd have died, Keith, but she saved me."

Confusion masked Keith's earlier confidence. "I thought you saved her."

Her eyes closed against her will, but Erika managed a smile. "I did. She didn't get out of the car. I had to drag her by the hair through the window... I think. She must have run out of air."

It took a moment, but she felt him shift, his lips press against her forehead, his breath as he whispered, "Love you, girl," and the emptiness when his hand released hers and he left.

Alone in the semi-dark room with its pings and beeps and buzzes, prayer kept her tethered. *Okay, I probably should thank You for a lot of things. And apologize. I kind of neglected You while I fumed at Flynne. Um, sorry. Thanks for getting us out of this mess—all of it. Especially for catching Knupp. Not sure what his deal is, but thanks for keeping us safe from him. Please heal Keith... and Flynne... and me. Thanks for helping me get Flynne out. Feels like I've got at least a concussion and a couple of broken ribs. Don't know how I swam with those, unless You had something to do with that. Thanks again.*

Though she tried to stay conscious, Erika felt everything drift away until she couldn't think at all.

0000 01 000 0000 1 01 110   010 111 110 001 0

They lay there asleep. Erika on the bed and connected to monitors and an IV, Keith in the chair-bed shoved as close to her as he could get it. A chest tube drained into a canister already filling with a frothy pink liquid. Mark's heart squeezed as Erika whimpered when she shifted.

Keith's eyes shot open, and he gazed at her, reaching for her hand, ready to do whatever it took. When she continued her rhythmic breathing, he leaned back on his chair and met Mark's gaze. "Hey..."

The curtain ruffled in his wake, but the metallic scratches on the track didn't rouse Erika. "How is everything?"

Keith rose in slow, ginger movements and carried his cannister. "Out here." They'd barely stepped from the room when a well-rounded woman sent a piercing gaze down the hall. Keith grinned. "I think that's Molly-speak for, 'Go in the waiting room and don't wake my patients.'"

"Dragon nurse?"

"Heart of gold's more like it," Keith murmured.

The waiting room held two men—one old, bent, wrinkled, and drooling out of one corner of his mouth. The other young, muscular, handsome, and drooling out of the other side of his mouth. Keith stood just inside the door and pointed. "Morgan—Flynne's friend."

"How is Flynne?"

"They won't say. Tyler said you'd handle it so we could get news." Keith jerked a thumb at Morgan. "You'll want to get them to let him in, by the way. They're... close."

"Uh, oh."

The sigh told it all. "I didn't tell Tyler. Didn't know how." Keith rubbed the back of his neck, sagging a little against the door frame. "I figured it was her business, anyway."

It might be true, but Mark couldn't risk it. She'd have to work with Tyler. He'd have to trust her. Now he wouldn't—not deep down. That could get people killed.

And what happens if you and Claire don't work? Will that make her not trust you? You not trust her?

Mark beckoned Keith to follow and moved down the hall closer to the elevators. "Tell me. What do you think? When this is all over and Flynne is back home, then... what?"

Keith's shrug said everything.

"Okay, thanks. I'm going to go get an update on her and get approval to bring him back there." Mark hesitated with a glance back at the waiting room. "Do we like him?"

"So far, so good."

"Okay. And Erika's still hanging in there? No water in the lungs or...?"

The pained expression on Keith's face told a lot more than he'd meant to. "They're pumping antibiotics into her to combat any bacteria she may have swallowed. She has two broken ribs on the left side and severe bruising all over. Concussion... I think she'd have sprained wrists or shoulders—even a broken arm—if she hadn't been bound with duct tape. That probably saved her." He glanced around as if looking for the "dragon with a heart of gold" and added, "I think she's favoring her knee, too. Can't be sure."

"I'll watch for it. Okay. I'll let you know what I find out."

He'd taken three steps before compassion overrode business. Mark returned, gave Keith a gentle hug, and said, "Thanks for being here—for putting yourself out there."

"Erika..."

"You'd have done it for Corey even on the day she went off on Erika. You might not have wanted to, but you would have." Mark didn't wait for a reply. He took off for the elevators at a quick clip and rode two floors up to the

ICU, ready to deal with the woman at that desk.

It was a man—six foot, seven if he was an inch and built like Paul Bunyan's brother. Dark skin, dark hair, dark eyes, bright smile—right up to the moment Mark stated his business. Dark expression. "You're not family. You can't go in."

"Call Dr. Levoski."

Narrowed eyes and pursed lips challenged him. Mark didn't back down. After a few taps on the keyboard and a few more of the mouse, the man held out his hand. "ID, please."

Never had anyone asked for ID before—not at a hospital. Not when he wasn't a patient. Mark passed over his driver's license and waited.

"You're not family, though?"

"I'm her boss. She doesn't have family here, and she was on the job when she got injured. Dr. Levoski—"

The man's huff could have intimidated a Navy SEAL. "People who throw around connections disgust me."

"People who allow patients to suffer alone without people who know and care about them disgust me."

Eyes locked, the two men didn't blink or budge. Only the screaming of a machine sent the nurse bolting from behind his desk and into a glass-walled room. A few steps toward the door was all he needed to know it wasn't Flynne—much too old. And the wrong gender.

Mark spun in a circle, looking at the rooms that served as almost wedges in a pie around the center station. Flynne was two doors down. A glance into the room where another nurse now bolted—where a few more people flew—told him he could go to Flynne. They couldn't stop him now. Prudence told him to wait. He needed these people on his side.

Ten minutes later he heard the solid tone of a flatline. How? How could he hear it so clearly from fifteen feet away? The team kept working until the antithesis of Nurse Bunyanator stepped back in an obvious show of resignation. A lovely woman, tall and Nordic, also stepped back from the rest and made a discreet *signum crucis.*

I could have prayed. Didn't even try. At that moment, it also occurred to Mark that he could pray for Flynne. *Okay...* The temptation to cross himself formed, but he'd never known which direction what happened. Some of those things were offensive if done backwards—devil worship and all that. *Might not be a Christian, but I'll choose that over the alternative.*

Still, Keith never made gestures when he prayed. He just grew silent, eyes cast down when possible. Mark had seen it enough to know that much.

In movies, they address You as a 'heavenly father' or 'God' or 'Jesus.' Not sure which one is best, but that prayer Jesus prayed mentioned 'Father in Heaven' so... Why was it so difficult? He'd been to church. He'd listened to TV preachers and pastors at weddings and funerals. Still, he couldn't remember a single prayer that wasn't in a movie or in that place in the Bible. Not one.

Keith always says, "Faith isn't a formula, it's a relationship." Maybe that meant casual, respectful deference would suffice. Mark started there. *It seems presumptuous to throw scattered thoughts at You now and then and then appear here asking for something. Well, if You're Who I think You might be, You might also be the only One Who can help. So here goes. That man in there? Please help me know if I can do anything for him or his family. If not, please be a comfort to everyone who loves him. Flynne...?* He choked back emotion. When it didn't help, he gripped the counter of the nurses' station and worked to steady himself.

The Bunyanator appeared at his side. "Are you all right?"

Mark nodded.

"Give me a minute. We—"

"Go ahead. I'll wait." And he did—waited for the man to finish what needed to be done and for a moment of privacy to continue that prayer.

I want both of them well and healthy, of course, but Flynne... Once more, he fought back fears he couldn't even name. *She was right about all this. I was wrong. I put her here.* His hands shook at that thought. *I put her here. Please get her out—alive and well. And if it's possible at this point—after it's already been done... I'd really appreciate it if there's a good reason for that Cayman account.*

Peace followed those thoughts. Mark hoped it meant something. He'd just decided that an "amen" was in order when a thought came out of nowhere and released itself into the cosmos. *And please protect The Agency—especially my agents. We're under attack. Amen.*

Two shoes appeared in his line of sight just as the thought, *"Attack? Where'd that come from?"* occurred. A glance up showed The Bunyanator watching him.

"Are you ready to see her?"

He nodded. "What can you tell me about her condition?"

The man froze, pivoted, and retraced his steps. "I was checking for that when I got interrupted. Just a moment."

The Bunyanator obviously found what he needed, because he began speaking before he even stood. "She's doing as well as we can hope at this point. The EEG looks good, so we don't have signs of severe brain damage, but we can't assess beyond that until she's more alert."

"Is she in a coma?"

"No, no. Her body is just working hard. We were dealing with mild hypothermia, arrhythmia, fluid in the lungs, her kidneys started failing—"

"Nooo…"

The Bunyanator led Mark to Flynne's side as he explained how things were. "They're doing better now. If her heart and lungs can stabilize, I'll feel a lot better, of course, but…"

"Will she make it?"

"I can't promise anything…"

Mark glared at the man. "I'm not asking for a promise but for an opinion. Do you think, with all your experience, that this girl will live?"

Only a short nod followed. "If I have anything to say about it, she'll thrive."

"I need to go get her boyfriend."

"Whoa…"

Mark refused to back down. He stood there, feet planted apart, arms folded over his chest in his best Keith imitation, and refused to break eye contact. "She needs the people who care most about her. I can start making calls and make an enemy of you, or you can assume that Levoski trusts that I have her best interests at heart."

"Can't have both of you in there at once. Even Dr. · Levoski won't break that one."

"That's fine. I'll go get him." He took two steps before looking back. "Thank you. For everything. Just save my girl."

TWENTY-SIX

Bleary-eyed, Tyler stared at screens that meant nothing and flicked the balls of the Newton's cradle with little interest. The clock rolled over to two a.m. With a wicked sweep of his hand, he sent the contraption flying across the room. It crashed against the door to Mark's office with a satisfying clinking-thud.

The tangled mess on the floor created an adequate representation of Tyler's mental state, and he might have perfected it with a few swift kicks and a toss into the wastepaper basket if the phone hadn't rung. His hello echoed in the room before he even snatched it from the cradle. "Is she okay?"

"From what I am hearing them imply but not say, Flynne will likely recover fully and without any lasting negative effects."

Never before had Tyler sworn in utter gratitude. "I thought it was taking so long because…"

"Because of weather. I got in late. Look, I need to talk to you about something. I need your opinion on Flynne's trustworthiness."

That knocked him back in his chair. "Huh?"

"She went rogue, Tyler. It doesn't matter if she was right or not. Next time she tells agents that I said to do something, how will they trust that it's true? She lied."

That wasn't something he'd thought of. He'd been

proud of her initiative—her drive to do "whatever it takes," just like The Agency motto said. But Mark had a point. While agents sometimes had to lie to one another for the good of their clients or The Agency itself, they needed to trust the word of the one holding their intel. "I don't know."

"If she tells you to kidnap me and ignore everything I say, will you do it?"

Though he ran a dozen scenarios through his mind, Tyler couldn't think of a single reason he would trust her... and yet he still couldn't say he wouldn't. But why? The answer came just as Mark started to ask another question. "I think—yeah. It depends on if she promised not to do it again."

"You... what?"

The disbelief would have been bad enough, but being frosted with a thick layer of amusement just made it that much worse. Still, Tyler stuck to his assertion. "I mean it. Flynne is not above manipulating the truth and the rules to her advantage, but when she says she won't, she won't."

"I wasn't aware that you were that much in love with her."

The words hung there, as if a bomb waiting to be activated. Through each miserable second, Tyler grappled with the idea of being truly in love with Flynne. Sure, he cared about her. He wouldn't have been tormented for the last few hours if he wasn't, but in *love*? Maybe a bit premature. *Then again, do you ever feel like you love the person you love... enough*? He didn't know.

"Am I?"

"It sounds like it to me."

A new thought changed Tyler's perspective a little. "Even if I'd say the same thing about Keith? Or even

Erika?"

"Are you saying you're not in love with your girlfriend?"

That he couldn't say either. "I don't know. I just—well, we never talked about it. I don't see her enough to know. I think that's the thing."

"So, I'm curious about something."

Why are you so chatty?

"If you and Flynne broke up, how much would you trust her to have your back then?"

"Why shouldn't I? That's just weir—oh." His gut clenched as understanding gripped it and twisted a knot. "Morgan."

"If it makes it any easier, it sounds like it happened in the course of trying to divert him from realizing Erika was there."

The knot twisted tighter. "It doesn't." He'd have hung up if he didn't have a message for Mark. "Got a call from Corey."

"And?"

"They found the niece—traffickers, they think. At a rest stop, she managed to sneak out of the van they had her in and climb into a trucker's cab. He called the police."

The dead line told him that something was up. He just didn't know what. *Other than the fact that my girlfriend apparently... isn't.*

0000 01 000 0000 1 01 110   010 111 110 001 0

"St. Louis commuters are shaken after a bizarre accident today. A car plunged off the Eads Bridge and into the Mississippi. Witnesses say that another car rammed the vehicle multiple times before it hit another car and flipped through and over a section of the safety railing. Police have the man they believe to be responsible in custody after two other drivers blocked his car and held him until police could arrive..."

A hand stirred a small dollop of honey into a sturdy mug in slow, lazy circles. *Clink, clink.* As the newscast droned on, a phone rang. "G'day. What do you have for me?"

"He's in custody. Being questioned. Not talking yet."

"Let's keep it that way." The teaspoon tapped again. *Clink, clink.* "Did the girl make it home?"

"She's still giving a statement, but the mother is there with her."

"Excellent."

The grotesque sounds of a throat clearing preceded the next question. "Do I let him know she's home?"

"Not necessary. Mendina will ensure that." Another stir. Another clink. A sip. "You're good for now. Pull everything back. I have a call to make."

Starting a call relayed through multiple servers and locations around the globe—a nuisance but necessary. Time consuming, too. Between sips of hot, black, honeyed tea, the teaspoon made its synchronized clinks. *Clink, clink.* Sip. *Clink, clink.*

Five minutes passed. *Clink, clink.* Sip. *Clink, clink.*

Ten.

The phone rang at almost fifteen minutes on the dot. "Hello, Secretary Jehnson."

"Who is this? How'd you get this number?"

"Are all your bad guys present and accounted for?"

"Wha—?"

"Better check on that."

266

Click.

A smile formed. The spoon swirled. A sip. *Clink, clink.*

0000 01 000 0000 1 01 110   010 111 110 001 0

Corey answered with the first ring. "What's going on, Mark? We got a call that Brent's been arrested!"

"He has. He ran Erika Polowski and Flynne off the Eads Bridge."

After a gasp that almost hurt to hear, she protested. "He *wouldn't!* Brent is *the* most mild-mannered man. He catches mice and takes them out to the country and lets them go. It drives Marci nuts!"

Everything Mark had found said the same thing. "Look, if Erika and Flynne hadn't seen him in St. Louis— obviously following them. If we didn't have him on CCTV stalking her, I'd be agreeing with you. I'd assume that people stopped the wrong car somehow, but they didn't. So, what do I need to know about your brother before I go in and talk to him?"

"His family is everything to him. None of this makes sense, but in case he knows Alyssa was missing, tell him she's back first thing. It might help... somehow." She huffed in that way she always had when needing to steady herself. "I told them he didn't take her."

"He couldn't have. We knew that. I'll do what I can to get him out. Erika and Flynne won't press charges if I can find out what he was doing. There'll still be criminal charges, but they'll be easier to get dropped if the girls refuse to cooperate. It's safe for Marci and the kids to go home now, though. I've got surveillance on their house— just someone in training, but I think that's all you need

267

right now."

"I'm on my way to St. Louis now."

"Don't go into the station without calling me, first. I want to use you if the situation warrants it, but it'll be more effective if you appear unexpectedly."

"Okay." The huff sounded wavery this time. "Mark, he didn't do this. I mean, maybe he did, but *he* didn't. You know?"

It was the first thing she'd said that did make sense to him. "Just get here, Corey. Somehow, this is going to be all right. I just don't know how yet." Once she disconnected, he added in a sigh, "And I don't promise you'll like how, either."

An officer led him to an interrogation room, giving him sideways glances all the way there. Inside, Brent sat with his hands cuffed to the table, staring at the opposite wall almost unblinking. "Just knock if you need out. I'm going to lock the door."

Mark nodded. As the door closed, he pulled up a chair to the end of the table and sat there in an attempt to avoid the feel of an interrogation. "Are you all right, Brent?"

The man didn't move.

"You should know that this room is being visually and audibly recorded."

That got him a blink and a slight shift but no real response.

"You should also know that I am not with any state or government agency."

The man's hands clenched. His jaw twitched. He looked over at Mark.

"My name is Marco Mendina, and while I'm not a lawyer, I'm your best shot out of here. Do you understand that?"

This time, not a twitch.

A glance around the room did little to help Mark. It was all standard fare. Plain walls, table with restraint bars, three chairs, and two tiny cameras peering down, watching. Always watching. *They don't even need the mirrored windows anymore.*

Mark started with the best chance at cooperation. "Marci and the kids are worried about you." The way the man stiffened gave away much. "Did you hear about Alyssa's disappearance?"

Tears rolled down his cheeks.

"I know you didn't have anything to do with that."

The movement was so slight, Mark didn't know if he'd really seen it, but the man looked like he shook his head. Barely.

"She's home now—safe."

Brent sat up straight. "Safe?"

It might have been the wrong move, but Mark couldn't help but smile. "Safe. Untouched. She got away."

The man sobbed. Before Mark could even request tissues, his phone rang. Suresh. "Yes?"

"The man who gave Liv Todd the information about her sister? I found him."

"Who was it?"

"His name is Brent Knupp of Dolman."

Things clicked into place. "Thank you. Payment will be sent tonight." Without waiting for a response, Mark clicked the phone off and sent a text message. Then he turned to Brent. "Liv Todd is safe, too."

That stopped the tears. "What?"

"I can get you out of here. It won't be easy, but I can. Your daughter is safe, your targets are all alive. But you have to tell me who you're working for."

All visible signs of discouragement or distress vanished, and a hard look that Mark suspected no one knew he could manufacture appeared. "Marco Mendina?"

"Yes."

"Do your employees call you Mark?"

He smiled. "Yes, Brent. They do."

Silence reigned again. The jaw worked, his eyes flitted from Mark to the cameras to the cuffs on his hands, and back to Mark again. At least ten minutes passed before he spoke. "My family needs protection. No matter *what* you do with me, they are not safe."

"I have a guard—"

"*They are not safe!*" The voice reverberated against the walls until the whole room screamed them.

"Indefinite or temporary?"

Brent's jaw worked again. "Long-term. At least until you get the creep."

Creep implies man. That validates a lot of presumptions. Good... Good...

"Can you do it now?" Brent leaned forward, hands clasped together. "Even if you don't help me. Get them out." His eyes narrowed. "Tell Corey—"

"We'll talk to Corey later. Right now, we need to talk about who you're working for."

The man's jaw clamped shut so fast it should have broken teeth. He leaned back as far as possible in the chair and stared at the wall again. Silence.

"Mr. Knupp, we're going to help your family."

Still, nothing.

"Is this about where *you* are, or where your *family* is?"

For a moment, Mark thought he still wouldn't answer, but the half-whispered word came eventually. "Both."

That's all it took. Without even turning away, Mark

called Claire. "Hey, love, time to move. Get the Knupp family to the Harbinger apartment ASAP. Destroy your phone now."

Ignoring Brent's bug eyes, he made the next call. It rang... and rang... The third try got an answer. "Mark, I don't have time—"

"I need Brent Knupp released to me. St. Louis police. ASAP."

"We're kind of in the middle of a huge mess over here. I don't know if I can—"

There wasn't time to play the "whose Daddy is tougher" game. "Don't make me go to the press."

"Don't make *me* go to the press. Do you have any idea who is missing from federal custody?"

"Do I care?"

"You should. Now what's up in St. Louis?"

A smile formed. *You can bark, but you've got no teeth.* "Check the news. Brent Knupp was just arrested for forcing Erika Polowski and Flynne Dortmann—"

"*Your Flynne?* And... Polowski... Hang on."

Two minutes dragged out longer than half-time at a football game. Jehnson's voice sounded strained when he returned. "I'll make the call. Give me twenty."

TWENTY-SEVEN

Sunshine streaked through the vertical slats of the window blinds, teasing her with the day outside. Every bit of her ached, from the hangnail on her toe to the rogue eyebrow hair that always grew away from the rest, as if it considered itself too important to associate with common hairs. Her head, however, pounded like nobody's business.

Keith still slept in the chair beside her bed. His hand dangled over the arm, just a couple of inches away from her mattress, as if he'd fallen asleep touching her. *Probably because he did.*

An aide entered, carrying a tray with two meals on it. She smiled and gestured at the bed tray. Erika could have cried when she realized the woman wanted her to move—to remove Keith's phone and make room for the tray. Wincing, she grabbed it and allowed it to drop to her lap. That hurt, too. Her eyes closed in pain-filled defeat.

By the time Erika managed to convince herself to open her eyes again, Keith was awake—watching. "Did you sleep?"

She nodded. "I know you did."

"Might be a dumb idea, but I thought it was a risk worth taking."

He's getting pretty good at talking with his mouth wired shut.

"I overheard one of the nurses say that they're

probably discharging you this afternoon—no pneumothorax for you."

Erika eyed him, uncertain if *he* was ready to leave yet—if it was safe for him. "And you?"

He checked the canister at his side and grinned. "About where it was last night. I think I'm drained. Can't take a good breath, still, but that might be the whole broken · lung thing."

Erika didn't believe him until he threatened to show her the nasty cannister. "Okay, show me."

And he did. She couldn't be sure it hadn't increased any. She hadn't paid *that* close of attention to it, but either he'd become a better actor in the past few days, or he wasn't lying. "Good."

They ate in silence. Oatmeal, scrambled eggs, bacon. Orange juice for her. Milk for him. The white, dry toast lay there getting colder and more disgusting with every passing minute. Eventually, a woman twice the age and size of the last one came in to take it away. "Have you decided what you want for lunch? I recommend the roast beef with *au jus*."

They just nodded.

"For two, right?"

Another nod.

"Mashies and raw veggies?"

Keith didn't move, but Erika nodded.

"He's not a veggie guy?" The woman winked. "I'll add an orange on there."

They stared at each other until Keith finally spoke. "Do you feel like half your age all of a sudden?"

To Erika's utter disgust, she giggled. "Yep."

He rose, shifted that infernal cannister onto the floor, and leaned over her, searching for something. If the smile

274

that formed meant anything, he'd found it. "Hey…"

Those eyes staring into hers… if she hadn't been in love with him already, that look right there would have done it. "Hey, yourself."

"I could have lost you."

"God said no to an early entry to eternity."

His fingers brushed back her hair, and his hand cupped the back of her head. With his gaze locked on hers, the whispered words washed over her. "Thank You, Lord for saving Erika… again, and now we ask for healing."

"For him, too," Erika added.

A wink. "Okay, for me, too. Can't take care of her if I'm a mess anyway."

The kiss should have made him gag—what with the vomiting, the Mississippi river water, the no brushing of the teeth… Instead, he lingered as if she'd gargled in Listerine and washed it down with mint water. For half a second or two, he even made her forget that she should be mortified.

"I love you."

The words proved to be too much. Tears formed. "Endorphins."

Keith grinned. "Fine, I endorphin you. I'm dopey on dopamine. Seronading you with serotonin. Your moxie gives me oxy… and an incurable desire to hold you indefinitely…"

"I think you nailed it with the dopey one."

Once more, he brushed his hand over her cheek. "I'm good with that." He swallowed—twice, his eyes never blinking. "I could have lost you," he repeated.

And once more, she disagreed. "Nope. Sorry, it wasn't possible."

With his cheek pressed to her forehead, he murmured,

"Care to elaborate?"

"It's basic theology. God numbers our days. I'm alive. That means my number wasn't up. Therefore, I could not have died. Basic theology."

"Your dad's going to love that one."

It was time to give in before she chickened out. A compliment sandwich might not work, but what about a love sandwich? Erika decided it couldn't hurt to try. "That my father even cares about theology still baffles me. And I love you, too. Oh, and did I tell you that he actually said he loves Jesus? He's found theological proof of his love, regardless of his emotionless state."

Keith stood up and shoved his hands in his pockets, considering. "Agape?"

"Yep! Good one."

She'd just allowed herself to think she'd gotten away with it when Keith sat on the lengthened chair bed and winked at her. "Don't think I didn't catch that four-letter word you threw at me."

The morning nurse came in before Erika had a chance to manufacture a retort. *Thank goodness.*

Blood pressure, new IV bag, and an order to take a shower—one right after the other. "If you need help, you can call him or—"

"I'll call you."

Keith snickered. He turned his attention to the nurse and said with a complete deadpan expression, "Apparently my help isn't good enough for her."

"Or the fact that you're injured? I mean—"

Before it could go any farther, Erika broke in. "Or, it could be that we're not married, and there's no way he's seeing me naked for the first time when I'm all black and blueeeoooohno. I did not just say that out loud."

"You did."

From behind her, came Keith's response. "Said what?"

"Keep this one."

"That's what everyone keeps telling me." Erika couldn't help the snarky edge that crept into her tone. "It makes me want to dump him and find me a nice toxic narcissist."

Keith growled at that one. Without even looking the nurse's way he snapped, "Seriously, if you mess this up for me, I'm suing you for breach of possibility."

That earned him a laugh and the order to wait there. "I'll remove your canister and add a bag to your tube — easier to carry around. Maybe this time you'll leave it in?"

Despite the pain that sitting up, standing up, walking, and undressing caused, when the lukewarm water hit her, all tension released, and with it, emotions she didn't know she held back. One hand gripped the IV trolley just outside the shower enclosure. The other clung to a rail on the wall. Feeling like Samson between pillars, she held on and sobbed out every fear, every hurt, everything she couldn't name. By the time she'd sobbed out all the tears she felt sure she had left, Erika didn't have the strength to turn off the water. Instead, she plopped down on the shower bench and sobbed more.

The nurse, whose name Erika hadn't bothered to ask or look for, arrived almost the moment she pulled the aid cord and began the mortifying task of washing hair, rinsing her, and drying her off. Mesh, post-surgical underwear might not be as effective as her preferred Jockey brand, but they were a sight better than the filthy ones she'd been relieved of when she arrived and definitely better than none. The hospital gown had been washed enough to be soft as butter, and Erika almost didn't resent its less than fashionable and modest qualities.

Almost.

Though Erika leaned heavily on the nurse's arm and the IV trolley, the moment she stepped out of the bathroom door, she found herself wrapped in a hug so gentle she almost didn't believe it. "Ke—ark!"

Mark winked. "A guy with broken ribs shouldn't be lifting. And you shouldn't be walking. Bed or chair?"

The nurse answered for her. "Bed. She'll crash soon. She's wiped out."

"Looks like bed." He almost made lifting her seem like nothing. Only a bit of tightening around the lips and a bulging vein in his temple gave away the exertion.

The process of lifting her and then laying her down again prompted a few unwelcome whimpers and air sucked through clenched teeth. "I officially regret making Flynne tie me up."

Both men stared without saying a word. The nurse blinked, pulled up the blanket, and shot a look at Keith. "Sorry... I thought you were the boyfriend. Brother?"

"Boyfriend," he corrected. "Long story. Flynne was researching how someone would kidnap someone, and Erika made her use duct tape for authenticity."

"And that means you weren't buckled. It's a wonder you're not dead, girl. Tell your writer friend to research existing cases next time." And with that, the woman strode from the room.

"Sorry. It came out before I thought. Good with the story there..."

Mark shushed her. "We're prepared." He reached down and fumbled through a gift bag. "No... that's Flynne's replacement Burberry backpack. I figured it was the least I could do." He picked up the other bag. "So, I went shopping for something that would be easy to get into to wear home. The woman who helped me recommended that."

Erika dragged a dress from the bag—longish, flowing… a wrap dress, no less. "Thanks. It's beautiful."

"She said you wouldn't have to lift your arms or bend over. She also added other things you might need… including flip-flops." He lifted the other bag. "I'd better get this to Flynne. Morgan's with her now."

He'd reached the door before a memory hit her. "Hey, Mark?"

"Yes? Need something?"

A shudder ran through her, in spite of herself. "When Flynne was trying to kick out the window, I heard her say something about how she'd better get Burberry *stock* this time."

Staying awake was harder than trying to get a toddler to go to sleep. Even awake, Flynne found the effort of keeping her eyes open nearly impossible. Morgan never moved—didn't seem to care that she hardly spoke to him. He just sat there, and when she even hinted at trying to be awake, he talked.

Tired of the noisy silence of a room full of hushed machines, she stirred. The sounds of silence didn't change. Flynne propped open one eye and saw Mark sitting where Morgan should be. She couldn't help herself. "Just sayin'. I was right."

The words came out in a rasped whisper. She'd

forgotten that part. Not being able to talk with the ventilator tube had been bad enough. The angry throat, on the other hand—twice as bad… almost.

Mark handed her his phone. It took her a moment to see what it said, but then it clicked. "A hundred shares? Really? Coolio."

He held up a giant gift bag. "Clothes for when they let you out of here, and a replacement backpack."

"I think a lot of money is at the bottom of the Mississippi."

A hand closed over hers—she felt rather than saw it. That's when Flynne realized she'd closed her eyes again. "You're safe. Erika's safe. That's all that matters."

It was stupid to ask, but she had to. "Are shares, like, my severance pay, or am I, like, not fired yet."

"Not fired, Flynne. Not even close."

"I'm almost jellie of myself. Have totally, like, the coolest boss man ever."

The twinge of guilt she felt at knowing how expensive a hundred shares of any stock had to be vanished at his chuckle. "So, does that mean you still puffy heart working for The Agency?"

"It's eptastic." She sighed. "And the guilt is back."

"For what?"

Both eyes opened this time. "That's a lot of shares— and Burberry. I probably lost more money—"

"Stocks are twenty-three bucks a share right now. They'll go up again. It was an inexpensive but good investment."

"Our deffies of inexpensive are, like, polars."

She felt rather than saw his look. "Was what you just said intelligible to you?"

"Yeppers."

280

"Good. You're getting better. While we're on the topic of money, though, I have to ask…"

Flynne remembered something just then — remembered and flinched. "You found Uncle Greg's Cayman account."

"Uncle Greg?"

Though she suspected shame had more to do with it, Flynne allowed herself to believe exhaustion kept her eyes closed. "Check my tax file dates. That day or the next, Uncle Greg deposits money into my regular account."

Speaking took so much effort. It hurt. Flynne hoped that was enough to help Mark figure out all she hadn't said yet.

A moment later, he cleared his throat. "And if we redo each form without the interest income from the Cayman account, it'll equal that deposit, I assume."

"Yeppers."

"Why open the Cayman account at all?"

The answer wouldn't make Uncle Greg look good, but she wasn't lying to Mark — wasn't hiding anything from him. Never again. "New wife," she rasped out. "He's, like, sursies she's going to, like go all divorcies on him and take everything… like Aunt Zell tried to do."

"You have to admit, Flynne. The date you —"

"Uncle Greg."

Mark corrected himself as if she hadn't just barked at him. "Right. It does look odd when he just happened to open that account on the date you started working for The Agency."

Her eyes flew open again. "He did?" A nod prompted a sigh. "Coinkidinky, as far as I know. He didn't, like, tell me until the end of the year."

"Good. I figured there was an explanation, but I had

to ask."

"For sursies.

Things grew quiet for so long that Flynne suspected, irrationally so, she'd fallen asleep. But when she said, "Mark?" and he answered, asking if he could get something for her, she relaxed again. "I'm good. You're here."

"So… you don't want me to call Tyler in?"

That one stung, and she deserved it. But before she could find some way to explain, Mark kept talking.

"He knows, Flynne. I had to tell him."

"Thank you." She'd said it on robo-mode, but the moment she did, Flynne meant it. "I hadn't thought about, like, what to say, you know?" This time, she beat him to the speaking punch. "Is he, like, mad?"

Silence answered her question most eloquently. Flynne wanted to protest. They hadn't had enough time to be *that* close. That thought prompted another. "Wow…"

"What?"

"I don't feel any different about Tyler. I thought I was, you know, like, totally into him. But now I'm all confuzzled." By that point, words had become too painful to even consider, but she forced herself to ask the next question. "Why'd you tell him?"

Mark squeezed her hand again. "I needed to know if he'd trust you if you sent him on a strange mission."

This time, Flynne forced herself to meet his gaze. She left the silent question between them. Mark gave her a weak smile before nodding. "He said if you promised not to go rogue again, he'd believe you. He's hurt, though."

"Okay."

The last thing Flynne expected to hear Mark say was, "Don't feel guilty for discovering that he isn't the guy for you. Better now than after two kids to fight over and a dog neither of you want."

"I didn't mean... I'm not sorry, but—I am." She felt the tear slip down her cheek before she realized it had even formed. "That's just all kinds of messed up."

Again, the squeezing of her hand. "Sleep, Flynne. We'll fix it all later. Right now, just rest."

"You staying?"

Mark's chuckle—almost just like being at the office. "I won't leave until you tell me to go."

"Awesome sauce."

TWENTY-EIGHT

Mark paced the front of the hospital while Tyler rerouted a call from Doyle. The man began speaking without preamble the moment the call connected. "Sam's on her way to the office—quitting. I recommend you move operations."

"Sam's quitting?"

"We just missed an ambush funeral. I saw we were being followed, took us off on a dirt trail, we hid in a cave, and enjoyed front row seats to seeing the RV turned into a watering can."

"And that unnerved Sam?"

A cleared voice, a few seconds, and Doyle finally huffed—the most emotion Mark ever heard from the guy. "Mark. We aren't on detail. We were just on our way back from the thing with Schmatloch. If someone tried to take us out way out here, with everything else going on, we have to assume—"

"Right. Of course. Right." The fact that it was probably a drug-related hit that had nothing to do with The Agency meant nothing. Too much had happened to act on that assumption. "So, Sam's lost confidence in our intel?"

"Yes."

"Have you?"

Only the slightest hesitation hinted at the answer before Doyle said, "Yes. But I have confidence that you'll get us back on track. Flynne's safe?"

"And going to make it. She's also promised never to do that again."

"Sounds like she made a good call."

Ouch. Rub it in. If I'd listened, she wouldn't be fighting infections.

Doyle spoke again. "Mark, is Keith back?"

He hadn't asked it yet, but he knew if he told Keith what was up... if he asked... "He will be, yes."

A thought that had been percolating for a few days finally bubbled over. "How do you feel about training a new girl—more in surveillance and self-defense?"

Sirens that had been approaching now grew close enough to make it impossible to hear. Mark waited, still pacing, but around the corner and away from a man puffing away on a cigarette that wouldn't last a minute at that rate. The sirens cut out a moment later.

"The Todd girl?"

Someday, when I'm done, I think I want you to take over. Your instincts for the business side are killer. Aloud, Mark just said, "Yes."

"Tell her I'm coming. Where do I go?"

"Oregon."

"Got it." Silence hovered again before Doyle said, "You're doing a good thing here. Someone doesn't like that. But that shouldn't be a surprise to any of us." With that, he disconnected.

A glance up at the windows above him squeezed his heart, but Mark turned toward the street and called for his car. Once it arrived, he put up the partition and called the secure line of the Oregon house. "Let me talk to Liv."

She came on much more perky than a girl hiding out should be. "Did you find him? The guy who gave me the information?"

"I did. We know who to go after to protect you and your parents. You can go home, and you'll have answers later. Or, you can accept a job."

"A job?"

The explanation began. Liv listened to everything, from how her parents would be protected until they caught the person behind everything, to what she'd be trained to do—and almost without a word from her. When he asked, "What do you want?" however, she finally spoke.

"I want to know why you pretended to be a guy who they say is dead now."

That stopped him. "Pardon me?"

"You pretended to be Dan French."

"My name's—"

"Marco Mendina," she interjected. "Yeah, I know. But you arrange your words and inflections just like Dan French. He just didn't have the hint of a Spanish lilt on a few things, so I missed it at first."

Should I be terrified or glad my infusion of an accent is working? Mark cleared his throat and tried again. "Um…"

"Look, you can deny it, but I know it's true. If I'm going to work for you, I need to know—"

"I can't tell you unless you decide to work for me. But I would like to know how you picked up on those similarities."

Once more, she explained how she'd always recognized, and often accidentally imitated speech patterns. "People have a distinct way of speaking, even when they're trying to hide how they speak. It's just something I've always noticed."

He wanted her on his team now more than ever. *And with Sam gone…* "Well, you just solidified my decision to convince you to join us."

"Is it illegal?"

"We are an independent company, but all government agencies allow us to operate, even knowing we may step outside the law to protect someone."

A giggle followed. Of all the things she might have said or done, giggling made the least sense—at that moment, anyway. "That's probably true of anything. A baby is trapped in a hot car. Breaking the window is illegal, but you do it and no one cares."

"Excellent analogy."

"Will I be able to afford to quit my college classes?"

That's an interesting way of phrasing that. "If you want to keep them up, you can afford the time and money to do it. If you'd rather postpone—"

"I'm in. And I quit." A slight hesitation hinted her next request would amuse him. "Is there any chance you can get me a late withdrawal without it affecting my transcript?"

What have I gotten myself into? Still, Mark couldn't help but appreciate the girl's moxie. "I loved your sister's spunk, Liv. You've got it, too."

"Yeah, and I've got three inches on her."

"What does that make you, five-one?"

Her laughter made it sound like a challenge. "Maaaybeee…"

"Doyle's coming for you. Don't make his job easy."

"I would never!"

0000 01 000 0000 1 01 110   010 111 110 001 0

A new, handcrafted Newton's cradle sat in the place of Flynne's old one. The rosewood base and frame contrasted beautifully with the rose-gold spheres. Tyler swung the right one aside and watched the gentle, rhythmic swinging begin. *She'll love it.*

It would be a peace offering—an apology for ruining her stuff and a way to say he understood. "No hard feelings," he whispered.

If it were only true.

The phone rang—Mark's private line. Tyler snatched up the phone, and before Mark could say anything, he blurted out his rehearsed speech. "Flynne risked her job and her life to protect Erika. That proves that she'd go all out to protect any of us. Even me. I trust her."

"Good."

"So, what'd you call for?"

"We need to make plans."

Tyler pulled a notepad to him. "Okay, well I have been in contact with a lot of people—a *lot*, Mark. First, Schmatloch loves it in Niagara. He's talking about moving up there when this is all over."

"Get movers to his house, get paperwork to transfer the title to me, and have him go find a place to live there. It's done."

"Is it necessary? If we've got—" Mark just ordered it done, so Tyler moved to the next, trying to stifle his huff and a "never mind," but not quite succeeding. "I've got an update on the Kim-Park family. They're well, and Shin is actually liking his job as a teacher. Mrs. Kim-Park can't get over it. She is, however, annoyed at being on a Tarjay budget."

Mark's hesitation hinted at what would come next. However, that "next" arrived with a bonus. "Okay, my instinct is to send her a gift card to one of her favorite stores. Find out what that is and send it if you think it would be a help. Don't if you think it would increase long-term discontent. She's got to adapt, but this is pretty cold turkey for someone used to the finest of the finest."

"Someone who thinks she is, anyway." When Mark asked for clarity, Tyler hoped he hadn't overstepped. "It's just that she acts like her Coach and Spade are Prada—that her Banana Republic is Louis Vuitton."

"Good point. Tread carefully. If you send it, keep it reasonable and do it near a birthday or other special day. It's been close enough to extraction that we can let them think it's because they're just starting over. Maybe give it to Shin to give to her."

"Sure thing."

A call came before Mark could send out the next order. "Hey, Mark. It's Suresh. Hang on."

A minute later, Tyler stared at the phone, almost speechless. "Um…"

"He already told me about Knupp."

"He quit. Demanded his money and he's out. I'd guess he's moving to some place where money goes a long way."

Tyler knew this silence—this one that Mark did when all new plans got set in motion. Tyler just waited. The cradle balls bounced their *plink, clink, plink, clinks* while Tyler's eyes bounced back and forth with each *plink*.

A sigh, one Tyler suspected Mark didn't know he made, preceded a string of tasks. "Okay, get Paris and Henry to the Harbinger place—just until I talk to Knupp again."

"Gonna get him out?"

A moment passed… two. "That's where I'm headed. We need to do this now. Okay, so we've got Kim covered, Schmatlock is good, we've lost Sam—"

"What? What happened to Sam?"

"She's on her way there to quit. Do the exit protocol and deposit three months' salary into her account."

Tyler's throat went dry enough to make him croak as he asked, "Doyle?"

"Covering Todd. She's joining us."

"Does she know we're responsible for Lucy's death?" The moment he asked, Tyler regretted it. "Sorry."

"No. She doesn't. I'll talk to her once everything settles. We need to debrief Knupp before we decide if we offer the Todds a new life. Meanwhile, get Flynne's laptop to her."

"Courier?"

Mark's tone took on an apologetic but firm quality. "No, Tyler. You."

Insert expletive here—all the ones Keith would never say. Insert them here. "Yessir."

"Soon." Mark shifted as if he hadn't just thrown a sucker punch. "Okay, who's left?"

"Just Brent and maybe Sam."

A slow exhale followed. "That's what I'm hoping to get from you. Watch her. Ask questions about the thing— all of it. Then get to St. Louis." Only then did Mark add, "And sorry about this, Tyler, but let's rip off that Band-Aid now."

The aide hadn't steered them wrong. The French dip sandwich was better than you'd find at most restaurants, and the bun wasn't too thick. "I'm used to hospital food having no seasoning, but this…"

"I think someone knows how to pull flavor from and

into beef without it." Erika took another bite. "You'll fight for me, right?"

"Always."

She grinned at all he didn't say and flicked her straw wrapper at what he did. "You know what I mean. I'm going to see Flynne one way or another. I owe her."

"She nearly got you killed."

"Don't. Even. Start. With. Me." When he only quirked an eyebrow at her, Erika glared. "I mean it."

"So do I. But yes, I'll fight for you to get to see the unintentional attempted murderer." Adding a smile and a wink to that failed.

"For your information, I could be *dead* without her. Mark ignored the signs. Even I thought she was nuts, but who was right? Huh? Who was right?"

That, he couldn't argue. Somewhere deep inside, a thought poked and festered. How *had* Flynne seen what no one else did, unless…?

The curtain rattled and Mark's head peered around it. *Thought you weren't coming back for a while.*

Erika beckoned. "Come grab a bite of the other end of this. It's amazing."

"I've always considered hospital food and amazing to be incompatible words." But when Mark took a bite, his eyes widened. "Can I get one in the cafeteria?"

He heard the unspoken request for privacy. "Probably." Keith rose. "I'll be right back."

Mark glanced at the empty plate. "I suppose you want another?"

He kissed Erika's cheek and once assured she'd be fine alone, led Mark from the room. "We can eat outside."

They made it halfway through their sandwiches before Mark turned casual conversation on its head. "I need you back. Probably six months at least. I also need a replacement for Suresh."

Keith's gut twisted. "I have to be honest. This kills personal plans."

"You know I wouldn't ask…"

And he wouldn't. Keith knew that more than Mark probably did. "I have to talk to Erika about it. Sorry, but—"

"Do it. If she has any concerns, we can put her up somewhere secure for the next few months just to be sure."

He didn't want to ask, but there wasn't any way to avoid it. "What's with Suresh?"

"He quit today—said he's out. We need two people. When Ellison died, I didn't make it a priority, and now look where we are."

"Suresh is the best…"

"I've heard of an Armenian out of Fresno who we might need to talk to. I might need you to vet him."

Keith had no idea how to do that. "So, what…? I can't just ask for references."

"Have him check out Sam and find out if there's more to her leaving than just a lack of confidence."

A call came through—Tyler, if the gentleness in Mark's tone meant anything. Keith listened to half and frowned at the way Mark eyed the windows above them for a moment. "I'll go talk to her. I need this covered before you get here."

Tyler's coming? Uh, oh.

Disconnected, Mark turned. "Do you know about Detweiler?"

Keith nodded. "The one taunting Schmatloch?"

"Except she wasn't. It was all a sham. Flynne verified the trail for me, but it was a sham."

"Easy to do if you know what you're doing."

Mark gazed out over the street as if it had the answer to life's problems. "Yeah... well... there's just one problem."

"Hmm?"

"The car she used to go to St. Louis? It was Mona Detweiler's. Flynne's been house sitting for her for six months."

Lord? What's going on in The Agency?

Keith jerked a thumb at the doors. "Going in?"

"I have to now."

"Let's find out what else Flynne isn't telling us. I'll get Morgan out—drive him home so he can shower and eat."

They'd made it halfway up the elevator before Mark asked, "Scale of one to ten—give me your trust score for Flynne."

"Before that call? Nine and a half."

Mark nodded. "Me, too. And now?"

"Neutral—five. I don't know."

TWENTY-NINE

While Mark waited for Keith to lead Morgan from the room, a tougher feat than even he'd imagined, he reviewed every conversation they'd had about Mona Detweiler. He'd brought the case to Flynne for verification of facts. She'd done the research and verification, but he'd done the initial interview. He'd informed *her* of who Mona was. He'd *ordered* her to research.

But she didn't say she knew Mona. Not once.

Once Keith managed to get Morgan out of the building, Mark had to step out of the room to wait for a sponge bath, the changing of the linens, and all the vitals. All that did was make him even more unsettled. The fact that she looked done in by the time he returned to the room nearly made him rethink the visit, but he needed to know. He needed to *see* her reaction.

Her voice still raspy and painful-sounding, Flynne watched him as he pulled up a chair. "Is this when I get totes reamed for going all rogueified?"

"No." He pulled out his phone and zipped Tyler a message. CHECK FLYNNE'S RESEARCH ON DETWEILER. NEED ANY ANOMALIES.

A simple OK came a moment later.

"What's wrong, Mark? I know that expression. You're, like, so ticked."

"You need to know that Tyler is on his way with your

secure laptop." A choice word, "Flynne-ified," followed. *Do you have any idea that with your teen-speak, your cursing sounds like a cupcake flavor?*

"I knew I'd have to see him but not this soon. Can Morgan or Keith accept it and—?"

"No. I need this awkward moment over. I need you guys to get to work. We are about to put a stop to all this mess, and I need everyone in the game."

"What's going on?" At his questioning look, she scowled. "I know you. You, like, only use sports analogies when you're supes ticked."

"Right now, only confused. But..."

She closed her eyes. "What'd I do?"

The game began. Mark didn't say a word until she finally opened her eyes again and gazed at him. "Talk to me about Mona Detweiler."

Eyes closed again. "I was going to tell you."

"I'd rather know why you didn't."

The blood pressure cuff went off, and she winced. "These things are, like, for realz the worst things ever."

Mark didn't respond.

"When I saw her name, I had to know—for myself. I mean, I work for these people! So, I checked it out. They were totes guiltified—actually, I think just she is. With that new password, I doubt her husband ever logs on."

"Why's that?"

"It's, like, her boss's name. I think that's what this Bavaria trip is about—part of it, anyway. They took the kids for the first week and then sent them home. I think she's trying to save her marriage."

And...

A sigh followed. "You'd be proud of me. I totes didn't let on to Erika that I had ever been on that computer before."

"Why didn't you tell me? And why did you say you'd verified their activity if you knew it was fake."

Her expression—was it shock that he'd found out, or shock at what he'd said? Confusion followed. After a couple of sips of water, she tried again and sounded less raspy. "What's fake? It's all on the computer. I could totally take you there and show you."

"It's fake, Flynne. Otto got a threatening call when CCTV shows her only taking a picture of her breakfast and then chatting with her companion. She did nothing else, and that picture showed up just when it should have."

This time, he knew the expression meant shock. "How?"

He waited. Her eyes closed. They sat there in total silence. Mark felt better with each passing second. If she'd planned it, she'd have a "solution" or "explanation" by now. It's what Flynne did. That she didn't have one likely meant she believed what she said. *Or she's a better actress than you give her credit for.*

"It should be so obvi, Mark, but I don't know. I printed everything out. You saw it. That was on her actual, physical hard drive. I took it from *there*. I didn't connect remotely, and I know I should have told you that, but I can tell you how to get in and how to see it for yourself."

He passed his phone. "Call Tyler. Tell him how."

She stared at it for a moment and sighed as she accepted it. "I so deserve that."

Just as she swiped the screen, her face clouded. "Corey Knupp sent a text. She's at the station."

"Tell her to wait until I get there." He deliberated a moment before adding, "And tell her we're moving him."

Thumbs flew with speeds that Mark could only envy.

297

A moment later, she tapped the screen, tapped it again, and the ringing of a phone filled the space between them. "Hey, Mark? I—"

"It's Flynne. Mark's here. You're on speaker."

"Okaaay..."

She took another couple of sips of water before choking out, "Look, I heard you're coming. Can we talk then? Mark has a job for you, and I need to tell you how to get in."

"To where?"

"Mona Detweiler's." Flynne gave a wince as Tyler slammed a drawer. "Ready for instructions?"

"Let 'er rip."

Let's call this an assumed win.

Five minutes later, as he accepted his phone back, Mark eyed her. "I know you're still recovering, but I have to say it anyway. If you ever keep information from me like that again, you're fired. Going rogue was bad but understandable. This..."

"I thought you'd say no. I got to be, like, an agent without, like, any danger. It was supes fun. The real agent stuff...? It's awful. How do they stand it?"

You don't even see the danger, do you? Mark tried a Socratic approach. "So, what would you have done if you'd have gotten caught?"

Once more, the eyes closed. "Oh. Hashtag stupid dot com. Supes stupid. Like stupid cubed." She giggled—the nervous giggle of someone about to fall apart. "It's like that song if you say it all Bible-like." She began croaking, "'Stupid cube-ed, you're a real dumb girl!'"

He rose, kissed her forehead, and said he'd go. "Just... talk to me next time, okay? For the record, I would have said yes."

"But I'm just the office—"

He interrupted that one. "And my last office manager/tech person became an agent. I'm not unreasonable."

She smiled. "Thanks for not, like, yelling. My head hurts." If the whimper hadn't echoed at the end of it, Mark might have felt manipulated. Instead, he promised to get the nurse to come check on what they could do for her. "It's about time for her to come bug you and ensure you don't get any sleep anyway. Get well. We need you in Rockland. We have to move base."

Her eyes widened. "Really?"

"Yes. I want your input on stuff, and I can't get that if you're not recuperated." *But only if Tyler clears you.*

At the door, he promised to return before he left town. Flynne gave a little wave and said, "Later gator."

0000 01 000 0000 1 01 110   010 111 110 001 0

When they'd been led to a Bombardier Challenger at the St. Louis Downtown Airport, Keith realized that the debriefing they were about to begin would be bigger than he'd expected. Corey had walked beside her brother with the nonchalance of a former agent in her element. *It's too bad you had to go off like that. We could use you right now.*

Not until after the plane reached cruising altitude did Brent Knupp relax. "My family?"

"An agent has them at a secure location—for now, anyway. We need a more permanent solution, but I need information before I decide what that is."

"Pictures."

Of all the things Keith would have expected to open

the debrief, "Pictures" seemed the least important.

Mark nodded. "Threatening or incriminating?"

"Threatening," Corey snapped.

Brent just nodded. "Subtle, though. Just proof that the guy knew where my family was at all times—that if he wanted to, he could hurt them."

"That's how it began?"

A nod slowly turned into a shaking head. "I thought so—at first. Then I met the guy again."

"Again?"

"He'd come into the coffee shop one day when I was waiting for the girls. Sat at the table next to me. Nodded at Erika and said it must be nice to have a job where the biggest danger was a coffee burn. Where your family didn't have to worry about you not coming home."

Keith shot a look at Corey. *What did you tell your family?*

She shot a silent response back. *Nothing.*

"He knew about Corey's job then, did he?"

Brent shook his head. "I don't—well, I didn't think so. Not then. He just talked about Mark and how Mark sent him on these missions to protect people. Said he liked knowing he helped people, but he'd rather have Mark's job—safe behind a desk and all."

The airy whine of the engines sounded like someone vacuuming in the other room as Mark, Corey, and Keith all stared at Brent. Corey spoke first. "What was the guy's name?"

"Bill Vering."

While Mark urged Brent to continue, Keith pulled out Mark's laptop and signed into the aircraft WIFI. A Facebook search brought up a list of them, but only three anywhere near Rockland. He turned the screen around.

"Any of them?"

Brent shook his head.

After three more attempts, Keith went to Google image and tried every variation of Bill, William, Willard, Wilhelm—all of them. Eventually, the improvised "mug book" turned up a yes. With that, Keith went to work with his limited computer skills. Ten minutes in, he sent the few things he'd found to Tyler and requested what they needed.

Meanwhile, Brent talked. The words came out in full sentences, usually, but often with long pauses between them. Defeat, shame, and fear slashed across each word, leaving their marks behind. "I didn't see him again, but I remembered the guy who loved his job but wanted out—wanted his boss's job with better hours, better pay, less risk. I got that."

There, Keith had to interject. "Just need to point out that we *are* in danger every time we go on an assignment, but Mark's job has so much more long-term, constant stress. The guy clearly never worked for Mark."

Mark nodded. "I've never seen him before."

"Well, the next time I had contact, I didn't realize it was from him. I got back in my car after getting coffee at Java the Hut and found an envelope on my seat. Eight by ten pictures of my wife getting her nails done, washing the dishes, jogging. That one was obviously taken from inside a car. The driver could have swerved—" He shuddered. "They were all like that. A long, metal nail file at the manicurist's, a knife on the counter waiting to be washed…"

Keith's gut twisted. It'd be enough to make any man do anything. "Just your wife?"

A nod. "That time. A couple of weeks later, another

one appeared. Alyssa at cheer practice—flying in the air and in a toppled heap when a pyramid went wrong. She was laughing in both, but the pictures weren't funny. On the school bus... from *inside* the bus. Crossing in a crosswalk. Talking to a man. Someone who seemed sort of familiar, but..."

"Bill Vering?"

Another nod. Brent hung his head in his hands and shuddered. "I knew after he contacted me again. He came right into Java, seated himself at my table, and asked if I remembered him. Just as I started to say yes, I *really* remembered."

Mark stood and went to the micro kitchen at one end of the cabin. A minute later, the scent of coffee filled the plane. Brent just sat there wringing his hands, and Keith wondered if Mark wasn't being just a little cruel. However, when the mug appeared before the man, he wrapped his hands around it as if desperate for the warm comfort.

"This time, he just jerked his head at Erika and said, 'She's a person of interest. All you have to do is sit in your car and watch her. That's all. An hour a day—different times.'"

Corey sighed. "Why didn't you tell me? I could have helped, Brent!"

"I still don't know what you did, Corey! What *job*? We all thought you were in some top-secret government clearance thing, where you'd have to kill us if you told us. So, we never asked."

With that, Brent closed off. He brooded into his mug, staring at the depths as if it held some murky secret that would solve all problems. Keith knew better.

More coffee appeared, and as if some sort of subtle trigger, Brent began talking again. "That's all I did for ages.

And then he appeared and said I had to start calling this old guy from a phone he gave me. The stuff he made me say... the letters he made me mail. They were..."

Only the high, airy, vacuum-like whine of the engines broke the perfect quiet of the cabin. Corey looked ready to explode, but she took her cue from Mark and kept silent. Keith just watched. Everything the guy said fit... and his body language did, too.

"Then, a couple of weeks ago, I got a call. This was from someone else—southern accent, I think. Weird one, though—nothing like I've ever heard before. I think it was affected. Anyway, she said for me to drive up and down Rosewood in Rockland. To follow a certain car. Stay back. Don't be seen. Just follow."

Keith stared at Mark. The man nodded. "Flynne. She was staying at the house of the woman they had Brent pretend to be."

For a moment there, Brent looked ready to retch. "You're—that's—sick. That's just *sick*!"

"So, you did."

"I wasn't going to, but Bill called and said my daughter looked really good in her cheerleader's outfit. That men—" He shook as he tried to take a sip of the still-hot coffee. It splashed everywhere. "Men would pay—"

"You don't have to finish. We get it." Mark said his name several times until Brent looked up. "I would have done the same thing. And I'm glad you listened."

"*They took her anyway! They took my baby girl!* They—I don't know what they did to her!"

Corey stood and wrapped arms around him. "They didn't do anything. She got away."

After clearing his throat, Keith shook his head and eyed the vacant chair. Corey made a silent protest. He scowled. A moment later, she dropped into the chair, obviously confused. Mark nodded before asking, "What did Bill say after that?"

"Told me there'd be a packet for me to drop off—to give to a girl, Liv Todd. He asked me to take a good look at her—tell him what I thought of her. Would men pay well for her? That kind of thing. When I took it to the girl, I tried to warn her off. Told her to watch herself. That was right before I left for St. Louis."

The man looked ready to fall apart. Every word that took him closer to the bridge incident made him more despondent, more jittery, more... everything. Mark must have noticed, too, because he picked up the narrative. "From there, I might be able to guess. Stop me where I'm wrong."

"Yeah, okay."

"You got a call at some point, telling you where to find them and to follow them wherever they went but to stay back. Either that time or another, you were also informed that your daughter had been taken, and the police considered you a prime suspect."

A nod.

"After that, an actual address came through—and a license plate. Then a command to kill or your daughter would be sold."

Another nod.

"You should know that by that point your daughter had already gotten away."

Brent sagged for a moment, obviously relieved, and then tremors started in his hands. He tried to pick up the mug again, sloshed some on the table, and set it back down. Hands rubbed against his legs. He gripped the arms of the chair. Twice, he tried to speak and couldn't.

Mark took pity. "You had no way of knowing that. If she hadn't, and you hadn't—"

"I—" He shook his head as if to clear it. "I was willing to hurt other men's daughters to spare mine. What kind of person—?"

Corey shushed him. "A daddy who loves his girls. That's who."

"She's right, Brent. I can't say it's right, but I don't think there's a father alive who wouldn't understand why."

Keith snickered. "Maybe Erika's." He shot Brent an apologetic look. "Tom Polowski doesn't have emotions. No anger, no fear, no affection—not like most people do. Physical responses to life but not emotional ones. Logic all the way."

As if he didn't hear Keith, Brent stared down Mark. "My family is safe, right? I'll go to prison if I have to. It's only fair. But if they aren't—"

"You're not going to prison, and your family is safe. I've got Flynne working on new identities and backgrounds now. She'll probably want to know what area of the country you'd like."

For a moment, Keith thought Brent would say California. His mouth formed the shape, the "Ca—" released, and then he clamped it shut. Closed his eyes. Glanced over at his sister. Looked back at Mark. "Does it have to be in the states?"

"No... if it's affordable, we'll do it."

"Why?"

The question wasn't unreasonable. In fact, they'd all probably expected it. But right then seemed odd. Mark, however, just sat there. Waiting.

"Seriously. Why are you doing this? I *hurt* your

people."

"Brent," Mark began. "My job is to ensure the bad guys don't win. If you get out safe, if your family is safe and happy, they lose. That's why."

"Spain," Brent said at last. "Marci's always wanted to have a vacation home in Spain. I speak Spanish—could teach English in schools there. She could teach exercise classes. The girls could have a European high school experience before moving into their own lives."

Mark nodded. "Spain it is."

THIRTY

The small airport at Marshfield meant less traffic and a quicker getaway to the Harbinger apartment. A white Yukon sat waiting just off the tarmac, ready for them. Before they exited the plane, Mark pulled three guns from his attaché case and passed one to Keith and one to Corey. "Probably overkill, but better that than dead."

Corey checked hers twice and stuffed it in the back of her waistband. "That'll teach me not to wear a holster. Yikes!"

Keith agreed. Still, he pulled on a sweatshirt with a front pocket and kept one hand in the pocket with the gun—slightly safer.

Mark's went inside his suit jacket pocket.

The cabin phone rang. Mark jerked it up and asked the captain what the trouble was. An unfamiliar voice came through. "I want The Agency."

"What?" It was an idiotic response, but Mark couldn't help it.

"You heard me. I want it. Five million is my opening offer."

Mark tried not to laugh. "It's not for sale."

Foul words exploded through the handset. Keith, standing six feet away, winced. Corey pulled her gun from her pants and held it ready.

"Ten. I *want* The Agency."

"I heard something about people in hot places wanting ice water. Doesn't mean they're going to get it."

Laughter followed. "You are such a fool."

It had to be Bill Vering. "Look, Vering."

"The offer stands—indefinitely. The inducements, however... those will go up." The phone clicked.

Mark pulled out his phone and called Tyler. "I hate to do it, but you get Flynne to help you do everything you can to get the Knupps' identities done yesterday."

With that, he jerked his head toward the door. "Keith in front, Corey to the right. I'll bring up left rear. I'm calling for the Yukon to meet us at the bottom of the steps."

"You think he's *here*?" Corey tried to muscle in front of her brother. "Maybe we should—"

"We'll do as I said, Corey." Mark waited until her features relaxed before adding, "We have to assume that's how he knew what plane. Still, it's more likely he called every private jet coming in from St. Louis until he found this one. That doesn't mean he's *here*. We could have landed at Rockland or Brunswick, for that matter—Louisville."

The door opened without fanfare. Steps lowered as usual. Keith stepped out, the Sig Sauer now at his side, ready. Halfway down the steps, he gave the signal. Corey stepped out with Brent right behind her. "Keep low," she hissed as they began their descent.

Mark stood at the top, scanning the area for anything—anyone. Nothing. He took a step. Swept every inch within sight and stepped again. Once the Knupps reached the tarmac, he jogged down the rest of the way and began scanning again as they raced for the Yukon. Keith opened the door, Mark searched around the car and went for the driver's side. A shot rang out. He spun, ready to fire, and saw Corey and Brent on the ground. Keith stood with his gun still pointed inside the vehicle.

A second shot fired.

Mark raced for the driver's door, stood back, and flung it open. A man half-fell from it, blood oozing from the side of his head. He stepped into the open doorway and held his gun, ready to fire, but no one else was in the vehicle.

"What happened?!"

Keith laid his gun on the floorboard and pointed at the airplane. "Corey, get your brother inside."

They'd taken two steps when Mark stopped them. "Wait. Brent. Is this Vering?" He snapped a picture and passed it between the seats and to Keith.

By the way the man turned away from the phone, Mark had his answer long before he said, "Yes."

Thank You, God.

"Bunny" the nurse came in and whispered something to Morgan, and a moment later, he stood, kissed her, and left without a word. *Tyler's here.*

It took another ten minutes before Tyler walked through the door. "Hi."

Flynne stared. He shuffled his feet. Eventually, she ordered him to come all the way in. "They, like, don't want us yelling all the time."

"Mark has a lot of work for us."

Despite the pain of talking, Flynne decided to get the worst over first. "I have some 'splainin' to do first."

He shook his head. "No… no you don't."

"Huh?"

"I've been thinking about it. Let's just put it in the past, okay?"

Her pride protested, but she decided it didn't have a right to. "If—I can't say sorries?"

"Apology accepted."

It didn't seem like he cared much. Morgan had been worried. He'd cried. Tyler just gave her a smile and pulled out the laptop.

Suddenly, she felt a whole lot better. "Glad to know I didn't break your heart when I met someone else." When he didn't respond to that, Flynne switched to the job at hand. "What are we supposed to do?"

"New identities for—what'd you say?"

"I've been, like, feeling, like, totes the biggest jerkface ever after what happened with Morgan. But you don't even care. Makes it easier on me, I guess."

"Don't care?"

She sniffled. "Bet you weren't even sorries I almost died. But, like you said. All in the past." She pointed at the laptop. "What're the parameters."

Silence reigned while he pulled out his phone and created a hot spot. After that, his fingers clicked over keys until he'd done whatever it was he thought was so important. "Knupps are going to Spain. What do we do?"

"IDs take the longest—that and photo modification. Let's start with names so we can do both of those. Oh, and start downloading their entire social media presence. All of it. Anything they're tagged in. It's all got to go poofs."

"Nothing ever disappears on the web, Flynne. You know that."

"But if people don't know it's there to search for, they won't search. We have to do everything we can and then

310

hope for the rest."

For twenty minutes they argued, until they settled on Albany for the surname. First names followed. Tyler tried calling to ask if the girls had favorite names, but the call never connected. "Must be busy."

"Do you know where they have the girls?"

"Is it important? Why can't we just call them Sarah and Emily and be done with it?"

"Names are important. And they're totes old enough to get to choose."

He grabbed the phone and called Claire. Ten minutes later, the Joe Albany family had been renamed. "Are you happy?"

"Totes."

In that moment, Flynne decided honesty was an overrated commodity and she should be glad she'd never converted to any religion. *But, I sorta promised to do the God thing...*

"That makes one of us," Tyler muttered under his breath. In his normal voice, he added, "Okay, what—?"

"What's that's supposed to mean?"

"Don't want to talk about it, Flynne."

"Then *stop* doing it! *You're* the one who wouldn't talk, and then you get all whatevs on me. So, just *yell* at me!"

The nurse came in and tried to calm her. "He's being supes stupes!"

That got Nurse Bunny hopping. "Look, if you're going to upset her, you'll have to leave."

"I'm *trying* not to. I'm *trying* to just do some important stuff so I can get out of her life, and she can go back to swooning over lover boy."

Bunny eyed her. "Ex-boyfriend?"

"Very *ex*."

"Last to know," Tyler added. "Even after her *new* boyfriend."

That stung, and something told her it should. "You're the one who was all, 'Whatevs' about it, and now you're acting like you even cared!"

"I did care, Flynne!" He jumped up and slammed the laptop onto the bed tray. "I sat there listening to scanners talk about how they weren't getting a response from you, freaking out, and you'd already *replaced* me!"

With that, he stormed out. Flynne watched until she couldn't see him anymore and looked up at Bunny. "I guess that maybe went, like, as well as could be expected? Under the curcs?"

"Curcs?"

A sigh escaped. Flynne closed her eyes, reached out, and shut the laptop. "Circumstances." She rested a moment before adding, "When he comes back, let him in and tell him photos. He'll know what I mean."

"You think he'll come back?"

"We're, like, co-workers. He has to."

0000 01 000 0000 1 01 110   010 111 110 001 0

Everyone who could be there was—Keith and Erika, Flynne and Tyler, Doyle, Brian and Karen. Corey. Claire. Liv and Erika locked in the office upstairs. A much smaller group than the last time. His gut twisted at how much they'd lost.

One by one—or in the case of Keith and Erika, two by two once Keith picked her up from the office—they left. Everything seemed in order. All reports in. All observations noted. Even Paris and Henry had left statements before going to guard the Knupps during the debrief.

Mark stared at the papers before him, flipping through each one to be certain he hadn't missed anything. Five whole days of nothing—not a single blip on any radar. The relief nearly overwhelmed him.

Claire paced, silent and fuming. Only after he pressed her twice did she began ranting. "Keith lied to me."

"About?"

"The Agency. I asked if he was coming back just yesterday and he gave me the same line about how he's retired and is just an instructor. But he knew he was back at that point, didn't he?"

"Yes."

She slammed her stainless-steel water bottle on the table as if it would solve her problem. "He *lied* to me then. Why would he do that?"

"To protect himself, me, The Agency..."

"From *me*? I'm an agent!"

Mark stood and pulled her close. After a brief hug, he sighed and sat down again. "Claire, he has to say whatever he has to say to keep this agency, the agents, and even his family safe."

"I know... but why me? It's not like I'm a threat to The Agency."

C'mon... you should be able to figure that out. Aloud, Mark just said, "Without my okay, he'd never do it."

"But..."

This was it. How she responded to him would define what kind of relationship they could have. "Claire, I'd lie to you in an instant if it would protect any of my agents or this agency. You have to decide if you're okay with that. If not, tell me now."

313

Before it makes being your boss even more impossible than it is now.

Claire moved behind him and slipped her arms around his neck. "Why does that not bother me but Keith lying to *me* does?"

"Would you lie to me to save this agency or one of my agents?"

"Like Flynne did?"

Ouch.

Before he could respond, she began kneading his shoulders. "I guess that depends on if you want me to."

"If it protects lives or The Agency, yes. Avoid it where you can, definitely. Living in lies is never good, but think of it like that woman in Jericho in the Bible. She lied to save those lives and the lives of her family. Keith told me once that it's how he can justify it to himself. He said that woman became some kind of great grandmother a few times over to Jesus."

"Rahab. That's right. Okay. Well, I just hope I don't have to. I won't like it, and you might be able to figure it out."

You could always quit being an agent and start being my partner—kind of a trial run for a longer-term partnership. A closer one.

To keep himself from blurting out thoughts he probably shouldn't be having, Mark spread out the paperwork before him. The summary pages he laid on top and began reading. Pacing. Reading some more. He sat. Stood. Paced. Read.

Claire said nothing. When he sat, she stood close and offered whatever comfort and support she could. As he paced, she leaned against the table with her arms folded and that secret smile that made him feel twelve again on her lips.

No matter what he did, Mark arrived at the same conclusion every time. "Something isn't right here."

"Not right, how?" She leaned against his chair, one arm around him, her chin propped on his head.

"That's just the thing. I don't know."

"Can I read them? Maybe I'll see something."

No agent had ever been privy to the notes before—not all of them, and certainly not the private ones meant only for his eyes. Those contained details about other agents—even about her. She'd not like everything she saw. But perhaps if someone else had been reading all along, the recent mess wouldn't have happened.

I can trust her. She's Keith's cousin!

A latent doubt—one he'd shredded ages ago, in fact—resurfaced and pasted itself together. The surface, though bumpy, was still legible in his mind's eye. *She was with Anastas. Trafficking. Brent's daughter. It was so easy to get to her that time. What if someone else...?*

The idea—ludicrous. He dangled it over his mental shredder again, but new thoughts burned into the page. *Wouldn't have to be a new group. They know who she is—who I am. Or, rather, was. They might know she works for me—even with Keith "dead."*

"Mark? What is it?"

He gazed up at her and tried to read something duplicitous in those eyes. Tried and failed. "Just thinking. It'd be a breach of protocol. Does the situation warrant it?"

She shrugged. "I don't know. It doesn't have to be now. If you want another pair of eyes, I'd do it. Or..." Her eyes brightened, and she kissed him before saying, "Really, you should have Keith look at them. He knows way more than I do. I just want to help, but he actually *can*."

And that just wiped out one irrational fear. Mark smiled. "Let's see if we can catch them before they get out of town. We'll do dinner. I'll ask if he thinks it's too much for you. I'm probably being paranoid."

They'd made it to the parking lot where Keith and Erika sat against the hood of Keith's '39 Packard and watched the sun set before Claire spoke again. "I think it's good that you were concerned—looking for trouble. You'd be crazy if you didn't."

"How do you figure?"

She stopped him just behind a commuter van and kissed him until he'd almost forgotten what she said. "Your agents were targeted. Someone was trying to buy you out with fear and intimidation. If you didn't keep looking for threats..."

"I wouldn't be doing my job." He tugged her forward and handed her the security case. "Let's drop this off at Wexfield before we go eat. We'll go over them together tonight."

"I thought you were getting Keith's input. He's still with The Agency, after all."

Mark wasn't one for public displays, but at the sight of her smile, he stopped in the middle of the parking lot. Cars coming and going slowed and honked. Keith and Erika probably gawked. He didn't care. As much as he *had* shown her what he hoped for, he hadn't. And he hadn't told her. "If you haven't figured it out, I'm in love with you."

"I had." She kissed him without any of the awkwardness a public place like that should cause. "I promised myself I wouldn't say it first. I always do, and then when I do, I always regret it."

"Well, I took care of that for you..."

She kissed him again. This time, he deliberately lingered. A wolf whistle from a passing car prompted a giggle, but she didn't pull away. Another horn blared, making them both jump. He didn't step away, either. When he'd said all he could without words, he pulled her into a hug and buried his face in her hair. "I meant it."

"I know. I love you, too."

Seconds passed, and this time he didn't hear the horns that probably still blared and the curses that were probably hurled at them as cars passed. This time, he just waited for some shift in her—something that hinted at the regret she spoke of.

It came in a faint sigh. "In case you're wondering," she whispered, "for the first time, I don't regret it."

"That's probably because you didn't say it *first*."

AUTHOR'S NOTE

Whew! It's been a while since we've visited Mark and his crew, and I'm sorry for that. When I got the idea of Flynne going "rogue," I knew it had to be a thing. And it had to be epic. Or is that "eptastic"? To ensure that happened, I called in my torment expert, Clark.

We talked. We schemed. We brainstormed until book five became books five, six, and seven. These three books are all connected to each other and the overall series, but each stands alone, too. (At least I hope they will!) If you don't read the next bit, you can end the series here. Flynne saved the day, they caught the bad guy, and life is good.

But if you dare, I invite you to read the opening scene of book six (and book two of the miniseries) and get a tiny look into, *Pointed Suspicion.*

0000 01 000 0000 1 01 110   010 111 110 001 0

Despite the full moon outside, darkness shrouded the room. A lone desk lamp bulb illuminated a fuzzy-edged circle in the middle—a spotlight on the center stage of unfolding plans.

Click—click. The pen served as a diversion more than a writing instrument. *Click—click.*

One sticky note occupied the center of that circle. It was green, and on it, one name. JEHNSON. The pen clicked open and a check mark appeared beside the name. *Click.* It closed again.

A few taps of the keyboard prompted a password box. Another few taps brought up a file. Inside, another file. *Click.*

An image opened. The entrance sign to Mayflower Trust filled most of the page. But behind it two people leaned against an antique car. The man wore a beard. The woman—Erika Polowski. *You're supposed to be dead.*

With a few clicks, the image grew until that bearded face filled the screen. The hand reached for the pen again. *Click—click.*

So are you.

The green sticky note was, once again, set aside. The hand fished through the wastepaper basket on the side of the desk. A crumpled, pink sticky note appeared.

Long fingers worked to smooth it against the table until the circled name could be read again. AUGER.

Leaning back in the chair, pen still in hand, two eyes stayed trained on that paper. On the circles around the name. *Click—click.*

The edge curled up a little too much. The green sticky note was moved to overlap it enough to hold it down. *Click—click.*

"Let the games resume."

CHAUTONA HAVIG'S BOOKS

The Rockland Chronicles

Aggie's Inheritance Series

Ready or Not
For Keeps
Here We Come
Ante Up!

HearthLand Series: A Serial Novel (Six Volumes)

Past Forward: A Serial Novel (Six Volumes)

HearthLand Series: A Serial Novel (Six Volumes)

The Vintage Wren (A serial novel beginning 2016)

The Shopkeepers of New Cheltenham

The Ghosts of New Cheltenham
Something Borrowed, Someone Blue

Marriages of Conviction

Blessing Bentley
Tempting Tait (Coming 2020)

The Hartfield Mysteries

Manuscript for Murder
Crime of Fashion
Two o'Clock Slump
Front Window
Silenced Knight (A Christmas Mystery "Noella")

**

Argosy Junction
Discovering Hope
Not a Word
Speak Now
A Bird Died
Thirty Days Hath…
Confessions of a De-cluttering Junkie
Corner Booth
New Year's Revolutions
Premeditated Serendipity
Random Acts of Shyness
Operation Posthaste

The Agency Files

Justified Means
Mismatched
Effective Immediately
A Forgotten Truth
Hashtag Rogue

<u>Pointed Suspicion (Coming 2020)</u>

Sight Unseen Series

<u>None So Blind</u>
<u>Will Not See</u>
<u>Ties that Blind</u>

Christmas Fiction

<u>Advent</u>
<u>31 Kisses</u>
<u>Tarnished Silver</u>
<u>The Matchmakers of Holly Circle</u>
<u>Carol and the Belles</u>
<u>Christmas Stalkings</u>
<u>Christmas Embers</u>
<u>The Second Noel</u>
<u>Silenced Knight</u>
<u>Merri's Christmas Mission</u>
<u>The Ghosts of New Cheltenham</u>
<u>Sand & Mistletoe</u>
<u>Tangoed in Tinsel</u>

**

Meddlin' Madeline Mysteries

<u>Sweet on You (Book1)</u>
<u>Such a Tease (Book 2)</u>
<u>Fine Print (Book 3)</u>
<u>Dead Letter (Book 4)</u>

**

Ballads from the Hearth

Jack

**

Gold Diggers Collections

The Trouble with Nancy

**

Legacy of the Vines

Deepest Roots of the Heart

**

Journey of Dreams Series

Prairie
Highlands

**

- ## Heart of Warwickshire Series

Allerednic

**

The Annals of Wynnewood

<u>Shadows & Secrets</u>
<u>Cloaked in Secrets</u>
<u>Beneath the Cloak</u>

* *

Not-So-Fairy Tales

<u>Princess Paisley</u>
<u>Everard</u>

* *

- ## **Legends of the Vengeance**

<u>The First Adventure</u>

Made in the USA
Lexington, KY
03 December 2019

58065621R00179